D1048912

"DO YOU UNDERS̶T̶A̶N̶D̶
WHAT IT MEANS
TO MAKE LOVE TO A MAN?"

"Yes," Elizabeth said haltingly. "It means that a man and a woman kiss each other. And perhaps put their arms around each other."

"Like this?" Lord Jonathan stepped forward and encircled her waist with his large hands. Then he bent his head and brushed his lips across hers. He straightened and stared into her eyes. "Is that making love?"

"I don't think so, my lord," she said uncertainly.

"Look at me, Elizabeth," he commanded in a voice that would brook no argument. "For your own sake, I am going to take you in hand and teach you about men and women."

He sat her down and stood there for all the world like a king issuing a royal decree. "Specifically, I am going to teach you about what happens between a man and a woman when they make love."

Desert Rogue

Suzanne Simmons

AVON BOOKS ◆ NEW YORK

DESERT ROGUE is an original publication of Avon Books. This work has never before appeared in book form. This work is a novel. Any similarity to actual persons or events is purely coincidental.

AVON BOOKS
A division of
The Hearst Corporation
1350 Avenue of the Americas
New York, New York 10019

Copyright © 1992 by Suzanne Simmons Guntrum
Inside cover author photograph by Watters Studio
Published by arrangement with the author
Library of Congress Catalog Card Number: 91-92436
ISBN: 0-380-76578-0

First Avon Books Printing: June 1992

AVON TRADEMARK REG. U.S. PAT. OFF. AND IN OTHER COUNTRIES, MARCA REGISTRADA, HECHO EN U.S.A.

Printed in the U.S.A.

RA   10 9 8 7 6 5 4 3 2 1

For R. R. G.
With love and gratitude

Chapter 1

First, he would seduce her. Then he would marry her if he had to.

The plan had sounded simple enough when he had proposed it to Prince Ramses. At the time he had not realized it would mean following his quarry through every bazaar in Alexandria. Apparently the lady liked to shop.

Black Jack moved from one shaded doorway to the next, squinting behind the folds of his headdress, making certain to keep his eyes well concealed.

If the truth be told, his eyes were both a blessing and a curse in this part of the world. Pure, shimmering cerulean blue, they boldly announced that he was no native to *Kemet*, the Black Land, Gift of the Nile, Egypt.

Indeed, had it not been whispered in his ear

by more than one lovely young maiden that his eyes were bluer than the River of Life on a cloudless day?

Beneath the mantle of spun cotton, his tanned face dissolved into a smile. Ah, the beauties he had known and loved since coming to the land of the Arabian Nights!

Black Jack pulled himself up short and muttered under his breath, "By the sacred blood of Osiris, you had best keep your mind on the business at hand, Jack-O."

The business at hand being one Lady Elizabeth Guest, youngest surviving daughter of Avery Guest, the Earl of Stanhope, according to his sources in England.

He kept to the shade afforded by the building at his back and watched the progress of Lady Elizabeth and her entourage as they moved from one colorful booth to the next, examining cheap trinkets, bolts of cloth, brass coffee servers, artifacts from a royal tomb—every man, woman, and child in Egypt claimed to have uncovered at least one such cache—and bottles of elixir made of mummy dust.

Black Jack wondered how long this particular "mummy" had been dead and buried before grave robbers had dug it up and sold it to an apothecary. Probably no more than a week or two if his was any guess.

As she picked up a gilded statue, made in the likeness of an ancient pharaoh, and turned it over in her daintily gloved hands, his attention focused on the lady herself.

She was tall. It was the first thing he had

noticed about her. Tall and regal. She carried herself like a queen. If posture was a barometer of good breeding, then it was no wonder she could claim kinship with her namesake, Elizabeth Tudor.

Her skin was milky white, nearly translucent, like exceptionally fine bone china. He would be willing to wager that the hands beneath the kid gloves were elegant, blue-veined and cool to the touch. As for the rest of her . . .

Black Jack let his imagination run wild for a moment. By the blessed Bast, he had forgotten how very fair English women could be!

Although her hair was tucked up beneath a rather whimsical chapeau concocted of woven straw, assorted fruits, and a ribbon or two, he pictured her tresses to be long and thick and silky. A few stray wisps at her nape revealed their color to be a rich chestnut brown.

He couldn't see her eyes beneath her hat and parasol, a bit of feminine frippery in pale pink silk. She was dressed in the height of London fashion—which was to say, Paris fashion—but the long sleeves, tightly cinched waist, and exaggerated bustle of her gown appeared restrictive, even downright ludicrous, when compared to the comfortable, flowing robes worn by the men and women of Alexandria.

Still, he had an impression of a cool, quiet, shaded glen amidst the hustle and bustle of the port city.

For one instant Black Jack felt a pang of regret.

England. If he didn't know better, he would have said he was homesick.

He brooded for a moment, whistling between his teeth, then watched as a small, dark monkey of a man scurried toward him. The servant stepped into the shaded doorway, made a small gesture of obeisance, and spoke in the ancient tongue of the pharaohs, although both men were conversant with many languages. "The *Star of Egypt* sails at dawn two days hence, master."

Blue eyes shimmered fiercely. "This I already know."

Eager to please, the man quickly went on. "The lady will be in the stateroom. Her maid in the adjoining smaller cabin. The Colonel and Mrs. Winters on the port side. The guide will be below deck sharing the first mate's quarters. Also there will be three, perhaps four, janissaries serving as escorts." He frowned as he counted the number of Turkish soldiers on his fingers. Then he exclaimed, "Ack! She is better guarded than Queen Victoria herself."

Black Jack's face took on a judicial, appraising look. "So it would seem."

The scrawny little man clicked his tongue disapprovingly and added, "I have seen the female, master. She is sickly and pale and what the English call an 'old maid.' "

He stiffened. "An old maid?" Surely not.

The one named Kareem wrung his brown hands in agitation. "Most assuredly. She must be seventeen or eighteen. Perhaps even older."

Black Jack bit a smile from the corners of his mouth. "That old."

"This female is not for you, master. Let me bring you the eldest daughter of my second cousin's nephew. She is nearly eleven and a true beauty. It goes without saying that she is a virgin and eager for the marriage bed. 'Tis best to train a female while she is still young and malleable, heh?"

He was not shocked by Kareem's frank talk. He had ceased to be shocked long ago. In the years since Lord Jonathan Wicke—now known only as "Black Jack"—had been in self-imposed exile from England, he had traveled through many lands and seen many customs that his countrymen would consider barbaric.

But then, he had also seen many wondrous things. And, although he was but six and twenty, he *felt* much older. He had had enough experiences, he reminded himself, for two lifetimes.

How different his life would have been if he had stayed in Northumberland as his father and older brother had desired.

He winced.

Well, perhaps not as Lawrence had desired. His brother would one day become the eighth Duke of Deakin, and he wanted nothing more than to have his black sheep brother out of sight and out of mind.

He finally answered his servant. "Your offer honors me, Kareem, but we must not forget that we are on a mission for Prince Ramses, and my involvement with the lady in question is part of a great plan."

Kareem bowed to the inevitable. "Since we must do as the Prince bids, 'tis a great pity the female is so old and so pale."

"Seventeen or eighteen is not so old in my country, and fair skin is much desired."

The native fellah shook his head in dismay and then said, puzzled, "Your country, master?"

He sighed. What was his country? He wondered even as he said the word aloud. "England."

There was a snort of disbelief, followed by an impertinent "England?"

Black Jack scowled and chided himself: How long has it been since you thought of yourself as English, Jack-O?

Kareem was unconvinced. "And does this English female know the secrets of her father?"

"Perhaps. Lord Stanhope has sent for her, that much is known. If he hasn't confided in her yet, he undoubtedly will."

"And you will take this unworthy female into your bed at the behest of Prince Ramses?"

He didn't bother to explain that the original plan had been his, not Ramie's. "Yes."

The man commiserated with him. "This will be a great sacrifice and a most difficult task, master."

Black Jack's eyes narrowed as Lady Elizabeth put the gold statue down and declared to the woman next to her that it was merely a reproduction, and a rather poor one at that. It seemed the lady knew her artifacts.

As Kareem jabbered beside him, Black Jack found his gaze drawn again and again to the figure of the young Englishwoman. He could not help but notice that her breasts were especially round and full for one her age. And her hips swayed in a surprisingly seductive manner beneath the ridiculous bustle.

"Perhaps not so difficult a task," he murmured.

The wiry, dark-skinned man beside him laughed quietly, knowingly. "You have been too long without a woman."

"Yes," he agreed with feeling.

"You know what they say, master."

He was curious. "What do they say?"

In the ancient tongue, his servant quoted the proverb " 'Egypt is like a man without a woman: hot by day, cold by night.' "

Black Jack laughed and then, only a moment later, swore softly under his breath. "Well, hell and damnation!"

The man beside him became agitated. "What is it?"

"It looks like the silly chit has managed to get herself separated from her entourage," he said. "She's turned down the wrong alley."

Kareem was immediately on alert; his hand went to the dagger concealed within his sashed belt. "The alley is most assuredly full of thugs and pickpockets, master. Do you wish me to go after her?"

He sighed, and shook his head. "You keep an eye on the others. I will see to Lady Elizabeth."

She was lost.

One minute she had been standing beside Colette and Colonel and Mrs. Winters, and the next she found herself quite alone in a dark alley. And all because she could not resist a closer look at the miniature black granite statue she had spotted in a booth she thought was just around the corner from the bazaar.

"I mustn't panic," Elizabeth said out loud, in an attempt to bolster her spirits. "These alleyways are not entirely unlike the labyrinth garden at home."

Home being the family seat, Stanhope Hall, with its thirty guest rooms, extensive park and gardens, numerous cottages, fourteenth-century chapel and surrounding graveyard—the final resting place of the Stanhopes since the time of the Conqueror—and all the land as far as the eye could see.

Home being one of Yorkshire's, indeed, one of the realm's, most magnificent estates.

Once she was old enough to comprehend the intricate pattern of "Lady Catherine's Folly"—her ancestress had apparently been foolish enough to get lost in the sculptured maze on numerous occasions, usually, it was noted with a lascivious wink, in the company of a young, handsome male houseguest—Elizabeth had often strolled through the tightly clipped yew hedges that grew well above head height, enjoying the challenge of wending her way from one end to the other.

Standing now in one of the chiaroscuro alleyways of Alexandria, she took a deep, fortifying breath and squared her shoulders. That was how she must regard her present circumstances: as a kind of maze to wend her way through, as a puzzle to be solved. Panicking was the last thing she could afford to do. She was in a strange country, and she did not speak the language.

Elizabeth started toward what she believed was the main street and the colorful, noisy bazaar beyond when she detected the scuffle of feet behind her. Without stopping, she brought her head sharply around.

There were two—no, three—of them: men of indeterminate age dressed in dusty robes and striped cotton *kuftans*. One had a filthy patch over his right eye. The others were wearing the traditional headdress that covered most of the hair and face. With furtive glances at one another, they chattered and gestured animatedly, but she did not understand a word they were saying.

"I do not speak Arabic," she announced with more bravado than common sense. "Do any of you understand English?"

One of the men smiled at her slyly; half of his teeth were missing in front, and the remainder were stained a dark tobacco brown. Another pointed and snickered rudely. Elizabeth felt the color flood her cheeks. She did not need a translator in order to comprehend the vulgarity of the remark.

The ruffians took a menacing step toward her, and for the first time since losing her way, she was genuinely afraid. Her heart began to pound wildly in her breast, and she was having difficulty breathing. Perhaps Colette had done up her corset too tightly.

She considered making an unladylike dash for the street, but before she could formulate an escape, she found herself surrounded. She opened her mouth to scream, but nothing came out. The din of the port city would have drowned out any sound she tried to make, anyway. Or so she consoled herself.

Her back was to the wall. She clutched her pink silk parasol in one hand and her matching reticule in the other as if they could somehow afford her protection from the thugs.

Unanswered questions flooded her mind. Were the men thieves? Was it her money they wanted? She had a handful of Egyptian coins in her purse— a few paras and piasters. The rest was in her trunk at the Victoria Hotel.

Or was their intent far more sinister than robbery?

The possibility sent a chill racing down Elizabeth's spine. One heard all kinds of tales, of course, even as far north as Yorkshire. Once she had been sitting quietly reading, unobserved, in a corner of the library at Stanhope Hall when her aunt related to Maman the lurid details of an unfortunate incident. It seemed to involve a titled English lady traveling through Istanbul, and a somewhat unsavory gentleman of her acquaintance. Elizabeth had not understood the entire story, but it had to do with the woman being "compromised" and eventually sold into slavery.

Dear Lord, she prayed these men weren't white slavers!

Surely after she had journeyed all this way, she wasn't going to end up in an exotic harem, wearing diaphanous veils and precious little else, the mistress of some rich pasha. Maman would have a fit of the vapors.

Elizabeth squeezed her eyes tightly shut and whispered a fervent, heartfelt entreaty to the almighty. After a moment she opened her eyes again, only to see a grubby hand, the nails black with dirt, clamp down over her mouth.

There was heavy breathing in her ear. Insistent fingers dug into her upper arms and forced her toward an even darker hovel farther along the alley.

"No—!" Elizabeth gasped.

She wanted to retch. The stink of sweat and unwashed male body was overwhelming. There was an awful laugh as someone clawed at her; her hat was knocked askew and her hair came tumbling down around her shoulders.

Despite the teachings that Nahny had drummed into her since childhood about what a wellborn English lady did and did not do, she hit at her assailant with her fists, harder and harder, again and again.

She kicked out with the toe of her shoe and caught another man on the shin, and heard, with a certain degree of satisfaction, a grunt of surprise and pain. But there were three of them and only one of her—and she knew she would eventually lose this battle of brute strength.

Then, out of nowhere, a robed figure appeared in the doorway of the darkened room. The newcomer was broad of shoulder and noticeably tall, standing half a head and more above her attackers. He moved swiftly, and with amazing grace and power. Like a flash of lightning, he struck: once, twice, three times in rapid succession. The first thug crumpled, hitting the dirt floor with a resounding thud.

There was another crack of a fist making contact with bone, then a groan, and a second man tried to make a run for it, holding his jaw in agony. The third assailant had already decided not to fight when the stranger spoke to them in a commanding voice in Arabic, but the intent was clear even to Elizabeth. They were the ones suddenly in danger. It was their lives that hung in the balance, not hers. And that was something they had not bargained for.

The thugs helped each other to their feet and ran from the dingy dwelling, leaving her alone with her rescuer. She could not see his face, it was concealed in the shadows, but his deep, sonorous baritone came to her in slightly halting English: "Are you all right?"

Elizabeth tried to assess the damage done to her person, and found it was more a sartorial matter than anything else. She was basically unharmed, despite the fact her hat was hanging by one ribbon and her hair had partially come undone.

She answered in a breathless but polite voice, "Yes, I'm quite all right."

The man seemed relieved, then muttered under his breath in exasperation, "In the name of Amon-Re, a female should not go wandering off by herself in a strange country."

"It . . . it was unintentional, I assure you."

He continued scolding her as if she had not spoken. "You allowed yourself to be separated from the rest of your entourage, Lady Elizabeth. That was most unwise."

Her ears perked up. "You know my name?"

The stranger hesitated. "Yes."

She tried to catch a glimpse of his face, but he was wearing a traditional desert headdress that revealed little and concealed much. "Who are you?" she boldly demanded.

"A friend."

Without thinking, Elizabeth blurted out, "But I don't have any friends in Egypt—except for my traveling companions, of course."

In a dangerously soft voice, the robed figure who had come to her assistance pointed out, "It is a good thing I happened along, then. You seem in need of a friend."

"What is your name, sir?"

He waved her question aside. "My name is of no consequence. Your safety is the only thing of import."

At that moment a dazzling ray of sunlight entered through a slit in the shuttered window and slanted across the man's right arm. His hands were clearly shown in detail. They were perfectly shaped, with large palms and long, graceful fingers. His skin was tanned a deep bronze color, and there was a smattering of fine hair that began at his wrist and ran up his forearm, disappearing into the sleeve of his robe.

But Elizabeth's attention was riveted on the object encircling his middle finger.

It was a gold ring.

Pure gold. Fashioned in the shape of an ankh, the ancient Egyptian symbol of life.

"How beautiful!" she exclaimed.

The man looked down, then jerked his hand back within the folds of the traditional long cloth coat he wore.

"Put yourself to rights, my lady." His instructions were given in a brusque tone. "It would not do for your chaperons to see you looking so much the worse for wear."

"How true," she sighed, and did as he bid her.

Colonel and Mrs. Winters had a tendency to take dear Maman's parting admonition—"See to Lady Elizabeth day and night, as if she were your own child"—too much to heart as it was. Heavens, they scarcely let her out of their sight.

It was most annoying.

She had hoped that once she was away from Yorkshire and Maman's watchful eye, she might have the chance to experience life to its fullest. Indeed, to that end, she had tearfully pleaded and cajoled, argued and reasoned, and finally finagled permission to visit her dear father in Egypt.

Life, in her opinion, should be filled with wonder and excitement, extraordinary people and places, and grand adventure. Especially grand adventure. Elizabeth had had precious little of it during her seventeen and a half years, but she had dreamt of it, imagined it, prayed for it.

Not literally, of course. It was unacceptable, according to Nanny, to pray for frivolous things, especially for one's self. One prayed for guidance, for the forgiveness of sins, for the queen's good health, for the souls of the dearly departed. These were the acceptable precincts of prayer.

Elizabeth gave a small sigh and went about the business of tidying her hair and straightening the fashionable bonnet that hung precariously to one side.

Once she had her toilette in order, the stranger

issued a final warning. "I think you understand that this little incident must remain our secret."

There was suddenly a different kind of danger present in the room. Elizabeth could sense it. Feel it. Almost reach out and touch it. She just wasn't sure she understood what the danger was.

Then it came to her: Perhaps *this* man was a greater threat than the gang of thugs had been.

He persisted. "Do you understand, Lady Elizabeth?"

She nervously fingered the drawstrings of her reticule. "Yes, I understand," she told him at last. "What happened this afternoon must be our secret."

"Then, after you, my lady," he said with an exaggerated politeness that did not seem to her in the least bit polite.

Elizabeth stepped out of the darkened hovel and into the bright sunlight. Her spirits lifted immediately. The sense of foreboding hovering over her disappeared. Surely this man was no threat to her. It must be an overactive imagination. Nothing more.

But what a grand adventure! Her first! She had been rescued by a tall, dark, and handsome stranger. Of course, she didn't actually know for certain that he was handsome since she could not see his face, but she imagined him to be so.

"Follow me." With that succinct command, he led her through the city's serpentine streets. "Turn to your right and you will find the bazaar and your friends," she was informed. Then, without further ado, her guide melted into the crowd.

Elizabeth took several steps and heard a familiar voice say, "There you are, milady. I have been searching everywhere for you. I was becoming quite *nerveux*."

She smiled and placed a reassuring hand on her maid's arm. "There is no reason to fret, Colette. I was just around the corner looking at some statues."

"Your maman would never forgive me if any *malheur* were to befall you," the mademoiselle said fretfully.

Elizabeth did her best to calm the girl. "Nothing terrible has happened to me. Please do not concern yourself."

Colette was very dear to her. The young Frenchwoman had become her friend and confidante in the years since Maman had brought her back from one of her annual shopping trips to Paris. The countess and the shopgirl had been forced to flee the city together when it was invaded by the Prussian army, an act that eventually felled the Second Empire and Emperor Louis Napoleon along with it.

More important, according to Lady Stanhope, it meant that she could no longer get her gowns from Worth's. That was where Colette had been a *couturière* when Maman had met her.

One delicate French brow now arched into an inverted V. "Your bonnet seems not quite right, milady."

Elizabeth quickly made excuses. "How silly of me. I bumped into it with my parasol. You will help me put my hat to rights once we return to our carriage."

"*Oui*, milady."

"I think I have had enough shopping for one day. Let us rejoin Colonel and Mrs. Winters and return to the hotel."

Suddenly it occurred to her that in all the excitement she had forgotten her manners and failed to thank her gallant rescuer for saving her from a fate undoubtedly worse than death itself.

Elizabeth quickly turned and scanned the crowded bazaar, but the man was nowhere in sight.

A wave of disappointment washed over her. It was too late. He was gone, and she would never see him again.

Chapter 2

"Qui *est-ce*, milady?" asked Colette. Then she repeated the question in English. "Who is he, my lady?"

Elizabeth stood by the steamship's railing and, with more than a modicum of interest, followed the direction of the young Frenchwoman's gaze.

There was a commotion on the dock as a fancy carriage pulled up alongside the *Star of Egypt*, and a gentleman leisurely got out. His servant accompanied him, two steps behind, a hefty leather valise clasped in each brown hand. As the man made his way toward the gangplank, a gaggle of porters and begging children quickly gathered about him in a circle.

While it wasn't polite to stare, Elizabeth reminded herself, gossip had it that even perfectly respectable society matrons had been known to stand on the gilt chairs of London ballrooms this past Season in order not to miss the entrance of the latest PB—professional beauty—Lillie Langtry. She was simply satisfying her curiosity as they had been theirs, she reasoned as she gave the newcomer her full attention.

"I don't know who he is, Colette." She deliberated for a moment and then said, "Perhaps he's the Englishman the Colonel mentioned would be traveling with us."

"He doesn't look like a proper Englishman, milady."

Elizabeth caught the tip of her tongue between her teeth. She agreed, but did not say so aloud.

Her maid lifted her shoulders, then dropped them again, speaking volumes as only a *parisienne* could with a mere shrug. "He is too handsome. And he is not in the least bit stuffed."

"Not in the least stuffed?" repeated Elizabeth, wrinkling her brow. Whatever could Colette mean? Then it suddenly occurred to her. "Do you mean stuffy?"

"*Oui*, milady. Stuffy." The slender woman beside her visibly brightened. "Perhaps he is a Frenchman." She began to chatter animatedly. "*C'est un bel homme. C'est un très bel homme. C'est un français, certainement.*"

Elizabeth tried not to laugh, but it was impossible to maintain a dignified manner when Colette was determined to be so deliciously French and so *très amusante* at times.

In the end she couldn't help herself; she laughed right out loud, in what Maman would have deemed was a most unladylike fashion. But the sound of her laughter, thankfully, was lost in the cacophony of dockside Alexandria. Shouting sailors and scampering beggars, frantically gesturing Arabs, "surely the busiest and noisiest people in the world," according to what she had once read in Florence Nightingale's Egyptian journal, all served to cover the sound of her merriment.

She regained control of herself and remarked to her friend and confidante, "Somehow I don't think the gentleman is *français*."

Not that he looked like a proper Englishman, either. Colette was right about that. It wasn't that he was too handsome—although he was the most beautiful man she had ever seen—no, it was something else. Something she couldn't quite put her finger on.

Elizabeth's brow furrowed in thought. There was a look about the man that suggested he hadn't been in England recently.

There were his clothes, for one thing. They were splendid and they fit him beautifully, only straining slightly at the confines of his broad shoulders, but the style wasn't quite Bond Street. His appearance was more that of a wealthy continental type. The type one saw on the streets of Paris, or perhaps in the European hotels of Alexandria.

He was tall. Three or four inches taller than any other man around him on the dock, and far taller than the small, dark servant who followed in his footsteps, instructing the porters on the loading of their luggage.

The gentleman removed his hat, and the hair beneath was revealed to be a beautiful tumble of black curls, blue-black like a sleek Arabian race-horse. His features were cut from a bold pattern. A strongly defined, yet patrician nose dominated the middle of his face. A slash of jet black brow slanted above each eye. Well-shaped ears were tucked close to his scalp. A hard, angular jut of granite formed his chin and jaw. *C'est un très bel homme*, as Colette had said.

Then he raised his eyes, and seemed to stare straight into hers, and for a moment Elizabeth's heart stopped beating.

Blue.

She felt as though she were drowning in an endless sea of blue. She had never seen eyes that particular color. They were the summer sky at dawn. They were the same glorious shade as the wisteria that vined up the trellis beneath her window at home. They were clear and intelligent and mesmerizing. . . .

She didn't even realize she was holding her breath until she began to gasp a little for air.

The boarding party started up the gangway. The Englishman was some eight or ten feet from her when he stopped dead in his tracks. He seemed surprised—indeed, stunned was not too strong a word—at the sight of her.

Was there something wrong? Elizabeth wondered self-consciously. Was her hair mussed? Her bustle askew? A smudge of dirt on the tip of her nose?

That had happened to her more than once back in Yorkshire when she couldn't resist doing a bit of gardening. Maman claimed gardening—she disdainfully called it "digging around in the dirt like a common scullery maid"—wasn't a proper pastime for a young lady in her position.

Well, bother being proper. And bother her position in Society. Gardening was the perfect pastime. She loved working the rich, dark earth with her own hands. Planting the delicate seedlings and watching them grow. Seeing the results of her labor come to fruition. Even their gardener, Trout, claimed she had perhaps the greenest thumb he had ever seen, and Trout was old enough to have seen many a thumb indeed in his day.

Elizabeth reached up with her monogrammed hankie and tried to wipe the tip of her nose, just in case there was a smudge of dirt on it.

Muttering under her breath, "Oh, bother," she stuffed the hankie back in her reticule and straightened her back. At least no one could complain about her posture.

The tall, handsome man continued up the gangplank. He was only a step or two from where she and Colette stood when he hesitated. He opened his mouth as if he were about to speak to her, then shut it again without uttering a word.

No doubt he'd thought better of initiating a conversation, Elizabeth decided. Any gentleman would be as aware as she that they had not been properly introduced.

With a barely perceptible nod of acknowledgment, he strolled past them to where the ship's officers stood ready to salute him.

"Welcome aboard the *Star of Egypt*, my lord." Elizabeth heard the captain greet the newcomer.

Then he said something in Arabic, and the gentle-man answered in kind.

An Englishman who spoke the native language fluently. Somehow she was not surprised. But what happened next *did* surprise her.

As if on cue, the noonday sun came out from behind a cloud and shone down on the deck of the steamship and all who waited there. Just as she raised her parasol to ward off the intense sun-light, Elizabeth caught a glimpse of something bright and unusually shiny.

Gold.

Pure gold.

The breath was snatched from her lungs. The Englishman was wearing a gold ring on his mid-dle finger. A ring in the shape of an ankh, the ancient Egyptian symbol of life. A ring she could have sworn was identical to the one worn by her mysterious rescuer in the bazaar.

She was a child.

A mere infant.

Bloody hell, Black Jack swore silently as he turned to speak to the captain of the *Star of Egypt*.

Somehow the hole he was digging for himself seemed to be getting deeper and deeper.

At the sight of Lady Elizabeth standing by the steamship's railing, he had been confounded. He had stared at her openly as if he had never seen a beautiful woman before. He corrected his own observation: a beautiful girl. For in the clear light of day, without a ridiculous basket of fruit on her head and a parasol shading her face, he could see that she did not appear to be more than fifteen or sixteen.

What was worse was his reaction to her. He had immediately felt the stirrings of desire in his body. The same stirrings that were causing him discomfort even now.

He had one consolation. Lady Elizabeth had not recognized him. Of that, he was certain.

It was nothing short of a miracle since the incident in the bazaar two days before had nearly spelled disaster. He had made several mistakes, and he was not a man who usually made mistakes. He had kicked himself when he'd allowed her name to slip out. Very shoddy business. Amateurish. Unworthy of a soldier who had once spied with the best of them.

Then there was the matter of the gold ring, the symbol of his sworn allegiance to the prince. Had she gotten a good look at it? Would she recognize it if she saw it again? If so, why was he so loath to remove it from his hand?

Damn. It was almost as if he wanted the chit to guess his dual identity. . . .

Black Jack forced himself to make the appropriate responses to the captain and the crew as he was shown to his stateroom. While Kareem went about the business of acting as his personal valet, unpacking his belongings and stowing them in their proper place, he poured himself a generous glass of after-dinner port. He cared little that it wasn't even teatime yet.

"Bloody hell," he grumbled under his breath as he downed the glass of dark, aromatic liquor.

He knew from the detailed report he'd had

commissioned that Lady Elizabeth Guest was nearly eighteen. But the damn agent had said nothing about her being a wide-eyed innocent. He had hoped—he had *expected*—a woman. He had gotten a girl.

He poured himself a second drink and began to pace the floor of his stateroom.

What was the color of her eyes, anyway?

Not brown. Not green. Not yellow, certainly. But the most incredible combination of all three. And she had watched him as if she had never seen a man before. It was disconcerting. It was disturbing. And rather flattering.

His mouth twisted sardonically. "You had better watch yourself, Jack."

He must remember what was at stake if he failed: the honor of Prince Ramses and the people who had once saved his life, who had given him a reason to go on living when he had thought there was none.

Black Jack stood staring out the window of his stateroom, the glass in his hand forgotten. He thought back to the day he had first met Prince Ramses, the same day he had earned his nickname.

They were both scarcely sixteen at the time, and newly settled into their rooms at Christ's College, Cambridge. He had bragged to the prince that he—Jonathan Malcolm Charles Wicke—the second son, and therefore, unfortunately, *not* the heir of the Duke of Deakin, was considered the blackest of the black sheep of his family.

This was no small feat, he had gone on to explain with a perfectly straight face and in his youthful, swaggering manner, since the Northumberland Wickes produced a legendary black sheep every other generation, hand in hand, it always seemed, with the "wild Wickes" blue eyes.

Prince Ramses had laughed heartily, shaken his hand in a most civilized manner, and dubbed him "Black Jack" on the spot. It was not until months later that he found out that Ramie had neglected to mention several things the day they had been introduced. First, that he had been married to his consort, Ma'ya, at the tender age of ten, and second, that the very next morning he had arisen from the bridal bower and ruthlessly ordered the execution of a dozen men in a dispute over tribal water rights.

Such was the way of the desert.

So much for *his* wild, wicked ways, Black Jack thought with self-deprecating humor as he raised the glass of port to his lips. Nevertheless, the nickname had stuck all these years. Just as his relationship with Ramie had endured. They were friends; they were far more.

And he had a solemn promise to fulfill to his prince and his people. It was as simple as that. There was no personal animosity in his feelings for Lord Stanhope, or for the daughter.

Lady Elizabeth might be young and innocent and beautiful; he might desire her as he had desired no other woman; but what had to be done, would be done. That was the way of the desert.

"I understand that Lord Jonathan has made quite a name for himself in this part of the world, as well as a sizable fortune," commented Colonel Winters as their small party gathered in the ship's lounge for tea.

His wife lowered her voice so as not to be overheard by the other passengers. "Did you say he is the second son of the Duke of Deakin, my dear?"

He nodded and continued. "The elder brother is the Viscount Lindsay. I believe the family seats include Grantley Manor in Northumberland; Kendalstone Castle, Oxfordshire; as well as a fashionable Park Lane address in London." He stroked his chin in a gesture that only served to emphasize the jowls forming there. He was twenty years older than his pretty wife; he looked thirty years older. "Course, one day it will all go to the elder son," he pontificated, "lock, stock, and barrel."

Amelia Winters shook her dainty head and declared, "I don't agree with the policy of primogeniture. It seems particularly harsh on the daughters and younger sons who lose by it." She gave a quick sideways glance. "If you don't mind my saying so, Lady Elizabeth."

She chose her words carefully. "While I understand the need to keep titles and estates intact, of course, it does make it difficult for those who are not the firstborn son to marry where they might like."

"Very well put, Lady Elizabeth," complimented the colonel. "Not that the lack of a dukedom seems to have prevented Lord Jonathan from making his mark on the world, I must say."

"Perhaps he is a particularly unique individual," ventured Elizabeth. If her suspicions were correct, he was far more unique than either the colonel or his wife dreamt.

"He certainly is a handsome devil," murmured Mrs. Winters. "I wonder if he's married."

"Not to my knowledge," supplied her husband.

"Speaking of marriage . . ." Elizabeth felt she could broach the subject since it had been raised by her chaperons. "Why does everyone I meet ask if I'm married? When I answer truthfully that I am not, they seem surprised."

The answer came from behind Elizabeth, spoken in a deep, husky baritone that sent shivers down her spine. "Perhaps it is because an unmarried woman of seventeen or eighteen is unusual in the Black Land."

Hulbert Mathias Winters popped to his feet and snapped his heels together. "My lord."

"Colonel Winters, we meet again," the latecomer responded amiably.

"May I have the pleasure of introducing my wife, Mrs. Winters, and our traveling companion, Lady Elizabeth Guest."

The man politely inclined his head. "Ladies, the pleasure is all mine."

"I had the distinct honor of meeting your father once at his club in London," volunteered the colonel as they took their seats around the tea table. "How is His Grace?"

The reply was guarded. "My father was well enough the last time I saw him."

"And your mother, the duchess?"

Elizabeth glimpsed the shadow that flitted

across Lord Jonathan's features before he responded. "I'm afraid my mother died nearly six years ago."

Colonel Winters was nonplussed. "So sorry. Didn't know, of course. My condolences, naturally."

He echoed stiffly, "Naturally."

The military man cleared his throat with a cough. "And your elder brother, Viscount Lindsay . . ."

A slightly sardonic smile came and went on the man's mouth. A generous mouth, Elizabeth decided, but one that was quite capable of cruelty.

"Lawrence was engaged in his favorite pastime on the last occasion we were both at Grantley Manor." He went on to answer the colonel's unspoken question. "My brother was breaking in his newest stallion."

"Your family seat is in Northumberland, I believe," spoke up Amelia Winters.

"Yes, it is."

"Lady Elizabeth is also from the North," she offered.

For the first time since he had joined their party in the ship's lounge, Lord Jonathan looked directly at her. His expression was polite, nothing more. She felt a stab of disappointment. There was no recognition in the indifferent blue eyes, no hint of surprise, no spark of awareness. Perhaps she had imagined his earlier reaction to her.

She quickly glanced down at Lord Jonathan's hands. She had not imagined everything. For there, on the middle finger of his right hand, for all the world to see, was a gold ring!

Even as the beat of her heart quickened its pace, Elizabeth reminded herself it could simply be a coincidence. The rounded cross shape of an ankh had to be the most common of the ancient hieroglyphs. For all she knew, every man, woman, and child in Egypt wore such a ring.

Then, too, the man who had come to her aid in the bazaar had been a native of this land, robed in the traditional headdress and long, flowing *kuftan*.

Lord Jonathan blithely inquired, "May I ask where you are from in the North, Lady Elizabeth?"

"St-Stanhope Hall in Yorkshire," she managed without spilling her tea.

"A beautiful spot, I hear."

Her color deepened. "We think so, my lord."

He accepted a cup of tea and several small, sweet cakes, but Elizabeth noticed that he did not touch either one. Instead, he resumed their conversation. "Is this your first visit to Egypt?"

"It is," she replied, hoping that her own features revealed nothing of her distractions.

Something flickered for a moment behind Lord Jonathan's eyes. "And are you enjoying yourself?"

"Immensely," she said in a brisk tone. Then she impulsively added, "The day before yesterday we spent the entire morning shopping in the local bazaars."

"Lady Elizabeth is quite a shopper," laughed Amelia Winters.

Lord Jonathan crossed one leather-booted foot over the other and said in an amused drawl, "I assume it was not the shopping that brought you all the way to Egypt."

Was he having a bit of sport at her expense? If so, she did not care for it, not one bit. "As a matter of fact, my lord, I am journeying up the Nile to join my father."

"Indeed," he said with a spark of genuine interest.

"Lady Elizabeth's father is the renowned archaeologist, Lord Stanhope," interjected Colonel Winters on her behalf.

"I see," he replied coolly.

"Perhaps you have heard of my father," she said, suddenly eager for any news of Papa.

There was a noncommittal shrug of his broad shoulders. "Few people in Egypt have not at least *heard* of Lord Stanhope."

She leaned toward him. "Have you met my father?"

Her hopes were dashed when he admitted, "I'm afraid I've not had the pleasure."

Elizabeth blinked, sat back, and took a deep breath. Any word of her father would have been welcomed. It was regrettable that Lord Jonathan was unacquainted with him.

Amelia Winters did her best to pick up the threads of their conversation and carry on. "How far are you journeying on the *Star of Egypt*, Lord Jonathan?"

"All the way to Luxor." He went on almost without pause. "I have some farmland in the region where I raise cotton."

"Cotton," the colonel repeated thoughtfully. "Interesting."

"I believe that one day Egyptian cotton will be known around the world," Lord Jonathan stated in a businesslike tone.

Elizabeth heard herself say to him, "Perhaps you will meet my father, after all, for Luxor and the Valley of the Kings is where I am to join him."

An ironic smile touched his lips. "In that case, I will look forward to a formal introduction."

Colonel Winters cleared his throat and interjected, "Seems we're about to be entertained with our tea."

A small band of Egyptian musicians entered the steamship's lounge with their instruments. Without preamble, they began to play. The music was ethereal, free-flowing, with vestiges of ancient melodies.

After the last note died away, Lord Jonathan leaned closer to her and said quietly, "The larger flute is called a *nay*; the smaller is a *salamiyyah*, used in Egypt to accompany Sufi songs and dances."

"What is the long-necked instrument with the metal strings?" she asked even as his warm breath stirred the tendrils of hair at her nape, making it difficult, very difficult indeed, for her to concentrate on what he was saying.

He explained patiently, "That one is a *buzuq*. Next to it is an *'ud*. The large-frame drum you see is a *tar*."

"We heard the small brass finger cymbals played while we were in Alexandria," Elizabeth told him. "But I do not recognize what the last man is blowing on."

"It is a type of oboe called a *mizmar*."

"The music is haunting," she whispered as the band began to play another song, "and very beautiful."

"Like the Black Land itself," the handsome man murmured so only she could hear.

Then they gave the music their undivided attention.

It was not until later that afternoon as they were parting company to return to their appropriate staterooms—even aboard ship it was expected that they would change for dinner—that Lord Jonathan said something to her that would haunt Elizabeth for days, for weeks, afterward.

He looked intently into her eyes and warned, "On this journey up the Nile, which we call the River of Life, be careful what you seek, Lady Elizabeth. You may find more than you had bargained for."

Elizabeth felt her stomach tighten in an odd manner. Surely the man had not guessed her secret.

She smiled thinly and replied, "I will be careful, I assure you, Lord Jonathan."

For what she sought, Elizabeth alone knew, was the key to the past and to her own future.

Chapter 3

$\sim\!\!\!\sim\!\!\!\circlearrowright\!\!\circlearrowright\!\!\!\sim$

S he could not sleep.

Elizabeth pushed aside the cool cotton sheets, drew back the mosquito netting, and reached for the dressing gown at the foot of her bed.

There was no sense in trying any longer. She had been lying awake for what seemed like hours.

Without bothering to light the gas lamp on the table beside the bed, she slipped her feet into a pair of satin slippers and tied the sash of her dressing gown securely around her waist. Then she opened the door of her stateroom and stepped out onto the deck of the steamship.

The night was still. The *Star of Egypt* had dropped anchor until the morning.

She leaned her forearms on the ship's railing and gazed out across the Nile. The moon was ablaze, a brilliant sphere of light against a midnight blue sky. She could see the palm groves along the river's edge; the lush, green fields in the foreground and the desert bluffs beyond.

Between the fertile fields and the desert the landscape was studded with shadowy huts, pristine white villas, and the ruins of ancient temples. There was a trickle of silver moonlight on the water. The night breeze brought with it the scent of lotus and papyrus; acacia, tamarind, and eucalyptus.

Every now and then she heard the sound of a large fish splashing in the river, or perhaps it was a hungry crocodile hunting for its dinner.

Elizabeth felt a strange chill course down her spine. All around her were shadows of the past. Yet there was a sense of timelessness about this place.

How many men and women through the ages, she wondered, had stood thus and gazed out on the eternal landscape of Egypt? What had they been thinking? Feeling?

Perhaps Cleopatra herself had stood on the deck of a royal barge and gazed over the dark blue waters, and recited the words of the ancient hymn: "Hail to you, oh Nile. Sprung from earth; come to nourish Egypt. Food provider, bounty maker, who creates all that is good."

Surely in ages yet to be, another woman would stand here and look out over the blue waters and wonder who had come before her to this place. What would she be thinking and feeling?

The past, the present, the future: they were as one to the Nile, the River of Life.

Elizabeth shivered, and wrapped her arms tightly around herself. To think that she had very nearly been denied this journey to the Black Land. She thought back to the conversation she had had last summer with her cousin; it had been the turning point. . . .

"I am afraid you have had your head filled with fantasies," Horace Fitz-Hugh lectured his young cousin. "Egypt is a miserable place. It is hot and dusty, full of flies and mosquitoes, and the most primitive and appalling living conditions." He shuddered, remembering. "The sun is quite relentless. I was ill from it the entire time I spent there."

"But I so want to go to Egypt." Elizabeth's voice took on a dreamy quality. "It is said that the blues are bluer, that the sand sparkles like diamonds, that the sunlight is brighter than the sunlight anywhere else on earth. Papa once told me there is an old saying: 'In Egypt, you are closer to the gods.' " She added for good measure, "It has been three years since Papa was home. I do miss him so."

Her middle-aged cousin shifted his considerable weight from one foot to the other. "Of course, it is natural that you should miss your father. But for you to go all the way to that desolate, godforsaken land—"

She interrupted, "The landscape is splendid, is it not? And the Nile and the desert and the wondrous Pyramids of Giza and the great temple at Abu Simbel?"

There was a subtle change in Horace Fitz-

Hugh's expression. "Yes, there are wondrous sights to behold, that is true. The temple at Karnak. The Sphinx. The colorful *dahabieh* as they float up the Nile." He caught himself and quickly amended, "But it is not a place for a young lady of delicate constitution, like yourself."

Elizabeth was nearly out of patience. She had to go to Egypt. She had to see Papa. She simply had to. Her father had not only recently written asking her to come, but he had sent Colonel and Mrs. Winters to act as her official chaperons. There would be no better time or opportunity for her to go. If she could convince Cousin Horace, perhaps he would take her side and help persuade Maman.

An idea occurred to her. Unlike so many of the young ladies of her acquaintance—who suffered from everything from the vapors to melancholia, and secretly enjoyed every minute of it, in her opinion—she was as healthy as a horse. Nevertheless . . .

She touched a lace hankie to her nose. "But I understand the weather in the winter in Egypt is quite beneficial to a delicate constitution."

"The winter months are more favorable than the time of the Nile flooding, or the awful heat," her cousin admitted.

She studied her hands for a moment. "I suffered greatly last winter here in Yorkshire."

That much was true. It had been a dismal five months from the time of her sister Annelise's death until the promise and hope of spring. Her dear, sweet Annie gone in less than a fortnight;

it was still hard for her to bear the loss.

Cousin Horace was visibly uncomfortable at the reminder of Lady Annelise's passing. At fifteen, she had been the youngest child of Lord and Lady Stanhope; an angel with blue eyes and pale hair and a sweet disposition. He cleared his throat. "It was a most difficult time for our family. For everyone."

"Yes. And the weather was particularly cold and damp, do you not agree?" She sighed. "I do not think I could bear another winter in Yorkshire like the last."

There was a concession of sorts made. "Perhaps the sun and the dry warmth of Egypt would be beneficial to your health, Lady Elizabeth."

She sighed again and looked out the window at the gardens and the park beyond. "I am sure it would be. But Maman has said that I may not go."

"She . . . Lady Stanhope may not have considered all the benefits," he said carefully. "If the opportunity presents itself, I could speak with her on the matter."

A smile lit up Elizabeth's face, quite bedazzling her distant relation. "That would be most kind of you, Cousin Horace."

He coughed. "Not at all, my dear. Not at all. We must look to your health, after all."

"Indeed, cousin, life is short, is it not, and must be lived to its fullest."

He cleared his throat for the umpteenth time, obviously at a loss to understand the philosophical musings of one so young *and* female, and dutifully escorted her in to tea.

Within three days, Maman had given her consent, and preparations had begun for her journey.

Now here she was gazing out over the River Nile. Elizabeth was tempted to pinch herself to make certain it was not all a dream.

She must commit to memory the beauty of this time and place. She must savor each moment for both of their sakes: hers and Annie's. For her dear, sweet sister would never make the journey to this distant land; she had already traveled on that final journey to Heaven itself.

Elizabeth reached up and wiped at her cheeks; they were damp with tears.

It was some time later—it could have been minutes or hours, since time seemed to have no meaning on this magical night—that Elizabeth sensed she was no longer alone. Before she actually saw him, or heard him, she knew it was Lord Jonathan. She was not certain how this could be, it simply was so. His voice came to her through the night, its rich, sensuous baritone sending tendrils of awareness to every nerve ending in her body:

"Hail to thee, Nefetari, most beauteous
   of women,
Consort of the God, beloved of Him who
   wears the two crowns,
Thou art fair in face, graced with a body
   and spirit that is perfection.
Isis incarnate, how the Gods worship thee!
   Thy breasts art sweeter than honey,

Thy beauty greater than the fabled Nefetiri,
   Thy skin finer than the gold of Kush,
      Thy eyes darkest ebony.
Thy voice is more pleasing than the music
   of the harp, than the sound of the
   River of Life at dawn.
     Thou art favored by the Gods.
They call thee by name and it is Egypt.
And when They see thee come it is said, the
   Beautiful One comes!"

When he was finished, she said, just above a whisper, "How very beautiful even today is the love poem written by the Pharaoh Merneptah Seti to his beloved wife."

Lord Jonathan stepped out of the shadows and into the moonlight. He stared at her in astonishment. "You know of this poem?"

"I know of it."

"And of Nefetari?"

She nodded, her unbound hair brushing back and forth across her shoulders like a swath of silk. "Named for the wife of the Great Ramses, she and Merneptah Seti had four children together before she grew ill from the strange fever that appeared at the time of the Nile flooding, and died."

He looked down at her, and his expression was one of genuine admiration. "You're familiar with the ancient pharaohs."

"To some degree," Elizabeth said modestly.

She was not about to confess the extent of her knowledge. It would not do to inform Lord Jonathan, any more than it would Colonel and

Mrs. Winters, that she was well read on the subject of ancient Egypt. Such a claim, Nanny had drummed into her since childhood, would appear boastful and impolite.

But there was more to her reticence than mere modesty. Maman strictly forbade any discussion of Egypt, or its history and artifacts, within her hearing. It was the harlot Egypt, after all, who had seduced her husband, who had heartlessly taken him from her and from her children.

Her mother's detestation of the subject had not prevented Elizabeth from sneaking into the little-used library at Stanhope Hall and reading voraciously, of course. She had cut her teeth on Baron Denon's autobiography, *Voyage dans l'haute et basse Egypt*, before tackling Giovanni Belzoni's accounts of his exploits in the Black Land and Champollion's translation of the hieroglyphs found on the Rosetta Stone.

Lord Jonathan suggested softly, "It would seem that you are your father's daughter, after all."

With obvious pride Elizabeth declared, "I am my father's daughter."

It was only at that point she remembered she wasn't wearing any underclothes, just a sheer cotton nightdress and a light robe. Scarcely the proper attire in which a lady entertained a gentleman. A meeting such as theirs would be considered highly inappropriate, even scandalous, back in England.

Society's rules were very strict about what an unmarried woman could and could not do. She was carefully attended on each and every social occasion. She must never walk alone in London, take a hansom cab, or travel in an unreserved train compartment. She must be accompanied by her mother or a chaperon or, at the very least, her maid when traveling to and from a ball. She was never left alone with a man in the conservatory, the library, or any private place. Such rules were de rigueur, according to Maman, and Maman should know.

Of course, Elizabeth reminded herself, back home it was extremely unlikely that she would find herself alone with a man on the deck of a steamship in the middle of the night.

Lord Jonathan took another step toward her, and her pulse began to beat double. He seemed even taller than he had that afternoon. She could see his blue eyes clearly, and the stubble of unshaven hair on his chin.

He was wearing a long, exotic robe over a pair of dress trousers and a formal evening shirt. The shirt was collarless and had been left unbuttoned to the waist; the sleeves were rolled up nearly to the elbows.

The loose-fitting material of the *kuftan* did nothing to camouflage his broad shoulders, muscular arms, and lean torso. The open shirtfront revealed a column of deeply tanned skin. His forearms and the dusting of hair along them were bronzed to a golden brown, undoubtedly the result of hours spent under a hot desert sun.

Elizabeth found her stunned gaze at eye level with his bare chest.

He was magnificent.

Her hand came up, and she realized at the last moment that she'd nearly reached out and touched him. She had never seen a man in a state of partial undress. Even so, she knew he was more muscular, more masculine, more handsome, than anyone of her acquaintance.

And far more dangerous.

She was suddenly aware of how little separated her bare skin from the cool night air and the virtual stranger who was standing only a few feet from her. She shivered; gooseflesh covered her arms and legs. She could hear the sound of her own heart beating wildly beneath her breast.

He was observant. "Are you cold, Lady Elizabeth?"

"Just a momentary chill, my lord," she assured him. "I'm fine now. Thank you."

He gave her a long, measuring look. "You could not sleep?"

She knew of no reason to lie to him. "I could not sleep."

He was unexpectedly gentle with her. "You've been crying."

"A little."

"What do you weep for, my lady?"

"I weep for beauty, the beauty of the Nile and this land," she admitted in a small, choked voice. And for Annie, she thought to herself.

"This country can do that to a man—" he corrected himself "—or a woman the first time it is seen." There was an undertow of fascination in his tone. "Egypt is the land of legend, suspended between reality and myth. Everywhere a man looks, he finds shadows of the past."

"Yes, that's it exactly," she exclaimed, looking up at him, meeting his gaze head-on.

For a few electrifying moments, they both seemed to forget everything and everyone but each other.

Elizabeth's heart began to pound even harder and faster. Her lips were dry; she wet them with the tip of her tongue. The fine hairs on the back of her neck stood on end. Her stomach turned over in the oddest fashion. Her breasts seemed to swell; their tips were suddenly erect, sensitive; they rubbed against the nearly transparent material of her nightgown. She was tempted to cover them with her hands, for there was a sensual heat in Lord Jonathan's eyes that was unmistakable.

Her own experience with men was limited, of course, but she had overheard Society women, sophisticated beauties who'd had many love affairs, discussing the male of the species at the weekend house parties at Stanhope Hall.

There were some men—just a few, it seemed—who could look at a woman and make her feel desirable, cherished, singularly important. A man like that could make love to a woman and never touch her, never utter a word. That was the way Lord Jonathan was looking at her at that very moment, and it left Elizabeth struggling to put air into her lungs. She wanted to melt all over him.

They both heard a splash in the river nearby, and the spell was broken.

When he finally spoke again, Lord Jonathan smiled sardonically. "I have not been totally honest with you, Lady Elizabeth."

She noticed that his expression bore no trace of an apology. "Indeed, my lord?"

A muscle in his face started to twitch. "I'm afraid not."

She wondered what she was supposed to say after a gentleman—if, indeed, he was a gentleman—confessed to being less than truthful.

He moved restlessly along the ship's deck. "I may have led you, and Colonel and Mrs. Winters, to believe that all is well between my family and myself."

"It is not?" she blurted out.

"It most certainly is not," he said with a bitterness that surprised her. "I have been estranged from my family for many years. Indeed, I have not seen my father, or my elder brother, Lawrence, since the death of my mother."

"She died six years ago," she said softly.

"Yes, six years ago this Christmas Eve, but . . ." He was obviously at a loss to know how she came into possession of such a fact.

"You mentioned it at tea this afternoon," Elizabeth pointed out to him.

"I did, didn't I?" He shook his head from side to side as if questioning his own sanity for a moment. Then he went on with a hint of self-scorn in his voice. "There is more I feel I must tell you."

Elizabeth raised a hand to her throat. "If you feel you must."

This was a most unusual and unorthodox conversation to be having with a gentleman. Of course, it was a most unusual and extraordinary situation to find herself in.

Still, if it was the ordinary she'd wanted, she could have stayed home in Yorkshire, Elizabeth quickly reminded herself.

Lord Jonathan made a vigorous gesture with both hands. "It is well-known back in Northumberland that certain men of the Wicke family inherit their blue eyes along with a regrettable tendency for being a bit wild."

"A bit wild?" she repeated, at a loss to comprehend what he was trying to tell her.

He frowned—drawing together the well-shaped eyebrows that were the same shade as the hair on his head—and tried once more to explain. "Black sheep, Lady Elizabeth. Every other generation there is a black sheep."

Was the man quite mad? Discussing agriculture at this time of night? "Black sheep," she echoed, faintly dismayed. "I don't understand."

He stopped pacing the ship's deck, planted his feet squarely in front of her, and folded his arms across his chest. "I am the blackest of the black sheep of the Wicke family. It is the reason I left home. The reason that I have not seen my father, nor my brother, in six long years."

She finally understood, and she was sympathetic. "My lord, I know exactly how you feel," she said with great conviction.

He was taken aback. "You do?"

She nodded. "I have not seen my own father in three years. Even then it was only for a brief fortnight before he rushed back to Egypt."

"I hardly think—"

She held up one hand. "There is more."

He rested his fists on his hips and studied her. It made her more than a little nervous, Elizabeth acknowledged.

"More?"

It was painful for her, but she needed to tell him everything. It was the only way to prove to him that she understood. "I have always been a great disappointment to Maman."

He seemed surprised by her admission. "Good God, whatever has led you to that conclusion?"

"It is as plain as the nose on my face," she stated clearly and forthrightly. "I am too outspoken. Too headstrong. Too impulsive. And too tall."

A burst of laughter escaped him. "Too tall?"

She was wounded. "I cannot do anything about my excessive height, my lord. But I refuse to cower in the corner, or somehow try to make myself appear small and dainty when I am not."

It was obvious he was trying to soothe her hurt feelings. He said kindly, "I don't think you're too tall. I think you're perfect just as you are."

She blushed with pleasure. "That is only because you are a man of such great stature yourself, Lord Jonathan."

"Ah-hem."

He couldn't be embarrassed by the compliment; it was little more than an observation on her part, Elizabeth reassured herself.

She was determined, however, to be honest with him to the bitter end. She sighed and volunteered, "There is even more, I am afraid."

He couldn't resist teasing her. "Apparently your sins are without number."

She took a deep breath and plunged ahead. "I believe having a Season in London is a complete waste of both time and money."

The expression on his handsome face was deadly serious, but she noticed that his chest seemed to be moving up and down as if he were laughing. "You do?" he finally managed.

"Yes, I do. The whole business is degrading. It's designed to do nothing more than show off young, marriageable girls as if they were goods on display."

"You have a point," he conceded.

"Even if it were not, a debut is likely to be a disaster in my case. I wouldn't know what to say or do. I'm not very good at small talk. I don't dance at all well. I'm far too tall for most men. And . . ."

"And . . ." he prompted.

She couldn't stop now. "And I cannot bear the prospect of a future in which I am expected to marry the son of some innocuous earl, bear my husband an heir and a spare, and then blithely initiate a long string of love affairs as do the other members of the 'Marlborough House Set.' "

"The 'Marlborough House Set'?"

"Those who socialize with His Royal Highness, the Prince of Wales," she explained. "I'm not suited to that life, my lord. I'm simply not."

He seemed intrigued. "What kind of life are you suited for, my lady?"

Elizabeth supposed she was about to reveal herself to be a foolish romantic. So be it, she decided. "I want to live life to its fullest, to travel the world, to have many grand adventures, and then when I am older, I want to marry, settle down in the country, and raise a homeful of happy, healthy children. I don't need a grand house, or a large estate, but I would like a library for my books and land enough for a garden."

"A garden?" His voice vibrated with the word.

"Yes. Specifically a rose garden."

Lord Jonathan was no longer teasing her. "And have you met this man, this paragon of domestic virtue whom you will marry?"

She was unaware of the beautifully innocent gaze she turned on him. "Sadly, I have not."

His manner was suddenly brusque. "Such a man is nothing more than a dream, Lady Elizabeth."

"Perhaps," she retorted. "But he is my dream. And one day I will find him."

Black Jack shook his head. Good God, what was wrong with him?

Unable to sleep, he had come out on deck for some fresh air. The next thing he knew, he'd been spouting ancient love poetry to a child.

He scowled and thought: *This is no time to start lying to yourself, Jack. Lady Elizabeth is no child.*

She was young, yes. But she was not a child. Not with a lovely body like hers, and a sharp, intelligent mind to match. In her lace-trimmed dressing gown she managed to be both girl and woman, both demure and desirable.

It was the damnedest thing.

For a moment he allowed his imagination to run wild. He closed his eyes and he could almost feel the smooth silkiness of her skin beneath his touch; the long, luxuriant strands of her hair wound tightly around his hand.

The scent of her was subtle, unperfumed, enticing. The sound of her voice was pleasing to his ear: it was clear and melodious and slightly husky in a very sexy way she was obviously unaware of.

He opened his eyes and looked down into her face. Her mouth was moist and pink, the bottom lip slightly more generous than the top. He wondered if she would taste of honey, or perhaps of sweet red wine.

He imagined the sensation of his mouth on hers, the tip of his tongue tracing the delicate outline of her ear, his lips pressed to the vulnerable curve of her neck.

Her figure was surprisingly mature for a girl not yet eighteen. He found that his hands itched to touch her, to cup the fullness of her breasts in his palms, to feel her nipples grow hard and rigid as he ran his finger back and forth across their sensitive tips.

He knew her soft belly would quiver deliciously beneath his caress. There would be an inviting crispness to the chestnut brown curls nestled at the apex of her thighs. She was a virgin, but he would bring forth the hot, sweet essence from her body, and it would cling to his fingertips, his lips, his throbbing manhood, driving him wild, making him crazy with need until he spread her lovely legs and drove into her again and again, seeking his release, spilling his seed into her welcoming womb.

Black Jack nearly groaned aloud.

He realized he had allowed Elizabeth to see more than he had intended when she inquired, "Lord Jonathan, are you quite all right?"

He adjusted the *kuftan* slightly to prevent any embarrassment to either of them, and gritted through his teeth, "Just an old wound acting up, my lady."

She was very prettily concerned. She even reached out and tentatively touched his arm. "You poor man, what may I do to help?"

He was sorely tempted to tell her: Let me take you to my bed, pretty lady, and make love to you until neither of us can see straight. Instead, he said: "Nothing. It is nothing really. The pain will pass."

She would not drop the matter. "Is it a very old wound?"

He reminded himself to keep breathing. "Very old."

The words came from her almost unconsciously. "Have you fought in many wars, my lord?"

"Too many."

"Are you a soldier, then?"

He told her the truth. "Sometimes. Soldier, businessman, adventurer, explorer: I've done them all at one time or another."

Her cheeks became flush with excitement; her eyes sparkled. "How very thrilling. Sometimes I wish I were a man so I could go wherever I pleased and do whatever I wanted."

He wondered if Elizabeth Guest had any idea how refreshing and unsophisticated she was. No doubt she would be mortified to know that he could read her like an open book. She let everything show. There was no mystery, no artifice, no game playing, no female wiles. She was exactly what she appeared to be, unlike most people.

Unlike him.

Then another possibility occurred to Black Jack. What if she was one of those women who resented being female?

"Do you enjoy being a woman, Elizabeth?"

Her answer was direct. "Yes, I do. Of course, I would prefer to be independent as well. To have my own money and the opportunity to do what I like."

"To grow roses?"

"Yes. And to travel, to study, to live life."

"To its fullest."

She nodded. "To its fullest."

He couldn't resist asking. "Have you ever been alone with a man?"

She put her nose a little higher in the air. "Certainly."

"Indeed."

"Well, after a fashion. There was Trout."

"Trout?" he said in a low, mocking tone.

"The head gardener at Stanhope Hall. Or at least he was many years ago."

He controlled the flicker of amusement her words caused. "Just how old is this Trout?"

She thought for a minute. "Eighty. Perhaps eighty-one."

He dismissed the gardener from his mind. "I don't think Trout counts. Have there been any others?"

He could tell she was trying to appear unperturbed. "My brother, Franklin. Papa, of course. And Cousin Horace."

"Ah, Cousin Horace."

She mumbled something that sounded like, "But he is Maman's friend."

"Maman's friend?"

All of a sudden the usually clear pallor of Lady

Elizabeth's face was flooded with red. "Her special friend."

"Special friend." He was not normally so dense.

She blurted out, "Cousin Horace is my mother's lover."

He cleared his throat self-consciously. "I see."

The girl was quick to explain. "They are very discreet, naturally."

"Naturally."

"But I have known for years. I presume everyone has." She drew her delicate brows together. "You must not judge Maman too harshly, as I did in the beginning."

"I'll try not to," he said dryly.

"I came to understand as I got older that Papa's only real interest was in Egyptology. He would go off and leave Maman by herself for years at a time."

"She could have gone with him," he suggested.

"If Maman had accompanied him to Egypt, there would have been no one left to look after Stanhope Hall, the farms, the tenants, the lands, and the myriad details it takes to run an estate of that size. Eventually there were us children, too."

"I'm surprised that you've developed such an avid interest in Egypt when it is the very thing that took your father from you."

She told him feelingly, "Egypt fascinates me. It always has. Perhaps it is in the blood."

He found himself in the grip of an odd feeling of disquiet. "You are truly your father's daughter."

And he must never forget that. Not even for a minute, he reminded himself gruffly. He wasn't on the *Star of Egypt*, cruising up the Nile, for his own pleasure. He was on a sacred mission. He had made a solemn vow and he must keep it.

In fact, he'd been a damned fool for staying out here with the girl as long as he had. If the colonel or Mrs. Winters were to discover them together under the present circumstances, he would never be allowed to speak to her, or to see her again. Somehow the prospect of that left him with a tight, gut-wrenching feeling in his belly.

He was more abrupt with her than he meant to be. "It grows late."

"Indeed, it does, my lord."

He found himself repeating the words he had said to her once before. "You understand, Lady Elizabeth, that this little incident must remain our secret."

She repeated, "Remain our secret."

He was forced to be blunt. "Otherwise, I am afraid, it might compromise your reputation. I may not have been in England for a long time, but I know that even a chance meeting such as ours would be severely frowned upon."

"Severely," she echoed in a monotone.

Black Jack stepped back into the shadows. The light of the moon shone down on him and illuminated his arm. He watched Elizabeth's gaze descend on his right hand, and realized it was shown in every detail.

But her attention was fixed on the object encircling his middle finger, on the heavy gold ring he wore as a symbol of his loyalty to Prince Ramses.

Her eyes opened even wider, then narrowed. Her expression wavered between curiosity and anger. Finally she exclaimed with a sharp cry of recognition, "It was you in the bazaar!"

He took a deep breath and at last confirmed her suspicions. "Yes."

Chapter 4

"I do not like being deceived, my lord," said Elizabeth in a primly angry voice, realizing that was exactly what he had done: deceive her.

"No, my lady."

She lifted her chin, knowing there was a look of pure fury in her eyes, and not caring a whit if he saw it. "I do not like being lied to, nor made a fool of."

"No, my lady."

She was quickly running out of patience. "Nor do I care to be patronized."

"Yes, my lady."

She stamped her slippered foot on the ship's deck. "And I would appreciate it if you would stop responding to everything I say with either 'No, my lady' or 'Yes, my lady.' "

"Yes, my lady."

"There! You've done it again," she pointed out.

"My apologies, my lady."

"You, my lord, are a most exasperating man."

"Yes, my—" Just in the nick of time Lord Jonathan caught himself.

"You did, however, save me from those awful thugs in the bazaar." Elizabeth supposed she had to give him his due. Fair was fair, after all. He had come to her rescue. He had conceivably saved her from a fate worse than death itself. "I thank you for that."

With a small inclination of his handsome head, Lord Jonathan murmured, "You are most welcome, Lady Elizabeth."

She arched one skeptical brow in his direction and began to tap her foot in agitation. "I would like to know something, my lord."

He shot her a curious glance. "Yes?"

There was an underlying edge of suspicion to her voice. "That day in the bazaar, why were you following me?"

"Following you, my lady?"

"Yes, following me." Was he hard of hearing, or simply a bit dimwitted?

His expression was one of practiced innocence. "Whatever makes you think I was—"

She cut him off adroitly. "Do not take me for a fool, Lord Jonathan. I may be young, I may be a little naive, but I am not stupid."

He gave her a long, hard look. "I never thought you were."

Perhaps he didn't think so.

Just because she had been treated like some brainless half-wit by every other male she had ever met, just because it had been drummed into her head by Maman that gentlemen expected young ladies to be gay and witty and entertaining, and that being gay and witty and entertaining most certainly did *not* include a discussion of ancient Egyptian mummification methods—she had found that gentlemen could be so squeamish about embalming details like extracting the brain through the nose of the corpse—did not mean that Lord Jonathan was like all the others.

Indeed, he was the singularly most unusual man she had ever met.

Elizabeth placed her hands on her hips; her toe was still tapping. "Well?"

He took a step or two closer to her until they were separated by only inches. He towered over her, but Elizabeth held her ground. It took all of her courage and determination to do so.

"Has anyone ever told you that you are utterly irresistible and utterly beautiful when you get your dander up?" he murmured, reaching out to cup her chin.

Her mouth dropped open. No one had ever spoken to her as Lord Jonathan was. No one had ever touched her as Lord Jonathan was touching her.

"No," she said as last, and didn't recognize the husky sound as her own voice.

"Then the gentlemen of your acquaintance have been sorely negligent," he stated, and without warning, swooped down to capture her mouth.

They had all lied to her.

Every last one of them. Maman. Nanny. Her elder sister, Caroline. The gossiping housemaids she had overheard early one morning as they dusted the statuary in the hallway outside her bedroom. Even Colette.

They had all led her to believe that some-day, one day, a handsome young gentleman—her fiancé, to be sure—would draw her behind a potted palm in the conservatory, the music room, or perhaps in the orangery and, with great trepidation and very little skill, bend toward her and brush his lips quickly, tenderly, breathless-ly, across hers. Thus, they had said, would she receive her first kiss.

They had all lied.

One moment she was standing there on the ship's deck, gazing up at Lord Jonathan. The next he was thrusting his tongue into her mouth.

She was stunned.

This was no kiss; it was an invasion. An inva-sion of the most intimate sort. She was quite cer-tain she was going to faint dead away. Perhaps she would have, too, if Lord Jonathan had not at that moment reached out and caught her about the waist.

He was very strong and hard and unnerving, one tiny part of her brain acknowledged. The rest of her was reduced to a mass of quivering marmalade that had no brain.

Then his tongue was thrusting between her teeth again, tickling the roof of her mouth, teas-ing and entwining with her tongue, licking her lips, plunging halfway down her throat until a shiver raced along her body from head to toe and left her trembling in its wake.

She couldn't breathe. She didn't care.

She should have been repulsed. Instead, she found she only wanted more.

It couldn't be right to feel the way she was feeling; she prayed it wasn't wrong.

He brought her closer to him, and she could feel the heat pouring from his body, smell the distinctive scent that was his alone: it was a heady mixture of spirits and exotic spices, the strong Turkish coffee they had drunk after dinner and something she couldn't put her finger on, something she suspected was unique to this man.

She was vaguely aware of clutching the front of his shirt. She leaned into him, clung to him, hung on for dear life. She could feel his chest rise and fall in rapid succession; it was a wall of smooth flesh and rippling muscle. Through the thin material of her gown and robe, her nipples rubbed against the matt of crisp, dark hair. The sensations left Elizabeth reeling. Her hips thrust forward of their own volition, and she was acutely aware of something wedged between them: it was large and hard and alive!

First her heart was in her throat, then it tumbled all the way down to her feet. Her toes curled up in the most peculiar fashion. A tiny cry escaped her. She wanted him to stop. She wanted him to go on kissing her forever.

When in doubt, shut a woman up by kissing her, Black Jack told himself as he bent over and took Elizabeth's mouth.

It had worked before, it would work again. After all, the average female had any number of tried-and-true techniques in her little bag of tricks. A man had to "make do" with whatever he could find at hand.

A sardonic smile flashed across his handsome features. It would seem that *what* he'd found at hand this time was a tempting bit of baggage named Elizabeth.

The moment his lips touched hers, he knew it was the first time she had ever been kissed. She was caught completely off guard: her mouth was slightly open, her small pink tongue was touching the back of her smooth white teeth, his name was still on her lips.

She was so damn sweet and innocent, Jack reminded himself. Yet his desire for her drove him to continue the intimate kiss, to bury his hands in her hair—a glorious mass of fiery silk he loved to imagine in a wild tumble across his bare flesh—to bring her tempting body up against his.

God in heaven, she tasted like the night: all dark velvet, magic, and mystery.

He filled his lungs with her fragrance. He did not know how it could be, but she smelled faintly of wild roses. He could feel the pounding of her heart where his thumb skimmed the vulnerable spot at the base of her throat. He could make out the telltale hint of blue veins against porcelain skin.

He felt her draw in her breath, he felt her pulse race, and he felt the rising heat in his own blood.

He realized he wanted to do more than drive his tongue into her enticing mouth. He wanted to kiss her everywhere, to fill his hands with her and, in turn, feel her touch on him: stroking him, cupping him, adoring him, driving him to the brink of ecstasy and beyond.

His body thickened, his manhood swelled against his trousers, the friction between his body and hers nearly setting him off. He hadn't been this quickly or completely aroused since he was an inexperienced boy. It was hellish. It was heavenly.

Jack ignored all the warning bells going off in his head. He wanted very badly to lay Elizabeth down right there on the deck of the steamship, lift the soft lawn of her nightgown above her white thighs, and drive his flesh into hers, plunging into her again and again until he could not stand on his own two feet.

But he didn't.

It was her small cry that brought him to his senses. "Lord Jonathan—"

Bloody hell, he couldn't make love to her now. It was too much. It was too soon. He had to have patience. He had to stop or ruin forever any chance he had of successfully completing this mission.

Breathing hard, and with genuine reluctance, he drew back. "Yes, my lady?"

Her eyes were dazed, and she was obviously flustered. "I-I believe this is most improper, my lord."

"Yes, my lady."

"We shouldn't . . . we mustn't . . ."

"We aren't," he finished with a crooked smile.

She suddenly tried to be the very soul of propriety. She tugged at the sash of her robe and stammered, "I-I must say good night now, my lord. I would not want Colette to awaken and find me gone."

"Heaven forbid," he drawled.

She inclined her head slightly. "I take my leave of you, Lord Jonathan."

He imitated her action. "And I of you, Lady Elizabeth."

With her hand on the door of her stateroom, she hesitated and turned back to him with a delicately furrowed brow. "Is this what they mean when they speak of living life to its fullest, my lord?"

He wanted to laugh. He restrained himself, and simply said, "Not quite, my lady."

She frowned. "I see."

"Somehow I doubt very much if you do," he muttered under his breath as the cabin door closed behind her.

Jack swung around and made his way along the deck to his own stateroom. The pocket watch on the table beside his bed informed him that there wasn't much left to the night.

Perhaps it was just as well. He was uncomfortably aroused and he would only dream, he knew, of a beautiful young woman with innocent eyes and a lush, inviting body and the scent of roses in her hair.

Chapter 5

~ ∽◯◯◡ ~

S he had been duped.

Duped, pure and simple, Elizabeth decided over the course of the next three days.

That moonlit night on the deck of the *Star of Egypt*, Lord Jonathan had kissed her for one reason and one reason only: in order to distract her from the line of questioning she had been pursuing, a line of questioning that he obviously did not wish to answer.

The man was a clever devil.

A long list of other names for him came to mind as she lay in her bed at night, tossing and turning, unable to sleep, unable to forget his kiss. Cad. Bounder. Snake in the grass. Scoundrel. Seducer. Libertine.

Although Elizabeth wasn't actually certain she knew what a libertine was. She had seen the word in a book once, and had concluded it was something a true gentleman couldn't be, wouldn't be.

Of course, if Lord Jonathan's behavior suggested that he was something less than a proper gentleman, then surely her response to him made her a great deal less than a proper lady. For she had been thrilled by his kiss. Indeed, Elizabeth suspected that she had even been dreaming about it.

On several occasions, having finally drifted off to sleep in the early hours of the morning just before dawn, she had awakened to find her lips tasting of him, her nostrils filled with his scent, her body tingling with unnamed desires.

It was most disconcerting.

If she was truthful with herself, she had to admit she'd been willing enough. One kiss and she had completely forgotten the questions she'd wanted to ask Lord Jonathan: Why had he been following her in the bazaar that day? And why had he been garbed in native costume?

She still didn't have the answers. But at least she was on her guard now. She would not allow Lord Jonathan Wicke to use his considerable charms on her a second time. She would not be duped again. To that end she had avoided being alone with him since the night in question.

Elizabeth set her mouth in a firm line of resolve and adjusted the fine washing-silk of her under-garments as she finished dressing for the day. She was seeing to herself this morning. Colette had already gone ahead to organize the picnic luncheon being prepared for them by the ship's cook.

She would simply have to find another way to live life to its fullest, she lectured herself as the steamship prepared to dock in Cairo, a way not so wrought with perils and pitfalls.

A knock on the door of her cabin some minutes later cut short her ruminations on the subject.

"Lady Elizabeth," came the familiar voice of Amelia Winters. "We're ready to depart on our tour of the English gardens and the pyramids whenever you have completed your toilette."

"I will join you momentarily," she called back.

She quickly finished buttoning the bodice of her touring dress, one of a dozen or more she had brought with her to Egypt. Designed by Colette herself, and sewn by local women back home in Yorkshire in a dozen variations and colors, the split skirt was a rather ingenious idea that made the outfit eminently practical and well suited for walking, mountain climbing, and riding.

Somehow Maman had been convinced by the clever Frenchwoman of its propriety. Elizabeth was merely grateful that it did not require a crinolette or a bustle.

She slipped her feet into a pair of sensible walking shoes, and plunked a straw hat down on her head. Gathering up a pale blue sunshade and a matching reticule from the dressing table, she left the stateroom to join her companions.

Elizabeth knew her cheeks were flush with excitement; she walked a little faster.

It was only this morning that dear Colette had remarked in her native French, dark eyes flashing,

"I never thought I would see Egypt, the Pyramids of Giza, the guardian Sphinx, milady. The Emperor Napoleon himself once stood in awe of these ancient monuments. He said they appeared on the horizon as great mountain peaks."

Elizabeth had repeated to her friend and confidante, "There is an old Arab proverb that states: 'All things fear time; but time fears the pyramids.' "

Colette had clapped her hands together with glee. "And to think that we shall see these wondrous things before the day is out!"

"Before the day is out," she repeated now, feeling a rush of adrenaline surge through her veins.

This was a day she had waited years for, Elizabeth reflected as she hurried along the ship's deck to join her chaperons. This was the day she would see the Great Pyramids for herself.

"Alee has arranged for a large carriage to transport us to the gardens," explained the colonel once their party was assembled in the ship's lounge. "From there, anyone who wishes to continue on to the pyramids may do so."

With those final instructions, the group descended the gangplank and made their way to where the young, handsome Egyptian guide awaited them.

"Perhaps, *sitteh*, my lady, you will sit here in the front of the carriage where you can best see everything," he said to Elizabeth in perfect English.

"Thank you, Alee," she responded as he gave her a hand up into the horse-drawn vehicle.

Once they had settled themselves, Elizabeth was surprised and disturbed to find herself seated between Mrs. Winters and Lord Jonathan. Throughout the carriage ride she was intensely aware of his vibrant body next to hers. It was not an entirely unpleasant sensation, she had to confess.

"Good of you to join our little troupe, my lord," remarked the colonel, who was sitting directly across from him. "An extra man is always useful on these jaunts. Never know what you'll encounter in the countryside."

"It's my pleasure, Colonel. I haven't seen an English-style rose garden in years. I'm looking forward to it," commented the younger man.

"And the pyramids, my lord, are you also looking forward to seeing them again?" inquired Elizabeth.

Lord Jonathan turned to her, and his tanned face suddenly dissolved into a charmingly intimate smile, the very kind of smile she feared most. "Of course I am. But I feel it is only fair to warn you, Lady Elizabeth, no words or pictures can ever prepare you for your first sight of the Pyramids of Giza—the last survivors of the seven wonders of the ancient world. All the rest are gone. Long gone."

His words sent a strange chill coursing through her. Unbidden, tears pricked the corners of her eyes. She bit the inside of her bottom lip to stop herself from crying. "To think that the pyramids were already thousands of years old when Julius Caesar stood in awe before them."

"You are a student of history, then, Lady Elizabeth?" said the woman beside her.

"Only a little, Mrs. Winters," she admitted with a careful smile. "As you know, I'm far better versed on the subject of gardens and gardening." She was referring to an afternoon stroll the two of them had taken together around the park and grounds of Stanhope Hall last summer.

"That is precisely why my husband and I believe that you will especially enjoy our first outing of the day."

"You may have heard of Lady Charlotte Baker-Finch," said Colonel Winters as he sat rigidly upright, his hands resting atop his silver-tipped walking stick. *Once a military man, always a military man* was his motto. "Seems a few years ago the lady was advised for her health's sake to leave English winters behind, and settle here in Egypt."

"I understand she was a rather celebrated author and society hostess at one time," interjected his wife.

The man nodded. "Now she has a house in an oasis not far from the pyramids, and is known throughout the expatriate community for her hospitality and her rose gardens."

"She has graciously invited us to visit her this morning," announced Mrs. Winters as if it were a royal summons from the queen herself.

Elizabeth was delighted, and said so.

The colonel added, "Rumor has it that Lady Charlotte speaks fluent Arabic, and feels free to mingle with the natives, often administering medicines to their sick."

"The Egyptians regard her as a *Sheikha*, a wise woman," said Lord Jonathan, who was apparently well acquainted with the lady's reputation. "She is beloved throughout the country. People will often travel many miles to have her examine them."

"I have read her *Letters from Egypt*, published nearly a decade ago," admitted Elizabeth. "The tales of her life and adventures on the Nile have inspired many an Englishwoman to make the journey to Egypt."

"Did she inspire you to make the journey, my lady?" inquired the man sitting beside her. "Or do you intend to write your own book of adventures one day?"

Something in his tone made her glance at Lord Jonathan, but his expression told her nothing. Elizabeth tried to recall whether she'd spoken of her diary on the night they had met on deck. She clearly remembered the moonlight, the scent of lotus in the air, the glorious Nile, and a thousand other things. The sound of his voice. The golden skin on his chest and arms. The wicked smile. The sensuality in his deep blue eyes. The stunning kiss that had shaken her from head to toe . . .

But no matter how hard she tried, Elizabeth simply could not remember mentioning the diary in which she wrote every night before bed. Nor could she recall speaking of *Letters from Egypt*, which had, indeed, touched her very heart and soul. Nevertheless, she suspected Lord Jonathan was somehow well aware of both facts.

"I enjoyed Lady Charlotte's book," she finally answered him, "but it was not the only one I read in preparation for our voyage. The colonel was kind enough to choose several volumes from the library at Stanhope Hall for my edification. Perhaps he can expound on the subject since you seem so interested, my lord."

As if on cue, Colonel Winters proceeded to tell the younger man *exactly* which volumes he'd chosen and why, going on at great length on the splendidness of the estate's library.

Elizabeth bit a smile from the corners of her mouth. The colonel meant well, but he had a most unfortunate tendency to be a crashing bore.

It would do very nicely for him to "entertain" Lord Jonathan on their drive this morning.

Lady Charlotte Baker-Finch lived up to her reputation. Her whitewashed mud-brick house stood in the center of a lush oasis of clear blue ponds and towering palms. There was a huge carob tree by the front entrance, and roses everywhere; roses of every imaginable size, shape, and color.

The house was not large, but it wasn't small. They were shown into the formal parlor by a native woman, and found Lady Charlotte lounging on a cushioned bed that had once belonged to a minor pharaoh of the Nineteenth Dynasty.

The knobs of the bed's slanted wood frame were embossed with gold from the Nubian desert. The headrest and footboard were inscribed with the appropriate references to the god-king, the pharaoh, son of Amon-Re, son of the Lord of Eternity, Osiris. The sides were decorated with intricate inlays of ivory from Africa, silver from

Syria, and lapis lazuli—blue was the favored color of the ancient Egyptians—from Badakshan.

"Welcome to my humble home," said Lady Charlotte in greeting, waving an ivory fan in one hand and a small, black Turkish cigar in the other.

With its elaborate, carved furniture, richly embroidered wall hangings, and vast collection of statuary dating back several centuries, indeed, several millennia, her home was anything, of course, but humble.

"Please be seated and I will have the woman, Anhai, serve us coffee," Lady Charlotte said after the formal introductions had been made.

Elizabeth was the first to close her mouth and find a suitable chair.

"I understand from Colonel and Mrs. Winters that you are the daughter of Lord Stanhope," the woman went on after all were seated and balancing a demitasse on their laps.

Elizabeth fixed an appropriately polite expression on her face. "Yes. I am."

"Come, come, my dear child. You mustn't be put off by appearances. I admit I was last shopping in Paris—" the woman snapped her fan shut and tapped it against her lips as she thought "—in 1858, I believe it was. So I must make do, you see."

She didn't see, but Elizabeth took a sip of her coffee and tried not to choke on the thick, lukewarm concoction.

Lady Charlotte's attention had already wandered around the group and alighted upon the younger gentleman present. "You are . . . ?"

"Jonathan Wicke."

Her pale gray eyes were shrewd. "I dare say so. And where are you from, Jonathan Wicke?" she inquired with uncharacteristic directness for an Englishwoman.

"At one time I came from Northumberland," he said smoothly.

"And now?"

"Now I have several homes; one is in Alexandria, and the other is in—the desert."

Their hostess was far less surprised by Lord Jonathan's reply than she was, Elizabeth noticed as she listened to the exchange between them. He had never mentioned any homes to her other than his ancestral estates back in England.

It seemed there was a great deal about the man that she did not know.

"Your chaperons tell me that you are interested in my roses," Lady Charlotte remarked to Elizabeth as she ground out her cigar and dropped the stub into what appeared to be an antique canopic jar. "Would you like to see my garden now?"

"Yes, I would."

The woman rose slowly from the three-thousand-year-old bed and reached for a wooden staff propped in the corner. "You may give me your arm, child. I'm not as young, nor as agile, as I used to be."

Elizabeth quickly moved to comply and discovered that Lady Charlotte Baker-Finch was actually a slight woman beneath the many voluminous robes she was wearing. No more than skin and bone, really.

How sad to grow old alone and so far from home, Elizabeth reflected sympathetically. To be surrounded by strangers and curious travelers, those recently come out from England and those posted to the far corners of the Empire, instead of one's children and grandchildren. Her heart reached out to the tiny figure at her side.

"I have read your *Letters from Egypt* several times," she confided to their hostess as they slowly made their way outside to the gardens. "Your book has inspired a whole generation of English-women to travel to Egypt; to see this wondrous country for themselves."

Lady Charlotte was visibly pleased. She smiled and revealed her tobacco-stained teeth. "It was just a bit of scribbling I did when I was younger. Still, I like to think that someone has read my little stories." Cocking her head, she peered myopically over her pince-nez. "Tell me, my dear girl—" the word came out sounding like *gull* "—has your father come any closer to discovering the tomb?"

Elizabeth stiffened, but managed to keep her voice casual and light. "The tomb?"

"The tomb of Merneptah Seti," said the old woman, dropping the ancient pharaoh's name into their conversation as nonchalantly as she would that of an acquaintance.

She stopped dead in her tracks. "How—?"

"How did I know that Lord Stanhope was searching for Set's tomb?" There was a raspy chuckle. "Sooner or later everything that goes on in the English community here in Egypt comes to my attention."

"I didn't realize that my father's lifelong dream was known to everyone."

"Perhaps not to everyone, but certainly to me," said Lady Charlotte, pursing her lips with satisfaction. Then she added, "Of course, I don't believe in digging them up, myself."

Elizabeth's throat felt oddly hot. "Digging them up?"

"The Ancient Ones. I believe they have as much right to rest in peace in their graves as anyone."

She felt compelled to voice the question: "But is it not true that most of the tombs were robbed in antiquity?"

There was a nod of the white head. "It is true."

"Then if we don't excavate what remains, another generation of robbers will simply break in and steal any treasure they can find, and in the process destroy whatever historical facts we may have learned about the Ancient Ones, as you call them."

Lady Charlotte arched a pure white eyebrow in her direction. "I believe you sound like your father."

"I am his daughter, after all."

"Are you an archaeologist, then?"

"No," she said carefully.

"But I venture to say that you are an Egyptologist."

She smiled uneasily at her hostess. "I am merely a young woman who shares some of her father's interests."

After a moment, Lady Charlotte said, "I see."

Elizabeth sensed it was time to change the subject. She stepped onto the garden path and gazed out over the incredible sight in front of them. "I never thought I would see a rose garden growing in the middle of the desert," she said in hushed tones.

"It is the eternal paradox of Egypt," pointed out her elderly companion. "The rich and the poor. The desert and the Nile floods. The green fields and the brown sand. The hot days and the cool nights. Death and life itself. It represents the endless fascination some of us have for *Kemet*, the Black Land." With decades of wisdom written on her wrinkled face, she speculated, "You are one of those, are you not?"

After a minute or two had passed, she agreed. "Yes, I am."

The old woman smiled at the admission. But her voice took on serious overtones when she predicted, "Egypt may well change your life, Lady Elizabeth."

She thought about it. "It may." A moment later she added wistfully, "I can only hope so."

"Twenty-five years ago Florence Nightingale came to the Black Land and sailed up the Nile, much as you are now."

"Yes."

"She wrote home to her family: 'One wonders that people come back from Egypt and live lives as they did before.'" Gray eyes filled with the wisdom of the ages were fixed upon her. "I didn't, of course."

Elizabeth shivered. "Live your life as you had before?"

Lady Charlotte nodded, and said in a softly haunting voice, "Nothing was ever the same for me again. In fact, my first memory of the desert still sends chills down my spine."

She had to ask, "What is your first memory of the desert?"

And so the woman told her. "We were driving in an open carriage. I was with several traveling companions and my—and a young boy of about seven. We had heard that one of the French archaeologists had uncovered a pharaonic tomb, and like so many others before us, we were ghoulishly curious to see a royal mummy in its coffin."

Lady Charlotte nearly stumbled; Elizabeth steadied her as they took the stone steps one at a time.

She continued with her story. "The pharaoh's sarcophagus was to be loaded upon a barge and sailed down the Nile to the port of Alexandria. From there, it would be placed aboard a French ship and transported to Paris, leaving this ancient land forever."

Elizabeth declared, "But that wasn't right."

"No, it wasn't." The woman sighed. "As the Ancient One was removed from his final resting place, the men of the desert fired off their guns, just as they always did at funerals. The fellahin women gathered along the banks of the Nile and raised their voices in mourning, the eerie sound of their wails echoing through the Valley of the Kings."

"Sacrilege," whispered Elizabeth.

"Sacrilege," echoed Lady Charlotte, shaking her draped head in dismay. "The desert people believed the pharaoh's tomb had been desecrated by the infidels, the hated foreigners who had no respect for their dead. After all, the god-king had been buried beneath the sand and stone for centuries in that place which we call—"

" 'The Place of Truth.' " Elizabeth finished her companion's sentence.

There was a studied frown. "You know of this?"

"I know of this."

"You are truly one of us, are you not?"

"One of you?"

Gnarled fingers closed on her wrist. "One who understands deep in her heart and soul what makes the Black Land different from any other place on the earth?"

"Yes, I believe I understand," she murmured.

There was an expectant stillness all around them. Then the others in the party caught up with them, and Lady Charlotte urged, "Come, my dear, let me share my garden in the desert with you."

"How beautiful," exclaimed Elizabeth as they approached a multitude of yellow roses cascading over a low brick wall. Everywhere she looked, it seemed, there was another delight to behold. "I recognize the yellow banksian rose, but I'm not familiar with this one."

"That is the rambling 'American Pillar,' " said her willing guide. "It has wide-clustered flowers of vivid pink, as you can see."

The two of them continued on, walking and talking together, studying each variety of flower as they came to it.

There were pink China roses, scarlet 'Frenshams,' the crimson 'Rosemary Rose,' the prickly, white-flowered trailers, the climbing 'Madame Plantier,' the yellow form of the Scotch rose, *Rose pimpinellifolia*.

There were trellises overhead weighed down with pinks, reds, oranges, creams, and whites. Their fragrance filled the morning air and clung to Elizabeth's dress so that she soon smelled like a flower herself.

As Lady Charlotte and Lady Elizabeth strolled through the garden, a man watched them; a man with blue eyes the color of the sky at dawn.

He studied the figure of the old woman, bent with age and near the end of her life. Then the girl: youthful, supple, with her whole future before her. This, too, he knew, was part of the eternal paradox of Egypt.

Black Jack stepped into the flower garden, bent over, and inhaled the scent of a crimson rambler at his elbow.

One day, he promised himself, he would make love to his beautiful Elizabeth on a bed of roses.

Chapter 6

"I have seen quite enough roses for today," declared Amelia Winters.

"Yes, my dear."

"And I couldn't possibly ride one of those damn filthy beasts," she added with a sour expression that managed to detract from her otherwise pretty face.

The colonel let out a sigh. Apparently the woman was in one of her snits. Something he had rarely witnessed.

At least in public.

Within the confines of their cabin aboard the *Star of Egypt*, he frequently got an earful. Dear Amelia was not what he would call a "jolly good sport."

She gritted her small, white, pointed teeth. "Do you hear me, Hulbert?"

"Yes, my dear."

She lowered her voice and hissed at him, "I simply will not sit astride an ass."

"No, my dear." He managed not to crack a smile, but knowing it would annoy her, said; "I believe polite company prefers to use the term 'donkey.' "

"I don't care what polite company prefers," she snapped, although she did care, of course, very much, "the bloody animals stink."

"Hadn't noticed myself," he muttered.

In his opinion, a donkey couldn't hold a candle to a camel when it came to smell.

"I'll make our excuses," she informed him. "The others can go on ahead without us."

He furrowed his brow, and tapped his silver-tipped walking stick against the side of his boot as was his custom when he was agitated. "Do you believe it's wise to allow Lady Elizabeth to go off on her own?"

"She'll hardly be on her own, Hulbert, with Colette, Alee, and Lord Jonathan in attendance."

"If you think it's quite all right, my dear."

"I do," she stated flatly.

"Whatever you wish, then."

As the rest of their touring party joined them in the courtyard outside Lady Charlotte's house, he watched as Amelia took a lightly scented handkerchief from her reticule and dabbed at her upper lip. "It seems particularly warm this morning, do you not agree, Lady Elizabeth?"

The colonel doubted it. Elizabeth Guest appeared as cool as a shady Scottish glen.

"I must confess I thought it rather pleasant, Mrs. Winters." Nevertheless, the girl showed an appropriate amount of concern for her chaperon's well-being. "You seem a bit pale. Are you feeling all right?"

Amelia swayed slightly on her feet. "The sunlight is so intense in Egypt, sometimes it affects me adversely."

"Do you wish to return to the ship?" inquired Lady Elizabeth, trying her best, Colonel Winters could see, to conceal her disappointment.

Before she could respond, Lady Charlotte stepped into the middle of the fray. "Nonsense," she stated. "Since Mrs. Winters is feeling the ill effects of the sun, it would be far better for her to stay here with me. You may continue your tour of the pyramids without her." She spoke to Amelia. "I'm expecting a rather entertaining group of gentlemen for luncheon: a Hungarian count, a minor prince, and an ambassador or two. Frankly, I could use a gay, amusing, pretty woman at the table. Perhaps if you rest for a while, you'll feel up to gracing us with your presence later." Then she turned and looked directly at him. "And you, too, naturally, Colonel Winters."

"I would be delighted, Lady Charlotte," he said with a small bow of his distinguished head. Then he cleared his throat and added, with a quick glance at Amelia, "That is, if you think you'll feel up to it, my dear."

She fanned herself and murmured languidly, "If I lie down in a cool, dark room now—perhaps I could manage to join you for luncheon."

"It's settled, then," declared Lady Charlotte. With a sweep of her hand, she waved Elizabeth and the others toward the waiting donkeys. "Have a delightful time. We will be here when you return this afternoon."

"Ladies . . ."

With that, the colonel offered first one arm, then the other, to their diminutive hostess and the pale beauty at his side. He escorted both women toward the house in the oasis, leaving the rest of the party to continue with their sight-seeing.

Damn fine actress, Amelia, the colonel reflected. Attractive woman, too.

Of course, there was a certain lack of breeding that poked its ugly head up every now and then. He supposed that was to be expected. After all, Amelia had come from the bottom rung of London society.

You could take the guttersnipe out of the gutter, but not the gutter out of the guttersnipe, as his mother had always been fond of saying.

Amelia liked to think she was genteel because she spoke the Queen's English as well, perhaps better, than he did. But it was all a facade. Beneath the demure manner, pretty features, and fashionable figure was an alley cat—and she had claws.

Hulbert Mathias Winters was suddenly relieved that he had never actually gotten around to marrying the woman. . . .

She had never ridden a donkey before.

It was rather like sitting astride an overgrown pony, decided Elizabeth as she touched her heels to the creature's underbelly. For the donkey was very small, and she felt very large in comparison.

"Does my mount have a name?" she inquired of their Egyptian guide, Alee. Although it seemed ridiculous to refer to the wiry little animal as a "mount." Surely a mount was one of the Irish Thoroughbreds back home in the stables of Stanhope Hall.

"Yes, *sitteh*, my lady," Alee said with great dignity. He brought his own donkey up alongside hers. "Yours is called Zizinia, the English lord's is known as Kalaoon, and your serving woman's is Welee, which means, in our language, simpleton."

"And what is the name of your donkey?" she asked, enjoying the leisurely ride along the avenue of shade trees.

"My animal is called Tarboosh, because his reddish coat resembles the traditional tasseled hat worn by the men of my tribe," he told her.

Elizabeth inhaled a deep breath of air and said, "The desert climate agrees with me. It was cold and rainy and quite miserable when I left England."

Alee frowned. "It is difficult for me to imagine a country where everything is close together and green, everywhere green."

She supposed it was an accurate enough description of England if one were Egyptian and lived in a land where everything was brown and larger than life.

He went on. "I have seen pictures of your country, of course. But that is not the same thing."

"No, it is not," Elizabeth agreed.

It had been that way for her and Egypt, after all. No painting or picture could ever do it justice. This land had to be seen to be appreciated.

She jingled the reins and urged Zizinia into a faster walk. The strong taste of moisture on her tongue told her the Nile was just around the next bend in the road. Indeed, she turned and there was the winding river with a wide swath of verdant farmland on either side. They were soon following its course toward their destination.

She glanced back. Across the deep blue waters and behind them was the Citadel of Cairo, built in the twelfth century by the Sultan Saladin, and crowned by the minarets on the mosque of Muhammad Ali.

The white sails of a dozen or more *feluccas*—small sailboats—dotted the river adjacent to the roadway, carrying both passengers and freight along the Nile as they had since ancient times.

In the foreground, a local farmer called out to his oxen, urging the huge animals to draw a primitive wooden plow through the fields of rich, dark silt left by the flooding Nile. Two veiled women strolled alongside the road at a leisurely pace, their hips swaying beneath their robes, earthen jugs balanced atop their heads. In the distance was an oasis of palm trees and what appeared to be a family picking dates.

Egypt as it was then, as it was now: they were one and the same.

With a sigh of contentment, Elizabeth put her head back and gazed up at the natural canopy formed by the trees, savoring the instant relief their shade provided from the sun. "This road reminds me of an avenue of limes that leads up the drive to my home," she remarked to Alee.

"This home you call Stanhope Hall," he said.

She was slightly taken aback that he knew its name. "Why, yes."

The young man explained. "Your father, Lord Stanhope, has spoken to me often of this place." He gazed off into the distance. "I would like to see England, and this grand house that has the Stanhope name upon it."

"Perhaps you will travel to my country one day," she suggested kindly.

Alee's handsome profile was turned to her, and she was reminded for a moment of the pharaonic princes who had once ruled this land.

"Perhaps someday I shall travel to England," he speculated. Then he reverted to the role of guide. Pointing to the thick, green vegetation overhead, he said, "These beautiful lebbek trees were planted by Ismail Pasha so that the road to the ancient monuments would be shaded and delightful for all who choose to make the pilgrimage. The sun is most fierce in our land, *sitteh*, and shade is greatly prized."

"Indeed," she said, knowing it often meant the difference between life and death.

Alee leaned back in the saddle and said, with a promise of adventure in his voice, "As we ride, I shall tell you a tale, *sitteh*, an ancient tale of the strange, inscrutable beast which is called the Sphinx."

His words sent a chill down Elizabeth's spine.

He began. "Facing the rising sun, the great man-headed lion crouches at the foot of the Ancient Ones' tombs, those mysterious stone mountains that point toward the heavens themselves."

"The pyramids?"

"The pyramids," he confirmed. "The features of the Sphinx are said to be those of King Khafre, who ruled many thousands of years ago. But my story is of a young prince who was riding in the desert one day and stopped to rest in the shade of the mighty Beast."

Elizabeth knew the story well, but she was enjoying the version told by Alee.

His enthusiasm grew. "The weary prince sought relief from the heat and the sun, and chose to nap between the giant stone paws of the man-lion. As he slept, he dreamt, and in his dream, the Sphinx spoke to him, promising him the throne of Egypt if he would but clear away the sand that had piled up around the beast over the centuries."

"And when the prince awakened . . ."

"He had the sand cleared away, and one day he did, indeed, become Thutmose the Fourth, King of Upper and Lower Egypt, Uniter of the Two Lands, ruler of all he surveyed, Great Pharaoh of Egypt. This was, of course, many centuries ago."

"Many centuries ago," echoed Elizabeth.

"Indeed, thirty-three centuries ago," Alee said, "at which time the Sphinx was already ancient."

But Elizabeth had no more thought for shade or sun, for ancient tales or modern storytellers. For suddenly there on the horizon, sitting on the edge of the vast, yellow-brown sands of the Libyan desert, soaring majestically, inconceivably, into the otherwise empty desert sky were the Great Pyramids and their guardian!

She could not speak; she did not dare breathe.

The words of Lord Jonathan, spoken to her in the carriage earlier that morning, echoed in her head: *"I feel it is only fair to warn you, Lady Elizabeth, no words or pictures can ever prepare you for your first sight of the Pyramids of Giza—the last survivors of the seven wonders of the ancient world."*

He had told her the truth.

She had thought she would be prepared for this moment, that she wouldn't be overwhelmed by their sheer immensity, by the great stone tombs pointing to the heavens, great stone tombs constructed of thousands, millions, of huge limestone blocks.

She was wrong.

"Mon Dieu! C'est magnifique! C 'est merveilleux!" whispered Colette as she and Lord Jonathan trotted their donkeys up alongside hers.

In a reverent tone, Jonathan Wicke quoted the lines from Shelley's sonnet: " 'My name is Ozymandias, king of kings. Look upon my works, ye Mighty, and despair!' "

But it was not despair Elizabeth felt. It was wonder and awe and joy. Joy as she had never known it.

She blinked away the tears. Her heart was pounding within her breast, and she was driven to call out her encouragement: "Faster, Zizinia! Faster now!"

For she must see the Great Pyramids and the guardian Sphinx up close, knowing that once she stood before them, she would fade into insignificance.

Chapter 7

"**G**ive me your hand, Elizabeth."

Jack knew she wanted to refuse. She'd been avoiding him for the past three days as if he had the plague, or the pox, or worse. But the truth was, she needed his help in scaling the huge limestone blocks if she wanted to reach the entrance to the Great Pyramid, and they both knew it.

The girl looked up at him, hesitated for a moment, and then finally placed her gloved hand in his.

He flashed her a smile. It was a small triumph, but a triumph nevertheless. "That wasn't so difficult, was it?"

"No, my lord," she said stiffly.

He just managed to hold on to the thin thread of his patience. "How very sensible of you to wear a two-piece skirt, my lady. I wish all females visiting Egypt were as practical in their choice of attire."

"Thank you," she remarked, arching one elegant eyebrow in his direction as they continued to climb. "I think."

They paused at the next plateau, and Jack leaned back against the face of the great stone edifice behind him. Climbing pyramids was hot work, even in November. He wanted to shrug off the ridiculous suit coat he was wearing and don his desert robes—they were far cooler and infinitely more practical—but he didn't dare. It was difficult enough as it was to remember that he was supposed to be a proper English gentleman.

Instead, he said to Elizabeth, "We'll take a short rest and wait here for Alee and your French companion. They seem to have fallen behind."

She glanced back at the other man and woman, some forty feet below them, and murmured sympathetically, "I am afraid the climb may be too much for poor Colette."

He had to ask. "Too much for poor Colette, but not too much for you?"

"No," she answered frankly. "Not for me."

He was intrigued. "Why is that?"

He watched as, beneath the youthful straw hat plunked down unceremoniously on her head, Elizabeth pursed her pretty lips in thought. "Perhaps, my lord, because I walk a great deal."

"Walk a great deal?"

"Back home. At Stanhope Hall. I walk every day. Several miles; sometimes more. Up and downhill."

He was puzzled. "Why?"

She shrugged her shoulders. "I love walking and I love the gardens, so I walk in the gardens."

Jack supposed there was a kind of perverse logic to the idea of walking without a destination in mind. But it had been so long since he'd thought as an Englishman: he'd forgotten the concept of doing something simply for the pleasure of doing it. In the desert everything came down, in the end, to survival.

He removed a silver flask from his pocket and offered it to her. "Would you care for a sip of cool water?"

She shook her head.

He raised the flask to his lips and wet them, swallowing only a trickle, just enough to clear the dust from his throat. Again, it was a habit born of the desert, where water was as precious as life itself. Where water *was* life.

Then he stood there, arms folded across his chest, and studied her profile as she gazed out over the desert floor.

"You are staring, my lord," Elizabeth said, without turning her head.

"Yes, I am," he admitted, sounding almost savage.

"It's not considered polite to stare."

"No, it isn't," he agreed, taking a step toward her.

He noticed that she went very still.

He stopped. "You've been avoiding me since the night we met on deck, Elizabeth."

The color rose sharply in her face. "I wish you would not speak to me of that night."

He didn't understand. "Why not?"

"You shouldn't."

"I should."

"You mustn't."

"I'm afraid I must," he retorted.

"Please—"

There were times, Jack was forced to admit, when Lady Elizabeth was damned exasperating for one so young and so beautiful.

"I'm only saying aloud what we have both been thinking to ourselves," he pointed out with impeccable logic.

She glanced at him, then quickly looked away again. "You may speak for yourself, my lord, but do not presume to know what is going on in my mind."

He swore under his breath.

"I beg your pardon, sir," she said, her voice vibrating with indignation.

Jack expelled a breath of hot air and muttered, "Show me the man who understands what is going on in a woman's mind, and I'll show you a bloody genius."

"You are deliberately being offensive, my lord."

"I certainly hope so, my lady." This wasn't going at all as he had planned. Indeed, he'd completely forgotten what his plan had been. "Elizabeth, Elizabeth . . ." He said her name several times, softly, seductively. "Didn't you enjoy yourself that night on deck?"

She continued to stare straight ahead.

He wasn't ready to give up. Not by a long shot. "I could have sworn you enjoyed my kisses, the touch of my lips on yours, the sensation of my tongue in your mouth, the way our bodies fit together as if you were made for me."

She was obviously horrified. "Hush, my lord! Do not speak of such things. Someone may hear you."

Jack paused and looked around them. There was no one nearby except Alee and Colette, whose progress up the side of the pyramid was markedly slower than their own.

"Who will hear me?"

"Someone."

He persisted. "Who?"

"Anyone." She seemed to realize that there was no one to overhear his words. "I will hear you," Elizabeth finished.

"Have I not spoken the truth, then?"

"No, my lord." She reconsidered. "Yes, my lord. But some things should not be said out loud between a man and a woman. It isn't—proper."

"Do you always do what is proper?"

"I try to."

His mouth turned into a mocking smile. "How very tiresome it must be for you, my lady."

Elizabeth looked directly ahead, unblinking. Then she wet her lips with the tip of her tongue, swallowed with obvious difficulty, and admitted, "I have not been totally honest with you. I don't always do what is proper, Lord Jonathan."

"Jack," he said softly.

Caught off guard, she repeated: "Jack?"

"Please call me Jack."

"It—it doesn't seem proper somehow."

"You were just telling me that you don't always do what's proper," he reminded her.

Elizabeth sighed. "That's true. It is perhaps my greatest downfall."

"Or your greatest strength," he said in a deceptively mild tone. "Do not concern yourself; if there is anyone who must shoulder the blame for what happened the other night on deck, it is me. You are still 'as chaste as unsunn'd snow.' "

"Lord Tennyson?" she inquired, interested in spite of herself.

"Shakespeare," he replied, with a cold glint of satisfaction in his eye. "The advantages of a classical education. Or at least part of one."

She announced morosely, "I thank you for your kindness, my lord, but I'm afraid it isn't true."

"What isn't true?"

Her gloved hand floated to her breast. "That I am 'as chaste as—"

"—unsunn'd snow?' "

She bowed her head and nodded.

Jack held his breath. What in the bloody hell did she mean now?

The girl confessed to him in an embarrassed whisper, "I enjoyed it, my lord."

A slow, sensual smile slid across Black Jack's handsome face.

He'd thought so. He'd hoped so. Now he knew so.

Relieved, he blew out his breath. "There's nothing for you to be ashamed of, Elizabeth. Whatever has been drummed into your head to the contrary, it is quite nice when a woman enjoys a man's kiss, his caress."

Her eyes traveled reluctantly to his. "Would I enjoy any man's kiss, my lord, or just yours?"

The question caught him by surprise. "I beg your pardon, my lady."

"Does this mean that I am a Wanton, that I would enjoy any gentleman's kiss as much as I did yours?" Her face was scarlet. "You mustn't be afraid to tell me, Lord Jonathan. I want to know the truth."

Jack sputtered furiously for a moment. "I'm not afraid to tell you." He was simply astounded and a little taken aback. "Of course you're not a Wanton." He was skating on thin ice and he knew it. "I think we can safely say that your reaction to my kiss was sweet and innocent and untutored."

"Untutored?" Elizabeth frowned. "Does that mean I kissed like a schoolgirl?"

"Not exactly." He found himself between a rock and a hard place, a most precarious position.

Her eyes narrowed. "Do you mean that I don't know how to kiss?"

He shifted uncomfortably from one foot to the other. "You may wish to gain some experience and practice in the art," he said as diplomatically as he could.

An anxious expression flickered across her young face. "And how do you suggest that I go about gaining experience, my lord?"

There was an odd little silence as he found himself at an utter loss for words.

She hastened to inquire, "Do you recommend I try practicing with any willing gentleman who happens along? Or did you have someone specific in mind?"

Suddenly Black Jack wasn't certain if the girl was serious, or merely leading him on a merry dance.

She continued. "After all, I have said that I wish to live life to its fullest."

The skin on his jaw seemed to tighten. "I will be happy to oblige you, Lady Elizabeth, *if* and *when* you decide you must start *living*."

She arched one chestnut brown eyebrow in his direction. "Indeed, my lord?"

Was she laughing at him? The chit had her nerve. Well, they would see who had the last laugh.

A faint smile flickered and died on Black Jack's face. "Indeed, my lady."

"The climb was most strenuous, was it not, milady?" gasped Colette as she and Alee joined them near the entrance to the Great Pyramid. "*C'est bizarre!* Why did the ancient builders put the opening up here?"

Alee enlightened her. "Even in ancient times the pharaoh feared grave robbers would loot the treasure buried with him for the afterlife. So those who built the Great Pyramid tried to outwit the thieves by placing the entrance to the tomb twenty-four feet east of the middle and fifty-five feet above the pavement. Then they covered it with a single slab of stone let into the surface. That way, the opening was invisible from below."

"They were very clever," interjected Lord Jonathan, "but not clever enough. The tomb was still robbed in antiquity. Indeed, the entrance was known even in the time of Christ." He shook his head. "Somehow the knowledge of its existence was lost, and according to legend, wasn't regained until the ninth century."

Elizabeth was fascinated. "What is this dark hole?" she inquired, pointing to an area not far from them.

Alee was the one who answered her question. "The son of the famous Harun al Raschid, whom we all know in the *Arabian Nights*, forced an entrance into the pyramid for the sake of the treasure it was supposed to contain."

The name seemed familiar, but she couldn't quite place it. "Harun al Raschid?"

"It was to him that the lovely Scheherazade told her stories for one thousand and one nights."

Elizabeth clapped her hands together. "Of course."

"This hole is the forced passage made by his son, Caliph Siamun," said Alee.

Colette's face had become animated at the mere mention of the word "treasure." She repeated, "Treasure?"

Their guide explained. "It was rumored that an emerald of stupendous size was hidden inside the pyramid. Nothing was ever found, of course."

Lord Jonathan added, "There are still thought to be hidden passages and undiscovered tomb rooms."

Alee agreed. "That is true."

Jonathan Wicke chuckled. "There is also carved into one of the myriad stones one of the strangest hieroglyphs ever discovered in Egypt."

Elizabeth looked up into his face. "What does it say?"

"It translates to 'this end up.' "

She laughed. "Ancient graffito."

His laughter joined hers. "Precisely."

"It is time for us to enter the pyramid, *sitteh*, if you are ready," said Alee.

"I'm ready," she assured him, although her heart was pounding again, and beneath her gloves, she was quite certain that her palms were damp.

"You must be careful, my lady, and you, too, my lord, for the way is long and sometimes treacherous," warned Alee.

The Great Pyramid had been named one of the seven ancient wonders of the world for its outward size, but Elizabeth knew the interior—with its corridors, passageways, air shafts, Grand Gallery, and King's Chamber—was also an architectural marvel.

"First we must make our way to the Grand Gallery, which is very long and narrow," instructed the young Egyptian. "After descending nearly one hundred feet along one sloping passage and then ascending for another one hundred and sixty feet, all within the vast mass of the pyramid, we will reach the chamber into which they carried King Khufu."

With that, they entered single file through the opening.

It was cold inside.

Cold and dark, Elizabeth realized with a shiver as they began their descent deep into the heart of the Great Pyramid. In front of them, along the solid stone passageway, there was a cowled figure with a torch. Some thirty or forty feet along, just at the edge of the darkness, was a second cowled figure with a second torch. Farther along there was another, then another and yet another. They provided the only light inside the massive stone tomb.

Elizabeth tried to contain her excitement, and ignore the fear niggling at the edge of her consciousness. She could hear the drumming of her own heart, the sound of her breathing as she forced the air in and out of her lungs. Although the ceiling of the corridor was well above her head, she was acutely aware of the tons upon tons of weight bearing down on her.

She peered ahead into the shadowy passage, and in doing so failed to see that Colette had stopped dead in her tracks. She bumped into the back of the Frenchwoman, who was directly in front of her.

"Milady—"

"What is it, Colette?"

The young woman's voice quivered. *"R-Rien."*

"It isn't *nothing*. What's wrong?"

"I am afraid."

"Afraid?"

"Oui, milady."

Elizabeth found herself whispering. "What are you afraid of?"

"I do not know, milady."

She could feel Colette trembling. "Are you chilled?"

"Oui."

"Are you feeling faint?"

"Oui."

"Are you ill?"

"*Oui.*"

"Oh, dear."

"I am truly sorry, milady, but I believe I have the *maladie* that some suffer from when they are in an enclosed place. I cannot seem to breathe."

She patted the Frenchwoman's arm reassuringly. "Try to stay calm and take a deep breath."

Her companion wailed: "*C'est impossible.* My heart is racing in my breast, milady. My knees are like *gelée. Sacré coeur*, I have ruined your visit to the pyramids."

Elizabeth had always been excellent in a crisis. Back home it seemed she was forever consoling Maman or her elder sister, Caroline, or one of the myriad female servants at Stanhope Hall. She knew firsthand that some women went into hysterics at the slightest provocation. Thankfully, she wasn't one of them. Having both of her feet firmly planted on the ground would hold her in good stead now.

"Never you mind, Colette. It's not your fault," she said in a no-nonsense tone. "These things happen."

Alee backtracked to where they were standing, and Lord Jonathan came up quickly behind them.

"What is it, *sitteh*? Why have you stopped?"

"Are you all right, Elizabeth?"

"I'm fine," she told both men. "It's Colette. She isn't feeling well."

"It is this—place," gulped the Frenchwoman. "I feel as if the walls are closing in on me."

The young Egyptian guide exclaimed, "Ack, this does happen. Not everyone is comfortable inside the tombs."

"We'll have to go back," stated Elizabeth. "That's all there is to it."

"*Non*, milady," objected her maid. "You must go ahead. I will not ruin this day for you. I can make my way back alone."

"That's impossible," she said kindly but firmly. "The path is too steep and too slippery."

Lord Jonathan took charge. "Lady Elizabeth is right."

Colette was nearly frantic. "But, my lord—"

"The solution to our problem is simple, however. Alee will escort you outside, mademoiselle. You will wait for us in the village at the base of the Sphinx where we tethered the donkeys and had our picnic luncheon." He turned to the younger man. "There is a bottle of wine left in the basket. Give Mademoiselle Duvay a glass or two to calm her nerves."

Alee nodded his handsome head. "This I will do, my lord."

"I will escort Lady Elizabeth to the King's Chamber. We will rejoin you later."

"Yes, my lord."

"*A bientôt*, Colette," Elizabeth called out as her companion and Alee backtracked toward the entrance.

Even after they had disappeared from sight, she was still torn. Part of her was admittedly afraid to be alone with Lord Jonathan; part of her was thrilled at the prospect. In the end, her curiosity to see the heart of the Great Pyramid overcame her fear.

Lord Jonathan gave a small bow. "This way, my lady." Then he offered his arm. "Perhaps it would be wise to give me your hand. As you pointed out to Miss Duvay, the way is steep and slippery."

She gratefully placed a gloved hand on his to steady herself. "Indeed it is, my lord."

The two of them proceeded, speaking of the vast number of workers it must have taken to construct the Pyramids of Giza, how the builders had escaped through special corridors once the tombs were completed, the speculation that there were still rooms lying undiscovered after thousands of years. Then they entered the Grand Gallery and began their ascent to the burial chamber.

Halfway up the stone stairway, Lord Jonathan halted and took the silver flask from his pocket. "Would you care for a taste of water?"

Elizabeth nodded. She raised the flask to her lips, let the cool water slide down her parched throat, and returned it to him with a polite thank you. Then she watched as he raised the flask to his own mouth and pressed his lips where hers had been only moments before.

A chill of a different sort rippled through Elizabeth's body. She was aware of Lord Jonathan—could she ever bring herself to call him Jack as he had requested?—as she'd never been aware of a man before. She could smell him, taste him, *feel* him, without being anywhere near him. It was most disconcerting, and most disturbing.

"On the day of his burial, the body of Khufu was borne along this passageway and placed in the stone sarcophagus prepared for him, where he was to rest for all eternity," murmured Lord Jonathan as they entered the King's Chamber.

The room was of granite and surprisingly spacious, with a high ceiling cloaked in shadows. There were lamps along the four walls, and there, in front of them, was the empty sarcophagus of the mighty pharaoh.

The breath caught in Elizabeth's throat.

"The ancient tomb robbers broke away the corner of Khufu's coffin in their mad search for treasure," related her self-appointed guide. "In spite of all his precautions, the king's body was torn from its final resting place and plundered of its rich regalia and splendid jewelry. Then it was carelessly discarded. In the end, Khufu was left in dishonor, no more than a heap of moldering flesh and bone among the fragments of stone and tattered mummy cloth lying upon the floor."

"Sacrilege," whispered Elizabeth.

"Sacrilege," repeated Lord Jonathan.

Sacrilege.

Sacrilege.

The word echoed back and forth within the stone walls of the chamber.

She shivered and resisted the urge to wrap her arms around herself.

"Are you afraid, Elizabeth?"

Denial sprang to her lips. "No." Then a more truthful "Yes."

His voice was low and husky. "There are no ghosts here. There is no one here but us."

Her breath was coming hard and fast. "I-I know."

"Do you suffer from the same malady as your companion?"

"No."

"What are you afraid of, then?"

So many things, she wanted to blurt out. You. Me. Us. This place. This land. The spell it weaves.

"Come here."

Elizabeth didn't know why, but she obeyed, taking a tentative step toward him.

"Closer."

She took another small step.

"Closer still."

She was standing directly in front of Lord Jonathan now.

"I know you're chilled and frightened and feeling all alone in the world." His voice was low and husky; it wove a rich tapestry of sound, ensnaring her as surely as a hunter's net entrapped its prey. "All you have to do is reach out, and you will be warm and safe and no longer on your own."

She wanted to say that she'd always been on her own, only more so since her dear, sweet Annie had succumbed to consumption last winter.

"Don't be afraid of life, Elizabeth."

Her sister had not been afraid of life, and yet she had seen so little of it.

Elizabeth reached out and placed her gloved hand on Lord Jonathan's arm, just the tips of her fingers, but it was a beginning. Then she leaned toward him, took a deep breath, and lightly rested her head on his shoulder.

He was solid and strong. The steady rhythm of his heart beating beneath her cheek was reassuring. He was flesh and blood like everyone else, and yet he was like no one else. Just as he had promised, the heat from his body warmed her. The arms with which he held her made her feel safe and secure. She exhaled a contented sigh.

A few minutes later Elizabeth stirred, vaguely aware that something had changed between them. Lord Jonathan was no longer comforting her. She felt an unusually firm bulge in his trousers; it twitched in reaction when she inadvertently brushed up against his thigh. A low groan issued forth from his chest.

She quickly stepped away from him. "My lord—?"

A succinct and fiercely spat reply: "Yes."

"What is it, my lord?"

"What is *what*?" he ground through his teeth as if he were in pain.

Elizabeth was afraid to say more. What if Lord Jonathan had some awful affliction that he dare not mention in polite company? Of course, the only other time she had been aware of his affliction was the night they had been alone on the deck of the *Star of Egypt*. He seemed perfectly normal at other times.

She cursed her own ignorance and forged ahead. "Is it because I am a Wanton, my lord?"

He sucked in his breath. "You are not a Wanton, Elizabeth. I thought I made that clear to you earlier."

She was hot with embarrassment. "But this strange—affliction that seems to overtake you. I couldn't help but notice that it only happens when you and I are alone together."

He spoke with ill-concealed impatience. "Don't they teach you anything in the schoolroom?"

With quick pride she replied, "Of course they do. I have been taught reading and writing, a bit of history and geography, a smattering of Latin and French."

"And . . . ?"

Elizabeth wasn't certain what she was supposed to say next. She responded with the first thing that popped into her head. "Maman has taught me how to pour tea, sit at table, sip champagne—although I am not allowed to actually drink spirits until I come out in Society—how to judge the quality of pearls, the proper way to eat ortolan—"

Lord Jonathan interrupted her. "What do they teach you about men?"

"About men, my lord?"

"Yes, men."

"Nothing, my lord."

He groaned out loud. "That's what I was afraid of. Blasted bloody hypocrites!"

"Sir!"

"Well, they are."

"Who is, sir?"

"Society. Especially aristocratic English Society," he said, his voice heavy with reproach. He condemned them one and all in a single breath.

She reflected on this. "I'm afraid I don't understand."

With feet planted firmly apart and hands resting on his hips, Jonathan Wicke loomed before her like a man who truly did "bestride the narrow world like a Colossus."

"They teach you nothing about what happens between a man and a woman?"

"Only that a woman should submit to her husband in all things." She added as an afterthought, "Of course, I don't actually know any women who do."

He made a disparaging sound. "Do you understand what it means to make love with a man, Elizabeth?"

Her heart seemed to be lodged in her throat. "Yes."

"What does it mean?"

She felt another rush of heat to her face. "It means that a man and woman kiss each other. And perhaps put their arms around each other."

"Like this?" Lord Jonathan stepped forward and encircled her waist with his large hands. Then he bent his head and brushed his lips quickly, softly, undemandingly, across hers. He straightened and stared into her eyes. "Is that making love?"

"I don't think so, my lord," she said, swallowing hard.

He drew her nearer and held her firmly against him. His hand slid up and down her arm. With one finger, he traced the outline of her bottom lip. Her mouth opened.

"Is this making love?"

She managed to shake her head no, but she was no longer quite certain.

He buried his face in her hair, and she knew he was breathing in her scent. Her stomach did a somersault, her knees buckled, she couldn't seem to keep her wits about her.

She wanted something from Lord Jonathan, but she had no word for it in her vocabulary. She was on the brink of a discovery. She felt as if she were on the edge of a great precipice, teetering back and forth. The tension was unbearable.

"Lord Jonathan—"

"Jack."

"Jack, please."

"Jack, please, what?"

"I don't know. Just please." She was confused. She wanted more, but more of *what*?

"By the blessed Bast," he swore as he clasped her around the waist again and lifted her up until she was at eye level with him, "they should bloody well teach you English girls something useful, even if it's only how to protect yourselves." He gave her a little shake.

She let out a gasp. "Oh!"

"Look at me, Elizabeth," he commanded in a voice that would brook no argument.

Reluctantly she raised her eyes and gazed directly into his. "Yes, my lord."

His mouth thinned. "For your own sake, I am going to take you in hand and teach you about men and women."

She nearly choked. Surely he already had taken her "in hand."

"Men and women, my lord?"

He set her down and stood there for all the world like a king issuing a royal decree. "Specifically I am going to teach you about what happens between a man and a woman when they make love."

Chapter 8

Elizabeth was suddenly grateful for the solid stone floor beneath her feet.

"We will begin with a kiss."

She settled a suitably studious expression on her face; she would not want Jonathan Wicke to think her inattentive. "A kiss," she repeated.

He raised his eyes heavenward, as if indicating a need for patience. "We'll start with something simple. Brush your lips across mine."

She went up on her tiptoes, brushed her mouth across his as she had been instructed, and quickly stepped back.

"Too fast. Too fast," he judged. "Try again."

This time she lingered for a moment, inhaling the scent that clung to him, taking a small taste of him—Elizabeth admitted to herself that she rather liked the way he smelled and tasted—then she backed off.

"How was that?" she asked, trying not to appear too eager for his praise.

He frowned. "Better. But a kiss is something to be enjoyed, even savored, rather than merely endured."

She took his suggestion under consideration. "Savored? Like my favorite pudding?"

Jack laughed. It was a rich and totally masculine sound, slightly on the mysterious side, and it sent tiny tendrils of awareness to every nerve ending in her body.

"That wasn't quite what I had in mind, but if it helps . . ." He shrugged his broad shoulders. "Yes, then, like your favorite pudding."

This time Elizabeth rested her hands on the front of his elegantly tailored suit coat and hovered in the vicinity of his mouth. She felt a little like a hummingbird fluttering near a forbidden flower.

She avoided looking directly at him, knowing that she wasn't ready for those mesmerizing blue eyes of his. Instead, she studied his lips: They were firm without being hard, they were full without being overly generous, they were very near to her own. She came closer and slowly brushed her mouth back and forth across his, once, twice, thrice. He tasted of red wine and sweet dates and desert sun.

Her lips were suddenly dry, and she was forced to wet them. In doing so, she accidentally touched his mouth with the tip of her tongue. A strange strangled noise came from deep down in his chest.

She hesitated. "Am I doing it incorrectly, my lord?"

"No." His breathing was labored. "You're doing it correctly."

"Not like a schoolgirl?"

His response was low and fervent. "Not in the least. You are obviously a very adept pupil."

"Is that good or bad, my lord?"

"It's both good and bad," he said, sounding almost angry with her.

"Is that the end of my lesson in kissing?" she inquired.

His eyes glittered like sapphires; his handsome jaw was thrust out in determination. "The end?" Jonathan Wicke gave a well-done laugh. "It's just the beginning, my dear Elizabeth."

Her eyes widened. "There's more?"

"More than you can imagine," he promised.

More than she could imagine? A premonitory chill raced down her spine. There was danger here. She could feel it. And it wasn't just because she found herself alone with Lord Jonathan again; it was due to her own curiosity. Curiosity, after all, had killed the cat.

"It was, however, satisfaction that brought him back," she murmured half to herself.

"I beg your pardon, my lady, but your attention appears to be wandering," he pointed out with a touch of exasperation. "You are talking to yourself."

Elizabeth gazed up at the darkly handsome man looming over her. "My sincere apologies, sir."

"As I was saying, we will move on now to

Lesson Two." He bent over and brought his face to within a fraction of an inch of hers, his eyes gleaming with purpose.

"Lesson Two," she echoed.

"A kiss may be playful or passionate, obligatory or greatly desired, given or stolen—"

"As was my first kiss the other night on deck," she blurted out without thinking.

He cleared his throat. "Yes."

She mused, half-aloud, "It wasn't at all what I'd expected."

Jack frowned. "What did you expect?"

Her forehead creased in thought. "I was told that my first kiss would be sweet and tender, that it would be bestowed upon me by some handsome young man in the conservatory or *l'orangerie* or the music room." She shrugged. "I assumed it would be a pleasant experience."

She felt Jack draw in a long breath and let it out slowly. "Was it so very *un*pleasant, then?"

Her eyes flew to his. "Oh, no. I didn't mean to imply that. It was thrilling. Truly."

His face relaxed into a smugly satisfied smile. "Then shall we proceed with the lesson?"

"Oh, yes, my lord, let us proceed."

"As I was saying, a kiss may convey many things, *be* many things. For example, a simple expression of greeting or friendship." He illustrated by dropping an impersonal buss on each of her cheeks.

Elizabeth laughed lightly. "I have had many kisses of that sort from Maman and Caroline and the elegant ladies who come to stay at Stanhope Hall. Even from a few of the gentlemen."

"A few of the gentlemen?" he repeated a little gruffly, his black brows drawing together.

She quickly explained. "Old friends of the family, a distant relation or two, and Cousin Horace, of course."

"Of course."

She could tell he was displeased. "What is it, my lord?"

Reaching out, he spanned her waist with his hands as if he were measuring her for a corset. "I don't believe I like this Cousin Horace of yours."

"But you don't even know him," Elizabeth pointed out.

"I don't have to," he said, splaying his fingers across her rib cage. "He has been allowed to kiss you many times, and I have not."

"But that's different, sir."

"How so?"

She swallowed. "Cousin Horace kisses me like a—cousin."

"And how do I kiss you?"

Elizabeth found herself at an utter loss for words. How could she possibly tell Jonathan Wicke that he kissed her like a lover when she had no idea how a lover kissed?

He grew impatient. "Like this?"

Without further ado he swooped down and captured her mouth. His lips were hard and demanding; they ground against hers. He was insistent she surrender to him. Just as that night on deck, Elizabeth was given no choice in the matter. She parted her lips and he plunged his tongue into her mouth again and again until she couldn't think, couldn't breathe, couldn't even stand on her own two feet.

Just as abruptly as the onslaught had begun, it ended.

Jack fell back a step, and stood there staring at her with hooded eyes. His chest was rising and falling in agitation. As was her own. She was not the only one, it seemed, who was disturbed by what had taken place between them.

Elizabeth was trembling with emotion. She took a moment to collect herself. Then she lifted her chin and said, with a hint of defiance, "Yes."

He squinted. "Yes?"

"Yes, *that* is how you kiss me."

He quickly corrected her. "That is *one* way I kiss you. There can, there will, be many others."

Before she could object to receiving another of his lessons, Jonathan Wicke gathered her in his arms, lowered his head, and took her mouth with his. This time he was gentle, persuasive, tender to the point of bringing tears to her eyes. This kiss was as different from the first as night was from day.

He kissed her, and the shadows of the King's Chamber rushed in on them. Elizabeth could discern the slightest noise, the merest movement around them. It registered somewhere in the back of her brain that there were no doubt mice, perhaps even rats, living and thriving deep inside the Great Pyramid.

Then the room receded and there was nothing but the heat of each other's flesh, the scrape of her muslin skirt against his muscular thighs, the soft, seductive feel of his jacket beneath her

fingertips. She was aware of every nuance of
smell and taste and touch. It was the singularly most exciting and yet frightening moment of
her nearly eighteen years. She was no longer in
control of herself or the situation. Her head was
swimming with sensations. Jonathan Wicke was
right: There was more to lovemaking than she
had ever imagined.

Far more.

She tried to breathe. "Jack . . ." Under the
circumstances, it seemed ludicrous to continue
referring to him as Lord Jonathan. "I-I don't know
what we're doing."

He reluctantly tore his mouth from hers, but
only for an instant, only long enough to reassure
her. "I do."

When he finally came up for air again, Elizabeth
whispered, "Is this what happens between a man
and a woman when they make love?"

At first Jack didn't answer with words. Instead,
he slowly and seductively slid his tongue in and
out of her mouth in a most suggestive fashion.
Elizabeth could feel his breath on her face; it
was hot and sweet and intoxicating. It went to
her head; she felt as if she had drunk a dozen
glasses of champagne.

"Lovemaking is like that," he murmured
against her lips. Seeing the blank expression
on her face, he went on, "You really don't
understand what I'm talking about, do you?"

Elizabeth shook her head and confessed, "No."
But she suspected it had something to do with
the warm dampness between her legs and his
awful affliction.

Jack drifted back into the shadows, carrying her with him. He began to take little bites of her delicately shaped ears, the soft skin where the curve of her neck met the top of her dress collar, the outline of her chin. She wondered if he could feel her trembling. Surely so, for she was shaking from head to toe.

"Don't worry, my wild English rose," he muttered thickly, "we'll take it one step at a time."

Then his hands were on her back, caressing her from shoulder to waist, then lower to the small indentation at the base of her spine, then lower still to her derriere. Since she wasn't wearing a bustle or crinolette—none was required by the cleverly designed traveling dress—Elizabeth realized belatedly that there was no barrier to the liberties Jack was taking.

He cupped her bottom in his palms and deliberately brought her into the enclave of his thighs. She could clearly feel the changes in his body. She gasped in shock when something hard and thick and swollen was pressed into her belly, but Jack did not stop. His hands moved up and down her figure, lingering, enjoying, making her breathless with his touch.

She wanted to ask him if they were making love yet. After all, her blood was boiling, her skin was covered with a fine sheen of perspiration, and she was fighting an almost hysterical urge to laugh.

What did it matter? She had never felt like this before. She wondered if she would ever feel like this again. Dear God in heaven, she hoped so!

Then she heard a soft whimper of need and realized it was her own.

"Patience, my beautiful Elizabeth," Jack whispered at her shoulder. "We're getting there."

Getting *where*? Elizabeth wanted to ask. As it was, she was about to jump out of her skin.

His right hand insinuated itself between their bodies, brushing up against her breast, and in spite of the corset she was wearing, her nipples reacted instantly. They puckered and poked at her clothing; it was both pleasurable and painful.

Elizabeth closed her eyes and threw back her head. She saw herself for the first time as a sensual creature. She was aching with an overwhelming desire. She wanted it. She needed it. Craved it. Despaired without it. She just didn't know what *it* was. Then a vision of Jack bending over to take her naked breast into his mouth filled her mind.

Her eyes flew open. By the saints above, she was a Wanton! She must be to entertain such illicit thoughts.

Then she was distracted again by what Jack was doing with his hands. They were burning her flesh right through the material of her dress. Slowly, deliberately, evocatively, he caressed her breast, her softly rounded belly, her slender waist, then he slid one hand down to the juncture of her thighs and touched her where she scarcely dared touch herself. He pressed his palm against the sensitive mound.

"Jack!" Elizabeth gasped, and closed her eyes at the thrill that shot through her.

"Yes, my wild English rose, we're getting closer and closer," he said with a gritty chuckle.

The friction of his hand was driving her quite mad. She arched her back and instinctively drove her hips toward him. He removed his hand and ground his body into hers. She could feel the rigid length of him rubbing against her.

She was dazed, but still curious. "What is it, my lord?"

He was nearly shouting. "My desire for you."

She managed a shaky breath. "I don't understand."

"When a man and woman want to make love, certain inevitable changes occur in their bodies," Jack explained in a hoarse voice as he rotated his pelvis back and forth across hers. "For a man it is all out front: his member becomes hard, erect, and grows to several times its normal size. For a woman, it is far more subtle. Her breasts swell and her nipples become distended." Jack placed his hand on her, and her body reacted as he had predicted. "And here—" he placed his palm between her thighs "—she becomes hot and moist, and her essence flows like sweet honey. Then she is ready to open up and accept the man."

Elizabeth felt her eyes grow round as saucers. She choked on the words. "Do you mean that a man puts *it* inside a woman's body?"

He didn't bat an eyelash. "That is precisely what I mean."

She was dumbstruck. "But why?"

"Why?" A burst of laughter escaped him. "Because that is the way it is done."

Her tongue was thick in her mouth. "Is that making love?"

"It's *one* way to make love."

"There are many," she said faintly.

"There are many."

"Does it feel good?" she asked in a rapid, deep, unnatural voice.

"It feels wonderful," he said huskily. "It's like dying and coming back to life."

Elizabeth was still skeptical. "Are you telling me the truth?"

Jack was suddenly solemn. "I'm telling you the truth. I swear it."

She reflected upon what he had revealed to her. Then she demanded to know: "Why was I not informed of this before?"

Jonathan Wicke shook his handsome head from side to side. "Society doesn't see fit to educate sweet young virgins in the ways of the flesh."

Elizabeth bit her lip and looked about twelve years old, although she had no way of knowing how young she appeared. "You must not speak of such things, my lord."

He crooked a sardonic brow at her. "Don't you think it's a little late for modesty?"

He was right, of course, but she voiced her objection nevertheless. "Such things should not be spoken of between a man and a woman."

"In other words, I may place my hand on your breast and I may even touch the very heart of your femininity just so long as I do not speak of it aloud," he said without a shred of gentleness.

"My lord!"

He mocked her. "Oh dear, did I offend your

delicate sensibilities, my lady?"

"Yes. No." Frustration drove her to blurt out, "Damn you, Jack."

He appeared mildly surprised. "At long last, a totally honest reaction from you, my dear Elizabeth," he said indulgently. Then he smiled and reached out a lazy hand to cup her chin. "Has anyone ever told you that you are utterly irresistible and utterly beautiful when you get your dander up?"

Elizabeth had heard it all before. From him, as a matter of fact. Sputtering with ill temper, she declared, as, indeed, she had the first time, "You are a most exasperating man!"

He stroked his chin and seemed not in the least bit contrite. "Yes, I suppose I am."

"It is not something to be proud of."

"No, I suppose it isn't."

She stepped away, shaking her head in annoyance. "Do not play games with me, sir. I am not a child."

He brought her up short and stared down into her face. "Let neither of us play games then, Elizabeth. Let us always speak the truth to each other."

She raised her chin in challenge. "The truth always."

"The truth always," he vowed.

He was a fine one to talk about the truth, scoffed Black Jack as he stood towering over the frazzled girl.

Let us not play games then, Elizabeth. What in the bloody hell did he think he'd been doing for the past hour as he introduced an innocent into the pleasures of the flesh? Indeed, had he not been playing one great, elaborate game with Elizabeth Guest from that first moment in the bazaar when he'd followed her into the alley and rescued her from the thugs?

What had to be done, would be done. That was the way of the desert.

Perhaps it was, but he wasn't very happy with the ways of the desert at the moment. To add to his discomfort, he was in genuine physical pain. He was about to explode. It would take very little to set him off: a casual movement of her hand or thigh against his crotch.

He needed a distraction: that was the key.

He took a deep breath, and exhaled slowly, forcing himself to think of other things besides what he really wanted to do, which was to whisk Elizabeth off to his tent in the desert and make love to her for a solid week.

Damn it to hell, he swore silently. His manhood was not retreating in the face of defeat as he had hoped.

Suddenly he very much wished he had a bottle of fine brandy at his disposal. For as much as he wanted Elizabeth here and now, he wouldn't, couldn't, find his release in her lovely young body. That was for certain. This was neither the time nor the place.

But one day, someday, somehow, Black Jack told himself, she would be his.

With the patience and the iron-willed discipline of mind over body learned in the desert and on the battlefield, he forced his muscles to relax. He was rewarded, in due course, by feeling the tension slowly flow out of him.

Once Jack was quite himself again, he adjusted his trousers and bent over to retrieve Elizabeth's straw hat, which had fallen, unobserved, to the cold stone floor of the chamber. "We must be leaving. It's time we rejoined Miss Duvay and Alee, and returned to Lady Charlotte's."

She nodded and said nothing.

"You may wish to put yourself to rights by that torchlight," he said, pointing to the other side of the shadowy room.

She walked past him in silence.

"Your hat, my lady," he said a bit awkwardly as he held it out to her.

"Thank you, my lord."

He shot her a curious glance. "Are you all right?"

Elizabeth fussed a bit with her hair before replying, "Of course I'm all right." He watched as she plunked the straw hat down on her head and turned to face him. "Why shouldn't I be?"

He hemmed and hawed before answering. "I thought perhaps . . . I naturally believed . . . I just assumed . . ."

She arched an eyebrow, perfectly shaped by Nature herself, in his direction. "Yes, my lord . . . ?"

His lips tightened. "I thought you might be distressed."

She looked at him with big eyes. "I am not distressed. I am quite well. And you, sir? How is your affliction?"

"I must deal with my 'affliction,' as you call it, as best I can," he responded in a taunting voice.

He had never thought of it in those terms until the chit had happened along. Now he was beginning to believe that's exactly what the damned thing was: a cursed affliction!

The more he considered the foibles of his own flesh, the angrier Black Jack got.

By the pointed teeth of the jackal-headed god Anubis, this was turning out to be a pretty piece of work!

For one so young and so supposedly innocent, Lady Elizabeth was certainly blasé enough about the afternoon's activities. Either that, or she was a damned fine actress.

Before it was all said and done, he would get to the bottom of the matter, Jack promised himself. He would have his answers concerning his elusive quarry.

It was later that same afternoon—they had returned to the small village at the base of the Sphinx, rejoining the rest of their touring party— that Jack overheard Colette Duvay inquire of her mistress, "Oh, milady, was the Great Pyramid as exciting as you have always dreamt?"

"Yes, Colette."

"Was it splendid, milady?"

"It was splendid."

"Was it large?"

"Larger than I had ever imagined," confessed Elizabeth, the tips of her ears growing pink.

"Deep and dark?"

She nodded, and self-consciously fingered the strings of her reticule. "Very deep and very dark."

"Cold?"

"Not once you reached the heart of it."

"Were you afraid, milady?"

"At first I was."

"And later?"

"Later I found that I was no longer afraid," she declared dreamily.

It was at that moment Elizabeth looked up and found he was watching her. She hesitated—her foot half-in and half-out of the donkey's stirrup—and stared back at him.

Jack could think of only one word for the expression he saw on her beautiful face. The discovery shook him to the core; it haunted him for days afterward.

Desire.

Elizabeth desired him.

Chapter 9

"One day women will refuse to wear corsets," Elizabeth announced with a grimace as she was being laced into hers.

"Ack, I do not think so, milady. It would be the end of *civilisation* as we know it. Now, take a deep breath and expel it, *s'il vous plaît*," instructed Colette.

"I do not see," she pointed out to the French-woman with the last ounce of her breath, "how refusing to wear corsets will be the end of civi-lization."

"*C'est la mode*, milady. Where would any of us be without *la mode*?"

Where, indeed, would the world be without fashion? Elizabeth reflected with grim humor as she was being buttoned, laced, and fastened to within an inch of her life. By the time Colette was finished, she could scarcely breathe, let alone move.

"Maman says that 'dress is an expression of a woman's place in society.' "

"Your Maman is a wise woman. You should listen to her more often." Colette couldn't resist adding for good measure, "We must put our shoulders back and stand tall, milady. Our posture is of supreme importance, is it not?"

Elizabeth was thankful that an answer wasn't required. The importance of good posture had been drummed into her since childhood. First by Maman and Nanny. Later by Caroline and Colette. It was not a topic of discussion that she personally found of any interest. Now, if they'd wanted to talk about the ancient Egyptian custom of worshiping and mummifying the sacred Apis bulls—that would have been riveting!

"I'll wear the brown outfit today," she said as she stood in front of the cupboard in her stateroom and regarded the row of day dresses.

"The green dress is most becoming on you," commented Colette as if she hadn't heard her. "It brings out the color of your eyes. An excellent choice."

Elizabeth sighed and gave in without an argument. "The green it is."

Colette Duvay took the dress out and fussed with it, fluffing the skirt and muttering to herself in her native language that the creases really should have had a flatiron applied to them, but as usual, there had been no time to see to it what with running from place to place as they were from morning till night. Then she lowered her voice and gossiped, as she kept working. "Did you notice the beautiful moire silk Mrs. Winters was wearing yesterday when we toured the mosques?"

Elizabeth wrinkled up her nose. "I believe it was pink."

Her companion shook her head and countered with a very French sort of clucking sound: "*Non, non*, milady. Not just pink, but rose—the color of the tea roses that grow in the garden at Stanhope Hall. The ensemble emphasized the lady's complexion and hair to perfection, *n'est-ce-pas?* Even her stockings were of the sheerest pink silk."

"However do you know that?"

Colette tugged the green dress down over Elizabeth's head before answering. "There was a brief moment, as Lord Jonathan was helping Madame Winters from the carriage, when the tinest bit of ankle was revealed."

Elizabeth said thoughtfully, "I suppose Amelia Winters is considered very chic."

"*Mais oui!* You could learn something from her," said Colette, not unkindly.

She kept her eyes downcast. "Do you suppose that men find her beautiful?"

Elizabeth did not see the knowledgeable look that was cast in her direction. "Ah, *mon petit chou*, I believe that Lord Jonathan finds *you* beautiful."

She raised her eyes, and gazed at her friend and confidante in the mirror. "Am I that transparent?"

"Transparent? *Mais non*. You have always been the mysterious one, you with your nose in a dusty, dreary old book, and those great huge eyes that say much but reveal little." Colette finished fastening the bodice of the green dress and stood back for a moment to admire her handiwork. "I was speaking of Lord Jonathan. I have seen how he looks at you."

Her eyes widened perceptibly. "How does Jack—Lord Jonathan—look at me?"

There was a discreet smile. "Like you are a strawberry tart and he would like to eat you up in a single bite."

Elizabeth blushed right down to her roots. The French were so blasé about such matters. She wasn't sure she would ever get used to it. Still, she found herself asking, *"Vraiment?"*

Laughing lightly, Colette Duvay assured her, *"Ma foi, c'est vrai!* Truly."

She moistened her bottom lip and voiced the doubts that had been gnawing at her. "I'm not altogether certain that Jonathan Wicke is a gentleman."

Her companion patted her arm with a leisurely and studied grace. "The important thing, *chérie*, is that he is a *man*."

"Oh, he is that!" exclaimed Elizabeth.

A faint amusement flickered across the young Frenchwoman's features. "If you will please be seated, I will begin on your coiffure." She picked up a sterling silver hairbrush from the dressing table and set to the task of untangling the chestnut brown tresses that reached nearly to Elizabeth's waist. *"C'est magnifique!"* Colette announced, as she did every morning; it was all part of their daily ritual.

"Hair is hair," sighed Elizabeth, although she knew that wasn't entirely true. Most women of fashion were forced to augment what Nature had given them by intertwining elaborate chignons or braids with their own hair. She was lucky; hers was rich and thick and soft as silk.

Colette told her very much the same thing. "You are very fortunate to have such a splendid head of hair. I have known women who would have sold their souls to the Devil himself to have such hair as yours."

She frowned and pointed out, "Caroline says I mustn't be vain about it. And it's not as if it is any of my doing, after all."

"Your elder sister is undoubtedly *jalouse* of you," the woman said baldly.

That possibility had never occurred to Elizabeth. "Do you really think so?"

"Mais certainement."

"I can't imagine why. Caroline is very beautiful. Her husband and children adore her. They have a wonderful house, a more than adequate income, and many friends."

Colette cupped her charge's face for a moment, and they gazed at each other in the mirror above the dressing table. "But you, *chérie*, are beautiful on the inside, as well as on the outside. This is rare indeed."

She was embarrassed. "Pah, Colette."

Her companion shrugged her shoulders, as only a *parisienne* could, and speculated, "There is the matter of your ages. Lady Caroline is ten years older than you are. Nothing can change that. And she does not have your beautiful hair."

Elizabeth sighed with pleasure. "And she does not have *you* to brush her hair."

They exchanged an affectionate smile.

Then Colette was all business again as she went back to the task at hand. "Since we are going to trudge through yet another dirty old museum today, may I suggest that we braid your hair and secure it at the nape, so."

"Yes, that will do nicely," said Elizabeth, but she had other things on her mind. Picking up an ivory fan from the dressing table in front of her, she spread it open and immediately snapped it shut again. "How old do you think Lord Jonathan is?"

"Twenty-six," came the reply.

Her eyebrows rose fractionally. "How can you be so sure?"

"I was speaking with his servant, the one called Kareem, and he told me."

For a long moment, indecision held her, then Elizabeth asked, "And Mrs. Winters, what is her age?"

"That one is harder to say." After an interval, Colette ventured a guess. "Perhaps thirty. Perhaps even a little older. She is extremely well preserved, whatever her years."

Elizabeth gnawed on her bottom lip, and offered, "Maman says that gentlemen choose to marry women younger than themselves because they must have an heir. But they actually prefer a more mature lady for company."

The hairbrush paused momentarily in midair. "The countess is rarely wrong about such matters."

"Maman says that a mature lady is better at conversation—" Elizabeth swallowed hard "—and other things."

"I suppose that is true." Colette's tone conveyed a shrug as she deftly wove the long strands of chestnut brown hair into a single thick braid.

"Do you think Lord Jonathan prefers an older woman to a younger one?" she asked with an offhandedness she did not feel.

"Do you mean an older woman like Mrs. Winters?"

Her heart gave a leap. "Yes."

There was no trace of irony in the Frenchwoman's voice when she continued. "Young or old, it is apparent to everyone that Lord Jonathan prefers you. He does not even see other women, but especially a woman like Mrs. Winters."

Elizabeth just stared and frowned, leaving it to Colette to explain her own remark.

"Mrs. Winters dresses beautifully and she speaks beautifully, but there is something about her that . . ."

"What?"

"Troubles me."

Elizabeth tore a leaf of *papier poudre* from a little purple book on the table and quickly wiped the shine from her face. "Is it because she is a married lady?"

Colette Duvay made a dramatic gesture with her hands. "I fear it is because she is not a lady at all."

"Not a lady?"

"Not a lady."

"How can you tell?"

"*L'intuition.*" She seemed reluctant to expound further.

Elizabeth made a final perfunctory check of her appearance and rose to her feet. "Surely you are mistaken."

"*C'est possible.*" The subject was skillfully changed. "The green dress was an excellent choice. It is most becoming on you."

"Thank you, Colette."

"Are we ready for breakfast now, milady?"

She gave her companion a bright smile. "We are, indeed." And, in spite of the fact that properly brought-up young ladies were never supposed to admit to being hungry, Elizabeth declared, "I'm famished."

"Nothing but piles of junk," declared Colonel Winters as they entered the Egyptian Antiquities Museum later that morning after breakfast. "Reminds me of my grandmother's attic at Pelly House."

"Now, now, dear, let's not go into all of that," sidetracked Mrs. Winters as she swept into the dingy hovel and took a look around. It was filled with worm-ridden furniture, broken crockery, stacks of antique spears, wooden boxes falling apart at the seams, headless statues, and decaying mummies. "Although I must confess this isn't what I'd expected."

"Nor I," admitted Elizabeth with a terrible sinking feeling of disappointment.

Jonathan Wicke entered through the open door,

ducking his head to miss the framework, and announced to no one in particular, "We must have taken a wrong turn somewhere. This is a storage room."

Elizabeth immediately brightened. "Of course, that explains it."

"Nothing but piles of junk," repeated Hulbert Mathias Winters as they retraced their steps to the spot where they had left their carriage.

As they did so, another horse-drawn conveyance pulled up alongside theirs, and two gentlemen got out. They doffed their hats in recognition, and the more elegantly dressed of the pair came forward and greeted them. "My dear Mrs. Winters, and Colonel Winters, we meet again so soon and so unexpectedly."

"Count Polonski, how pleasant to see you." Amelia Winters was suddenly all charm and lightness as the man raised her gloved hand to his lips. She seemed flustered by this show of continental manners, and it was a moment or two before she remembered her own. "Forgive me, may I present our charge, Lady Elizabeth Guest, and another member of our touring party, Lord Jonathan Wicke."

"André Polonski at your service, my lady," he murmured as he gave Elizabeth a small, crisp bow.

"*Count* André Polonski," corrected Mrs. Winters.

The gentleman shrugged and displayed a self-deprecating smile on his handsome face. "It is of little consequence since those with titles and lands were thrown out of my country in the aftermath of the Revolution." Then he turned and shook Jack's hand with a degree of familiarity. "Wicke."

Jack nodded and responded in a neutral tone, "Polonski."

"You two know each other?" said Colonel Winters.

"We've met socially on several occasions," replied the count. "I'm only surprised that I haven't had the pleasure of making your acquaintance before, Colonel, and that of your lovely wife. I thought I knew everyone in the expatriate community."

"Ah-hem, yes," blustered the military man, tapping his silver-tipped walking stick against the side of his boot.

Amelia Winters quickly stepped in and explained, "We were in the Sudan until my husband's recent retirement from service in Her Majesty's army."

"Damn messy business, the Sudan," muttered Hulbert Winters prophetically.

The pretty woman ignored him and continued. "In fact, we have just returned to the region from England. We're accompanying Lady Elizabeth, in the role of chaperons, at the request of her father, Lord Stanhope."

Recognition lit up André Polonski's dark eyes. "Of course, your father is the renowned archaeologist."

Amelia Winters's next comment was directed at Elizabeth. "We were introduced to Count Polonski at luncheon the other day. He, too, was a guest of Lady Charlotte's."

"A most unusual and fascinating woman, Lady Charlotte," enthused Elizabeth. "I have read her book, *Letters from Egypt*, several times."

"As have I," admitted the elegantly attired gentleman as he turned his considerable charms on her. "Is this your first visit to Egypt, Lady Elizabeth?"

"Indeed it is, sir."

"And today you are touring the antiquities museum." With hat in hand, he gestured toward the hodgepodge of buildings and shacks behind them.

"Yes. At least we're trying to. We took a wrong turn on our first attempt and ended up in a storage hut."

The count laughed; it was a lighthearted, infectious sound that soon had them all joining in. All but Jonathan Wicke, that is. Out of the corner of her eye, Elizabeth noticed that Jack stood slightly apart from their group.

What was he up to?

He seemed to be studying them, each in turn, as if they were pieces of a giant puzzle and he was trying to imagine how they fit together.

She would have liked to give the matter further thought, but André Polonski reclaimed her attention at that moment. "I know the director of the museum, Lady Elizabeth, and I am certain he would be happy to arrange for someone to show you where the best exhibits are located."

"That would be greatly appreciated, sir. Our regular guide wasn't feeling well this morning and was forced to remain aboard ship."

"Yes, how kind of you, Count Polonski," purred Amelia Winters as she stepped up and placed her hand on his forearm.

"If I may, then. This way," said the newcomer, indicating the direction in which they should walk.

They trooped off toward the entrance in twos and threes: in front, Mrs. Winters with the count, followed by Elizabeth and the colonel, then the others, including Lord Jonathan and his servant, Kareem.

Elizabeth glanced back over her shoulder and spotted Colette speaking to the man who had arrived with Count Polonski. Leaning toward her escort—in order not to be overheard—she whispered, "Who is the other gentleman?"

The colonel stroked his chin, as was his habit, unintentionally setting his jowls into a kind of swinging pendular motion, and considered for a moment before answering. "A destitute relation of the count's, from what we could garner during luncheon at Lady Charlotte's. His name is Georges something-or-other, I believe, and he acts as Polonski's valet, traveling companion, and second-in-command."

"I see." How dreadful, she wanted to say, to be stuck in such a dubious position. Rather like being caught in Limbo; it was neither heaven nor hell. Not a close relation, but not an employee, either.

"Seem to recall the chap's a Frenchie. That could be jolly good for your Mademoiselle Duvay. One of her fellow countrymen, so to speak."

A censorious brow was arched in his direction, but the colonel missed seeing it, as he often did.

Actually, Georges seemed quite taken by Colette already. They had their heads together and were chatting animatedly in their native tongue. Then Elizabeth spied the first of what was to be dozens of life-size statues, and everything and everyone else, for a time, ceased to exist.

"It's magnificent!" she exclaimed in reverent tones as she approached the masterpiece of ancient sculpture.

"It is King Khafre," stated Count Polonski, coming up to stand beside her. "Son of Khufu and the builder of the second pyramid at Giza."

"Khafre—he was also thought to be the creator of the Great Sphinx," she added as she studied the hieroglyphs carved into the dark diorite stone.

"I see you know your Egyptian history."

Elizabeth dismissed her extensive knowledge with an offhanded, "A little."

She wanted to reach out and touch the lifelike statue, but did not dare to be so bold. After all, this was Pharaoh. This was the god-king. Khafre may have been a man, but he had been no ordinary man.

The count went on. "This particular statue dates from about 2500 B.C. and was discovered by workmen in the valley temple at Giza about fifteen years ago."

Elizabeth stood and stared at the seated figure with its ceremonial headdress and beard, symbol of royal dignity. The throne was flanked by two lions, symbolizing the power and the protection they conferred upon the king. From her vantage point, Khafre's gaze rested far away, beyond the ken of any mere mortal who would look upon him.

She shuddered. The Ancient Ones had believed that they would live forever. Perhaps, in a way, that was exactly what they had achieved: eternal life. For she was gazing upon the features of a man who had lived and breathed over four thousand years before her.

"Ah, here is our guide now," pointed out André Polonski.

"Good morning, ladies and gentlemen. Welcome to the Egyptian Museum," said their appointed escort in perfect English. "I will be happy and pleased to show you the most remarkable exhibits in the museum's collection of artifacts."

"How kind of you, sir," said the count.

"The first room we will visit houses the treasures of Queen Ahhotep, uncovered in 1859 by the agents of Auguste Mariette, the founder of the Antiquities Service and this museum. The treasures include the gold ceremonial ax and dagger that belonged to King Ahmose of the Eighteenth Dynasty; a gold and silver bark; bracelets, anklets, pendants, and necklaces of gold and silver with semiprecious stones; and a pharaonic gold collar that weighs over 8,640 grams."

There was a collective gasp of astonishment from the group. The guide smiled broadly. This was apparently a common reaction, and one he enjoyed.

"Please follow me, if you will."

One after the other they trotted along behind their guide, going from room to room, building to building. Elizabeth tried to take it all in, but it was more than even she could fathom, despite the years spent reading about these very artifacts and their original owners.

They ended up in a high-ceilinged vestibule filled with glass cases in which the museum's impressive collection of papyri were displayed.

Elizabeth bent over and studied the fragile piece of paper in front of her. It was a rare copy of the ancient Book of the Dead, that most sacred of all religious texts. Its mere presence in the tomb was enough to insure the survival of the pharaoh in the netherworld.

She was awestruck; she scarcely dared to breathe. And when she became aware of someone peering over her shoulder, she didn't have to look up to know who it was. She simply knew.

"Were they men or gods?" posed Jack, his voice deep and his words slowly spaced.

"Perhaps they were men who *believed* they were gods," she replied as they strolled to the next case.

It contained a letter written centuries before by a dutiful son to his father, from a loyal prince to his king, the pharaoh. There was a handwritten translation beside the papyrus in both Arabic and English.

They moved on to a smaller display case tucked into a corner of the vast hall. The light wasn't as good here, and it took Elizabeth several moments to comprehend exactly what they were looking at. When she did understand, she grew hot with embarrassment. For the papyrus described in both hieroglyphs and pictographs a god-king and his queen in the act of making love.

"Apparently they were like other men in some ways," Jack pointed out unnecessarily.

Elizabeth couldn't believe what she was seeing, but neither could she take her eyes off the erotic papyrus. For there in front of her, in its infinite variety, was lovemaking between a man and a woman!

The text depicted a royal male with a huge member protruding from his groin. The female's breasts were exaggerated, and their pointed centers were painted a bright cherry red. Indeed, she recalled reading in one particular manuscript in the library at Stanhope Hall that women in ancient Egypt were accustomed to using rouge on their nipples.

She stared in disbelief at the illustrations. There was an entire series showing the man inserting his rod into the woman from the front, from the back, while reclining over her, while standing beside her, with the two of them seated, with her kneeling, with her mouth wide open. And that was only the beginning. The text went into even greater detail, describing what a male could do to a female with his tongue and a vast assortment of foreign objects.

Elizabeth felt the air catch in her lungs. Her hand flew to cover her mouth. Surely a man and woman didn't engage in such unnatural acts!

Jack laughed and seemed altogether unconcerned by the explicit nature of the contents. "I have a feeling that the ancient scribe who penned this particular papyrus thoroughly enjoyed his work. Don't you agree, my dear Elizabeth?"

She didn't answer; she couldn't speak.

"Are you feeling all right?" inquired the handsome man beside her, his tone only half-humorous. "Suddenly you've gone as white as a ghost."

She shook her head—it wasn't a yes or a no—quickly turned, and dashed from the room.

Even as she raced down the corridor, her skirts flying behind her, the heels of her shoes clicking on the marble floor, she could hear Jack calling after her, "Elizabeth, where in the dickens do you think you're going?" Then he swore loudly. "Well, hell and damnation!"

She couldn't have agreed more. Hell and damnation, indeed.

Once she was quite certain that she was alone, Elizabeth slowed her pace and tried to breathe normally again. Never in all her life had she imagined that a man and a woman did such things together. It was shocking. It was wicked. It was—enticing.

She staggered back against the wall of the museum and squeezed her eyes tightly shut. Her heart was pounding in her breast. Her hands were shaking. Indeed, she was trembling from head to foot. For if she was honest with herself, it wasn't outrage she'd felt at the sight of the erotic illustrations; it was curiosity.

What would it be like to make love with Jack?

She gave herself a good shake. "I mustn't think about such things. A well brought-up young lady wouldn't, shouldn't, couldn't . . ."

Elizabeth straightened and took notice of her surroundings for the first time since running away from Jonathan Wicke. This was an unfamiliar section of the museum complex, and one that they had not toured today.

Dusting off her skirts, she peaked around the corner. There was a roomful of ancient chariots and elaborately decorated boats; ritual figurines and *shabtis*, those substitutes for the deceased, charged with working on his behalf in the next world; sarcophagus and gilded coffins.

Drawn like a magnet, Elizabeth took several steps into the midst of the haphazardly arranged collection, and found herself immediately enthralled by what she saw. There were so many wondrous treasures to behold, despite the dust and the dirt and the grime. She impatiently waved a few cobwebs aside and tried to ignore the sound of something underfoot skittering across the floor.

She bent over a magnificently preserved death mask encrusted with carnelian, lapis lazuli, quartz, obsidian, turquoise, and colored glass, and lost all track of time.

It was a crick in her neck that finally brought Elizabeth back to the present. She reached behind her to massage the sore muscle and only then realized that the storage room was quickly filling up with shadows. There was no window, and precious little light was coming in now from the corridor outside.

Her manner lost its absentmindedness and took on an air of practical concern. There was a slightly musty, decayed smell in the air that she hadn't noticed earlier, almost as if a pallor of death hung over the room.

She thought she heard footsteps in the hall behind her. "Jack?"

But she knew it wasn't Jack. And when she swung around, there was no one there.

"Hello, is anyone here?" she called out all the same, suddenly feeling nervous and not knowing why.

Dead silence greeted her.

Perhaps it was time, she told herself, to retrace her steps and rejoin the others. They were doubtlessly wondering where she'd gone. They might even be worried about her.

Her hand was already on the doorknob when she spied a dark, looming shadow on the wall. Adrenaline shot into her veins. She stifled a scream. Then Elizabeth laughed at herself: It was an upright mummy case behind the door that she simply hadn't noticed before.

She paused to study the hieroglyphs on the front, tracing the ancient lettering with the tip of her finger and reading aloud, " 'A curse upon any who would do harm or sacrilege to Rahotep, he who dwells within.' "

Peering around the half-open lid, she discovered the mummy case was empty.

The storage room, on the other hand, was apparently not. For the next thing Elizabeth knew, a heavy hand caught her between the shoulder blades and shoved her into the empty coffin.

A savage voice, which seemed not to be male or female, hissed, "Go away, Englishwoman. Go

back to where you came from before any harm
befalls you."

Then the lid was slammed shut.

She groped for a handle, for any means of
opening the coffin, and quickly discovered that
no one had intended for the dead to escape.

Elizabeth's blood ran cold. There was no way
out.

Chapter 10

S he'd come up missing again.

The last he had seen of her was the colorful swirl of a green skirt as she took off down the corridor of the antiquities museum and, turning the corner, disappeared from sight.

Damn fool woman!

Damn fool child!

For Elizabeth Guest was both: woman and child.

Black Jack drove a hand through his thick, dark hair and muttered under his breath, "Damn. Damn. Damn."

Rescuing the chit was becoming a habit with him. He'd better make quick work of it before the others returned and started asking questions. Questions he didn't want to have to answer. Questions like why had she run off in the first place.

He could hardly reply that they'd been gazing at an erotic papyrus together and the young lady had been shocked out of her lacy drawers.

The explicit nature of the image that popped into his head was scandalous—and quite stimulating: Elizabeth without her drawers. Now, *that* would be interesting. Very interesting, indeed.

Black Jack felt his groin tighten and the beginnings of sexual arousal stir his flesh.

"You'd better keep your mind on the business at hand, Jack-O," he complained as he took off along the hall, the heels of his boots ringing on the marble floor.

He had certainly become one randy son-of-Osiris since meeting the luscious Lady Elizabeth less than two weeks ago. Admittedly, he had been without a woman for too long, but there was more to it than that. *Any* woman would no longer do. It was Elizabeth he wanted, or it was no one.

"A fine state of affairs," Jack bit off sharply as he turned the first corner he came to. "Caught in a trap of your own making, you bloody idiot!"

For every time he thought of their dalliance in the Great Pyramid, and he seemed to think of it often—it had kept him awake three nights running, cursing the weakness of his own vulnerable flesh—with Elizabeth trembling passionately in his arms, her nipples protruding through her clothing like two fine pearl buttons deliberately meant to tease and provoke him, he started to get hard all over again.

It was the damnedest thing.

But it was no excuse. He shouldn't have teased her this afternoon. He shouldn't have stood by and watched the expression on her lovely face when it finally dawned on her what they were looking at. He'd known at a glance, of course. He'd also known that she would be shocked. Any innocent would be, and Elizabeth was as innocent as they came.

At least she had been until she'd met him.

"You've become an uncivilized bastard, Wicke!"

Briefly he wondered that he felt so little remorse. Of course, remorse was a luxury in this part of the world; something an Englishman would feel, and he was no longer English. Or so he told himself.

He knew what he must do. He must find Elizabeth. Apologize to her. Soothe her. Perhaps kiss her a time or two. Then escort her back to the others. And he must, above all else, be a gentleman about it.

Jack marched along the corridor, opening and closing doors, scanning empty rooms, perusing deserted displays. "Elizabeth? Elizabeth, where are you?"

There was no answer.

Not a sound.

He cut down another hallway and inspected the galleries on either side, and came up empty-handed. It was as though she had disappeared into thin air.

Black Jack planted himself in the middle of the main corridor, his feet a good eighteen inches apart, his hands forming fists, and glared into the fading afternoon light.

Where in the hell was she?

Maybe she was playing games with him. Getting a little of her own back. His next thought was that she'd better not be. Retribution would be rained down on her lovely head if that turned out to be the case. He was not a man to play games.

Unless they were of his own devising . . .

When another half hour had come and gone and still he hadn't found her, Jack became genuinely worried. Something—some sixth sense that he had learned to trust over the years—told him that the matter was no longer one of lost and found; it might well have become one of life and death.

A sense of urgency drove him. He turned in to a section of the museum they had not toured earlier that day. He stopped and cocked his head and listened.

Tap. Tap. Tap.

He listened again, but there was only silence. Had he heard the tapping, or merely imagined it? Following his instincts, the same instincts that made it possible for him to travel in the desert as if he were born to the burning sands, Jack came upon a dark corridor and was rewarded by hearing the tap, tap, tap grow louder.

"Elizabeth? Gad, Elizabeth, is that you?"

Jack was nearly running now. He burst into the storage room and took it all in in a single glance: the collection of ancient artifacts, the straw hat knocked to the floor, the two sets of footprints in the dust.

The rhythmic sound was coming from somewhere inside the room.

The mummy case.

He tried to pry it open with his fingers, but it
was to no avail.

"Elizabeth?"

There was a muffled cry. "Jack!"

Frantically he looked around, trying to find
some object to use as a lever. He spotted a
metal spear propped in the corner. He grabbed
it, inserted the tip into the crack between the
front and back of the coffin, and pried open
the lid.

"Jesus, Mary, and Joseph!" he exclaimed as
Elizabeth crumpled into his arms.

He held her.

Held her close and promised himself that he
would never again take her safety for granted.
He realized that Elizabeth was far more precious
to him than he had imagined. He thought of
how narrow her escape had been, how close he'd
come to losing her, and a rush of anger surged
through his veins.

Grasping her by the arms, Jack stared down
into her tearstained face. "What in the devil were
you doing in there?"

Her eyes were huge, the pupils dilated to twice
their normal size, as she tried to explain. "Someone . . ." she took a deep, fortifying breath and
began again. "Someone pushed me."

"Pushed you?"

Elizabeth nodded, and the movement of her
head set her braid to unraveling.

"He locked me in."

"Who?" he demanded to know.

She looked up at him as if he'd taken complete leave of his senses. "I don't know who. I never saw him. He came up behind me."

Jack felt his eyes narrow into slits. "Then how do you know it was a man?"

The girl thought about it for a minute. "It was the hand on my back; it was too large and too strong for a woman. Besides, the voice was masculine—"

His ears perked up. "Voice? He spoke to you?"

"Yes."

"What did he say?"

Elizabeth swayed back and forth on her feet, and recited by rote, "He warned, 'Go away, Englishwoman. Go back to where you came from before any harm befalls you.'"

"That's all?"

She shuddered. "That's all."

It was enough.

Gazing up at him, tears swimming in her lovely eyes, Elizabeth whipered in a frightened tone, "Is someone after me?"

Jack scowled. "I wouldn't say someone is *after* you. But he may be trying to frighten you a bit."

She gave a short, derisive laugh. "Well, he's succeeded. I am frightened."

"There's no need to worry, Elizabeth. I'm here now. No harm will come to you."

Black Jack heard himself say the words, and at least for the moment, he meant them. He realized for the first time since his mother had died, he felt protective of a woman. Then he realized something else. His mother, the duchess, would have liked Elizabeth Guest. Liked her and approved of her.

"I must look a terrible fright," said the girl. She reached behind her shoulder and attempted to do what she could to fix the frizzled braid.

Jack brushed her hands impatiently aside. "Here. Let me do that." He grasped the strands of silky hair expertly between his fingers and began to cross one over the other.

"Where did you learn to braid a woman's hair?" she asked in a low voice.

He shrugged. "I used to do it for my mother." He quickly finished and secured the end to her scalp with a hairpin. "But that was years ago." He bent over and picked up the straw hat; the crown was slightly crushed, the ribbon half torn off. "I'm afraid your hat's a little worse for wear."

"That's what you said to me that first day in the bazaar," Elizabeth murmured, taking the hat from his hands. "Do you remember?"

"Yes."

Her voice caught a little. "Why were you following me that day?"

He studied her mutely for a short, taut moment. He wasn't used to having his motives or his actions questioned by anyone, let alone a girl barely out of the schoolroom and just off the boat from England.

And he wasn't about to tell her of his sacred vow to Prince Ramses.

Jack's mouth twisted into a wry smile. "Word was out on the streets of Alexandria. There was a beautiful girl shopping in the bazaars. She was reputed to be a rare English rose." A faintly hard-boiled expression crept over his features. "I hadn't seen an Englishwoman in a long time. I was curious to find out if this one was as fair and as beautiful as the gossips said." It was the truth—as far as it went.

"And was she?"

"She was even more beautiful than they'd claimed."

Elizabeth casually dusted off her skirts as if she were used to being locked in mummy cases and receiving compliments of that sort from a gentleman every day. But the tremor in her voice, when she spoke next, gave her away. "Naturally, this incident must remain our secret."

He bowed his head. "Naturally."

"Not that we've done anything improper."

"Not this time."

She speared him with a look. "But my chaperons would never let me out of their sight, not even for a moment, if they were to find out that someone had accosted me."

The solution to the problem seemed simple enough to him. "Then we won't tell Colonel and Mrs. Winters."

"Nor Colette."

"Not even the ever-faithful Colette."

Elizabeth tapped a finger on her bottom lip. "We won't mention it to anyone of our acquaintance: not Lady Charlotte, not Count Polonksi, not Alee, not anyone."

He was in complete agreement. "We won't tell a soul."

She glanced furtively around as if to make certain they were alone. "It is never wise to let the enemy know any more than you have to."

"The enemy?"

What in the blue blazes was Elizabeth talking about? What would any seventeen-year-old girl of her breeding and upbringing know about the enemy?

Nevertheless, there was a firm resolve, one might even say stubbornness, about her chin that Jack had to confess he'd never noticed before.

She lowered her voice to a surreptitious whisper. "Someone wants me to quit Egypt, my lord. Mark my words, that was just a first warning. There will be others."

He was speechless. Was Lady Elizabeth quite mad? Had she gotten too much sun? A dish of bad dates?

He regarded her for some seconds. What if she was right? What if someone did want to frighten her away? Or discover whatever information she carried around in that lovely little head of hers?

Someone, that is, besides him.

It had come to her while she was locked in the mummy case: the final clue to the mystery, the missing piece of the puzzle.

Excitement brought a hot flush to Elizabeth's cheeks. Her stomach was doing somersaults. Her mind was racing. Her hands were trembling.

She paced back and forth in her cabin aboard the *Star of Egypt*. Why hadn't she seen it before? It was so clear to her now.

Wrapping her dressing gown around her, she

sat down at the writing desk beside the bed. It had been a long, exhausting day, but she was too keyed up to sleep.

She took out the diary she wrote in every night and turned to the back. With the edge of a penknife she carefully peeled away the leather binding. Inside were sheets and sheets of thin paper covered with meticulous writing penned by her own hand, detailed maps and translated hieroglyphs. She patiently sifted through each sheet, stopping every now and then to bend over one and study it closer.

Years of intensive scholarship and hard work were represented by the sheaf of notes in front of her. What had started out, at the tender age of twelve, as an attempt to understand her father's fascination, indeed, his obsession, for Egypt and all things Egyptian—an obsession that had taken him far away from his family, his ancestral home, even his country—had eventually become a deeply personal quest for her.

Her family had land, titles, wealth, and social position. She had nothing.

It was the study of ancient Egypt that took Elizabeth away from her otherwise humdrum existence, filled her waking hours, and gave purpose to her life. It was her father's dream to find the tomb of the Great Pharaoh, Merneptah Seti. In time, it had become her dream as well.

Elizabeth spread the topographical map out in front of her. It illustrated in every detail the hills and vales of the Valley of the Kings, and how every natural cranny and crevice had been exploited as a burial ground.

She unfolded a second map and placed it above the first: this was an epigraphical survey and showed the inscriptions found on dozens of tombs discovered since the first decades of the century by renowned and respected Egyptologists: Wilkinson, Karl Lepsius, and her father, of course.

A third map was done in her father's hand. It had accompanied one of his letters to Cousin Horace and marked the site of his latest excavation. A large red X marked the spot where Lord Stanhope and his associates had been digging for Merneptah Seti's tomb. At last report, they had come up empty-handed. Again. Now Elizabeth knew why.

Papa was looking in the wrong place.

Suddenly she wished the journey to Luxor were nearing its end, instead of only its beginning. She must speak to Papa. She must share with him her maps, the results of her research, her conclusions.

After it was all said and done, *she* and she alone would be the key to show her father where he would find the answer to his lifelong quest. He would be thrilled. He would be proud of her. He would love her, at last.

Elizabeth lifted her head from the writing table in her stateroom and looked around with heavy-lidded eyes.

It was late.

Indeed, the clock on the dresser told her it was the middle of the night. She must have dozed off while she was studying her notes.

She rubbed the sleep from her eyes, and lectured herself: "It was a stupid thing to have done, Elizabeth."

For if she was right—and she was right—then her father was about to make the greatest archaeological discovery of all time.

It was not a thing to take lightly.

Men would kill—indeed, had been known to kill for far less—in this sometimes savage land. It must, of necessity, remain a carefully guarded secret: her knowledge, her discovery, the fact that she was the key to the puzzle.

No one must suspect. Not the colonel and his wife. Not Count Polonski. Not Jack. Not even Colette. The secret would be kept close to her heart. No word of it would be whispered until she'd had the opportunity to explain it all to her father. He would know what to do. He would see that she was right. He would take his workers and dig where she told him Merneptah Seti was buried, and the treasures of the past would be opened to them. Treasures such as man had never seen or imagined. Treasures beyond belief.

Elizabeth quickly gathered up her notes and maps, and slipped them into their hiding place in the back of her diary.

There would be little sleep for her tonight, but she did not mind. What was sleep compared to the thrill of a grand adventure?

Chapter 11

"**P**olonski has done *what*?"

Kareem took the brunt of his master's ill temper in his stride. It was not the first time he had been the bearer of bad tidings; it would not be the last.

He repeated the latest tidbit of news learned from one of the deckhands. "Count Polonski has booked passage for himself, and the one called Georges, on the *Star of Egypt* as far as Luxor. He has taken the recently vacated stateroom next to Colonel and Mrs. Winters."

Black Jack slapped his leather gloves against the leg of his riding britches in displeasure. "Son of a she-devil! When did he come aboard?"

"His carriage was pulling up at the dock even as I returned to my cabin."

Jack began to pace back and forth. "What time do we raise anchor?"

"Just after tea this afternoon."

"Blast!" He had to think fast. "I am to meet Lady Elizabeth and the colonel in ten minutes to go riding. We're going to see the Serapeum this morning."

The attraction—nay, obsession was a better word—of visiting ancient tombs was lost on his manservant.

Kareem wrinkled up his face. "Why, master?"

He explained. "Because Lady Elizabeth is fascinated by the cult of the Apis bulls and wishes to see where the sacred animals were buried."

The small man's teeth flashed in a rare, quick smile. "The young lady is most unusual."

Jack couldn't agree more. "Most unusual."

"The colonel will accompany you?"

"Yes. He is, after all, the girl's chaperon."

"And Mrs. Winters?"

"She has temporarily taken to her bed." Jack stopped pacing the floor of the sitting room, or what passed for a sitting room on a cramped steamship, and stared out the porthole. "Something was said at breakfast about a nagging headache."

Kareem cut straight to the heart of the matter. "Mrs. Winters does not enjoy the tombs."

"That is entirely possible." Now that he thought about it, Amelia Winters did manage to miss most of the touring.

Kareem offered another opinion. "Perhaps she prefers the company of a charming gentleman like Count Polonski."

"Perhaps she does at that." Jack picked up his hat and his riding crop. "In which case, I'm afraid she is going to have an unpleasant surprise one of these days. Polonski is neither charming, nor a gentleman."

This was obviously news to the native fellah. "You have encountered him before, master?"

"Indeed, I have." He beat out a rhythmic rat-tat-tat on his boot with the tip of his riding crop, and icily condemned the man with: "Ruthless, cold-blooded bastard."

His servant wisely kept his own counsel. It would not do to point out that the identical words were frequently used to describe Black Jack. A man had to be something of a ruthless, cold-blooded bastard just to survive in this part of the world.

Jack's brows congealed into a scowl. "It is no coincidence, I fear, that Polonski is sailing on this ship," he muttered half to himself. Then he glanced up. "I have a task for you, Kareem."

His companion gave a respectful bow of his head. "Your wish, as always, is my command."

"You must get off the ship."

"I will leave immediately."

"You will pack first. Take what you need for several weeks."

"Yes, Most Exulted One," said the diminutive man as if he were making a mental note—indeed, perhaps he was—of the instructions given him, "several weeks."

"Maybe even longer. It is difficult to know the time it will take to acquire the facts and figures I seek."

Dark eyes snapped to attention. "There is no need to concern yourself. I will be prepared."

Jack had no doubts about that. Kareem was always prepared. "I want you to return to Cairo as quickly as possible and see a man named Azar at this address." He quickly jotted down a house number and a street on a slip of paper and handed it to his minion. "Tell him that I wish to know if André Polonski has been involved in illegally smuggling antiquities out of Egypt in the past three years."

His manservant's eyes widened.

"I also want to know the source of Polonski's income."

"Yes, my lord, the source of his income."

"And anything else that may be of interest to me."

"What must be done, will be done."

Jack looked down at the wiry little man who had been his constant companion for the past five years. "You have never failed me before."

"I will not fail you this time."

Loyalty of that sort could not be bought. He patted the man on the shoulder. "I know."

"May the gods rain fire and famine, pox and pestilence, down on my head for all eternity if I ever fail you, master. May the women of my family be barren for ten generations. May my eyes be blinded, my tongue silenced, my—"

"I don't think we have to carry it that far, Kareem."

There was a look of the zealot in the man's eyes. "I have never forgotten what you did for my family, Most Generous and Benevolent One."

"That is an old debt and long ago repaid," said Jack, matter-of-factly.

"I have never forgotten," declared Kareem.

"I could not leave them to die."

"Anyone else would have."

"I could not."

Kareem stated simply, "That is why I will never fail you in anything you ask, master."

It had been a small enough thing to do, Jack recalled now. He had come across a family caravan in the desert. They had been attacked and left for dead by a gang of thieves and cutthroats. Everything had been taken, nothing was left, not even the clothes on their backs. Jack had bound up their wounds, clothed them, given them food and water, and when they were able to travel again, he had escorted them to their destination. For that, too, was the way of the desert. . . .

Three weeks later, Kareem had shown up at his door, pledging his loyalty, his life, his eternal gratitude, to Jack for what he had done for the fellah's family.

They had been together ever since.

When they were ready to part company—it was already past the hour Jack was to meet the colonel and Lady Elizabeth—he said to his man, "May the gods be with you."

"And with you, master."

"Rejoin us at Luxor when you have what I seek. The *Star of Egypt* will be anchored there for several weeks. If need be, I will find a reason to stay behind with the party if you have not returned by that time."

Kareem nodded his head. "I will rejoin you at

Luxor." Then added, "Pah, these English are a strange lot."

"They are, indeed," Black Jack agreed, both having forgotten for the moment that he was English. Then he had another thought. "It might be wise to have Azar obtain what information he can on Colonel and Mrs. Winters while he's at it."

"Yes, master."

Jack rubbed his chin as he considered the implications of what he had just done. "Something tells me that neither of the Winters are quite what they seem to be."

Kareem laughed darkly, and opened the door of the stateroom for his lord and master. "Ack, are any of us what we seem to be, master?"

Hulbert Mathias Winters gave the adjoining door between the bedchamber and the sitting room of their stateroom aboard the *Star of Egypt* a single, perfunctory knock, and entered just as Amelia was stepping out of a large copper bathtub. He took a moment to admire her lush hourglass figure, generous breasts, and white, creamy thighs, then commented: "Bit late in the day for bathing. Nearly teatime."

Amelia took the fine linen bath sheet from the native woman acting as her maid on the voyage, and dismissed her with a curt nod. "You may go now, Hete." She waited until the outer door had closed. "Don't be an ass, Hulbert," she hissed.

"I try not to be, my dear."

"Well, try harder," she said, blotting at her skin with the toweling. "I am bathing at this hour because it took these infernal people all day to get a tub of water properly prepared."

She was lying through her teeth; he could always tell. "Bit of a snag, what?"

"Yes. They're completely incompetent, every last one of them," complained the pretty woman.

He sauntered across the room and deliberately poked at the rumpled bedding with his riding crop, enjoying the expression of consternation that appeared on her face. Then he plunked down on the edge of the mattress and casually crossed one leg over the other, his boot resting on his knee. "Spend your day in bed, did you?"

Like the four-legged variety of cat, Amelia had always had the ability to land on her feet. She did so now. She nodded. "I had a terrible headache, as you were well aware of before you left this morning."

But Hulbert Winters didn't miss the small, smug smile that flickered across the she-cat's face. He even had a pretty good notion what it meant. He wondered in *whose* bed Amelia had spent the day.

She dropped the bath sheet to the cabin floor and stood naked in front of the dressing table, assessing her figure in the mirror. Not an ounce of false modesty about dear Amelia. She knew intimately every inch of her body the way a soldier knew his mount. She cared for it in much the same way: feeding it, grooming it, diligently looking after it, even sneaking it little rewards. A soldier understood if he took proper care of his horse, it would always take care of him. Amelia followed the same philosophy with her greatest asset: her body.

He leaned back into the pillows and watched as she turned her back to the looking glass. Peering over her shoulder, she pinched the flesh on her buttocks, apparently testing for unwanted padding.

Obviously satisfied that all was well in that department, Amelia slipped into a loose wrapper, sat down at the dressing table, and picked up her hairbrush. "Did you enjoy your day?" she inquired as she began to untangle the strands of golden-blond hair.

"Very much."

Hulbert pushed himself up on his elbows, then came off the bed and stood behind her. The sheer dressing gown had slipped halfway down her arm, leaving one shoulder and breast artfully exposed. With his gloved hand he reached out and encircled her ivory neck, caressing the bare skin. "You're as lovely as ever, my sweet."

She ignored the compliment and wrinkled up her nose. "You smell like horses."

"Been riding all day. What else would I smell like?" He brought the short whip around and flicked it back and forth across her nipples, then trailed it down her belly to the bushy apex of her thighs. "Always enjoy a good ride."

She wiggled and laughed knowingly.

She could be quite playful, even inventive at times. He'd seen her do things that could make a whore blush. And although she had pretended to be a virgin when they'd first met, she quickly dropped the pretense when she realized he simply didn't care. Indeed, he preferred that she was already accomplished in the art of making love.

Hulbert leaned over to follow the riding whip with the palm of his hand.

"You need a bath," Amelia pointed out.

"Fortunate there's a tub here, then."

"I'll have Hete bring you some fresh water." She started to get up and was stopped by the handle of the riding crop being brought down on her arm. He didn't hurt her, merely made his point.

"This will do for an old soldier. Don't mind climbing in after you, my dear."

"Whatever you wish, Hulbert."

Her meekness didn't fool him. He arched a shaggy graying brow at her. "*Whatever* I wish?"

He could almost hear her purring. She moved into the crook of his arm—apparently she'd forgotten her disdain for the smell of horses—and began to rub up against him. "What would you like?"

"For you to undress me—" buttons popped before he could finish his instructions "—and bring me a glass of Madeira while I soak in the tub."

Her mouth formed a girlish pout. "I thought you had something else in mind."

"Know you did. But you were wrong, my dear." *As you so often are*, he added silently.

"I suppose you're tired from all that riding."

Hulbert Winters wanted to say the same must be true for her. Instead, he nodded his head. "Bit of a trip to the Serapeum and back, old thing."

He knew she hated it when he called her "old

thing." That's why he occasionally made sure to throw it into their conversation.

"How is our charge, by the way?"

"Damn fine horsewoman, Lady Elizabeth."

"Somehow that doesn't surprise me. She's always struck me as the overly large, athletic type."

He ignored her cattiness. "Sits well in the saddle."

Amelia sashayed around him and said in a coquettish tone of voice: "That's what you used to say of me."

Hulbert was not amused. All of a sudden the woman annoyed rather than aroused him. No subtlety to her. No class. Not like Elizabeth Guest, who had more grace in her small toe than Amelia did in her entire luscious, overripe body.

Some of his distaste must have shown on his weathered face.

"You've become quite fond of the girl, haven't you, Hulbert?" said Amelia.

"Suppose I have. She's an fine, intelligent young woman with a good heart."

She struck like a coiled, poisonous snake. "I didn't think you ever noticed anything like a good heart. Unless, of course, it happened to beat beneath a pair of fine, high breasts."

"Is that all you ever think of?" he inquired with an air of deepest disgust.

"It's why you married me," she said a little too loudly.

He got his own back. "Ah, but we never quite got around to taking care of the formalities, did we, my dear?"

She turned her back to him and carelessly tossed over her shoulder, "It's just as well. You've gotten old, Hulbert, and you've become a bore in bed."

He twirled her around and brought her pretty face up to his, using the tip of his whip. "I think, my dear, that you have gone too far this time."

The authority in his voice had its effect on Amelia. Tears immediately appeared in her eyes; small, white teeth bit into her lower lip, drawing a drop of bright red blood; her heart-shaped chin began to tremble.

She inhaled deeply and whispered, "I'm sorry, Hulbert. I didn't mean what I said."

"I know you're sorry, my sweet. You always are."

It was a scene they had played out many times before, always with the same conclusion, more or less. And he wondered, as he always did, whether she was truly contrite, or merely a better actress than even he gave her credit for.

"Let me help you with your jacket and boots," Amelia offered in a subdued manner. "You'll want to bathe before tea."

"Smell like the very devil, I daresay."

"It's a manly smell, and you carry it well," she said, singing an entirely different tune than she had earlier. She continued making idle conversation. "I understand from one of the officers that we'll be docked at Minya, near Beni Hasan, for several nights so we can experience staying in the caves."

They were back on neutral and comfortable ground: their common goal, their mutual role as chaperons to Lady Elizabeth.

"Indeed, Lord Stanhope was very specific about his desires in this matter."

Amelia brushed off his jacket and hung it up in the cupboard, then presented her shapely backside as a boost to removing his riding boots. "Must we sleep in the caves?"

"Afraid so. It's all arranged."

She shivered, and her fear was genuine. "I don't like caves and tombs and things underground."

"I know you don't, old girl. But you'll do what has to be done. As you always have."

"Yes, Hulbert."

"It will be worth it in the end."

"I know." She set his boots to the side. "I'll have one of the servants polish these right away."

Amelia did see to him quite nicely, decided Hulbert Winters. It was one of the reasons, perhaps, why he kept her around.

Chapter 12

For once Elizabeth found herself in complete agreement with Amelia Winters. There was something eerie, even daunting, about sleeping in somebody else's tomb.

True, the proprietor of the hotel called them "caves" for the benefit of the skittish among his guests, but they were tombs all the same. One was even reported to still have the mummy in it!

These were not the grand and glorious final resting places of the great kings and queens—for that reason alone, they were often in pristine condition—but tombs of overseers, workmen, government officials, and their families. Cut into the cliffs high above the Nile, and the cluster of small villages along its banks, they had been built to a standard compact design, often measuring no larger than a small bedroom.

As he escorted her through the terraced garden, fragrant with evening flowers, the hotelier informed Elizabeth, "Yours was the burial chamber of the Lady Isis, wife of a village overseer during the Nineteenth Dynasty. Therefore, it is one of the most beautiful of all the painted caves."

"It's truly magnificent!" she exclaimed upon seeing her room for the first time.

"Yes, it is." Then the proprietor spoke of more practical matters. "I understand that your maid unpacked for you during dinner. There are refreshments on the table beside your bed. If there is anything else you desire tonight, please use the bellpull. Someone will come immediately."

That brought a raised eyebrow from Elizabeth.

Her host explained with a smile. "We are very modern in some ways, my lady. There are servants on duty throughout the night to attend to our guests' needs."

"I see," she said. "I'm sure I won't be needing anything, but thank you. You have been very kind."

"Your slightest wish is our command, my lady." He salaamed several times at the door. "I will send your maid to you now."

Elizabeth acknowledged the man's departure and then took a good look around the chamber in which she would be spending the next two nights.

The walls and ceilings were alive with color. They were brightly painted with intricate designs: the night sky and the heavens with thousands of twinkling stars, favored gods and goddesses, the lush fields of Iaru with its cool streams, palm trees hanging heavy with dates, and fields thick with grain and flax.

A mural on the far wall showed a string of porters carrying the exotic products of tropical Africa, including gold, ebony, leopard skins, giraffe tails, ostrich feathers, incense, shafts for spears, even a live monkey or two, and a baboon.

A lavish offering table was depicted on another wall. It was laden with fresh meat, trussed ducks and geese, bunches of lush purple grapes, loaves of bread, baskets of onions and other vegetables, and sealed jars of beer; an endless supply of food and drink to feed the spirit of the dead woman in the next life.

There was also a picture of the Lady Isis herself: slim, lithe, and eternally young.

"You were beautiful . . . are beautiful," Elizabeth whispered reverently as she stood before the life-size portrait of the tomb's original owner.

Even after three thousand years, the classic Egyptian features of the Lady Isis were perfect in every detail: the kohl-lined eyes, the formal black wig, the flowing gown of deep blue, the exquisite gold and silver jewelry.

"I wonder what happened to your mummy," Elizabeth speculated aloud. Adding, "I hope you don't mind if I sleep in your tomb."

"*Pardon*, milady?" said Colette as she bustled into the room, ready to see to her mistress as she did every night.

"*C'est rien,* Colette. I was just talking to myself." She quickly turned away and prepared for bed.

It was some time later that the young French-woman reluctantly bid Elizabeth good night and left for her own tiny bedchamber, declaring, "I still do not *comprendre* the reason for sleeping in catacombs, milady. I will undoubtedly have the *cauchemar*, the nightmare, as a result."

"Try not to think about it, and I'll see you in the morning." Then she called out cheerfully, "*Bonne nuit*, Colette!"

Once alone, she sat down at an ancient table to write in her diary. But with the portrait of the Lady Isis facing her, Elizabeth found her mind wandering tonight.

She rested her chin on her hand and gazed up at the lovely woman who had lived thirty centuries before her. "I wonder if you had any grand adventures." She sighed. "Were you in love with your husband? Did you have any children?"

Love.

This past week she had been giving the subject a great deal of consideration. She'd decided that she was *not* in love with Lord Jonathan, Jack. She couldn't be in love with him; it would be unwise of her and far too dangerous.

But she did think she rather fancied him.

Jack had been very quiet at dinner tonight. The charming and very amusing Count Polonksi had done most of the talking. He had been every-where, done everything, knew everyone, and he was a naturally gifted storyteller. He even related a delicious and slightly naughty tale about the

Prince of Wales and a certain Mrs. L——.

Elizabeth had blushed at the details, but she'd enjoyed every scandalous morsel.

With a dramatic sigh, she put her pen down and closed the leather-bound book. "There's no use in fighting it, Elizabeth, you're not going to write in your diary tonight."

She prepared for bed, turning down the lamp and slipping between the covers, remembering to lower the mosquito netting around her.

Then, on second thought, she got up again, took her diary from the table, and stuffed it under her pillow.

Elizabeth assumed it was dreams of Jack that brought her out of another night of restless sleep. She sat straight up in bed and stared into the darkness. The only hint of light was through a small window added to the front of the tomb, And only then because there was a full moon.

She sat there, her heart beating wildly in her breast, and tried to calm herself. She could not hear anything but the thunderous sound of blood pumping through her veins and the air rushing in and out of lungs starved for oxygen. Her body was bathed in perspiration. Her nightgown was damp and clung to her skin.

Had dreams of Jack awakened her again? Dreams of his kiss, his caress, his muscular body, that part of him which made a man so very different from a woman, the alluring words he whispered in her ear, the enticing things he could do to her with just his tongue.

Elizabeth shivered.

Or was it an even darker and less appealing dream that had brought her out of sleep?

She had been having the same dream over and over since her beloved Annie had died. It was the same terrifying feeling that always awoke her in the dead of night, her body in a cold sweat, her heart pounding as if it would burst.

Someone was chasing her.

She never knew who or why, only that if he caught her, it would mean the end. Annie was always with her, needing her protection, slowing her down as the unknown pursuer mercilessly hounded them. She never intended to leave her younger sister behind, of course, but inevitably Annie's hand would slip from her grasp and they would be separated.

She never knew what happened after that, Elizabeth realized as she sat there staring into the dark, because she always awakened herself, crying, before the end of the *cauchemar*.

She wiped at the tears on her face. What had awakened her tonight?

Thump.

Thump. Thump.

Elizabeth nearly jumped out of her skin. The fine, infinitesimal hairs on the back of her neck were suddenly standing straight on end. Her scalp tingled. Gooseflesh covered her from head to toe. She was frozen in place, one hand among the bed pillows, the other about to stifle a sleepy yawn.

The realization hit her like icy fingers walking up and down her spine.

Someone was in the room with her.

She tried to swallow and discovered that her throat was as dry and parched as the desert during a sandstorm. Her stomach was filled with butterflies. She couldn't seem to catch her breath; she felt as though she were suffocating.

Fear.

For the first time in her life Elizabeth understood on the most basic level what that primitive human emotion really was. Nay, perhaps not for the first time; the first time she had been truly afraid was the night her Annie had died.

But this was fear of a different sort. This was the fear of the unknown, the hunted at the mercy of the hunter, the pursued stalked by the pursuer. Her hands and feet were ice-cold. Her mind was vitally alert, while her body seemed paralyzed. It was like a *cauchemar*, a nightmare, only she was wide awake!

Then she saw a shadowy figure in robes steal across the small chamber, and she stifled a startled gasp. Someone—or some*thing*—was there!

Was it a ghost?

The mummy of the Lady Isis come back to reclaim her tomb?

Elizabeth felt hysteria bubble up in the back of her throat. She could almost imagine the linen-wrapped body rising from its coffin and walking through the night. Surely she could detect the smell of resin, used in ancient times to coat the shroud of the dead, and the faint but unmistakable odor of decay.

She gave herself a good shake. This was no time for histrionics. Of course it wasn't a ghost or a mummy returned from the grave. It was a flesh-and-blood human being. It must be.

Through the mosquito netting, it appeared that her late-night intruder was headed for her travel trunk. Whoever it was intended to rifle through her personal belongings.

Think, Elizabeth. Think! She couldn't sit there and do nothing, playing the fainthearted maiden. No Sir Galahad in shining armor was going to ride up on his trusty steed and rescue her from whatever terror lurked in the shadows of her bedchamber. She was on her own. Whatever must be done, would be done, by her, and no one else.

Where was her mettle? Her strength of character? Her courage? Her courage was one of the things that dear, sweet Annie had always said she admired most about her. Wouldn't her younger sister be disappointed to see her now, cowering among the bedcovers like a weak, silly woman?

She heard the telltale sound of the lid squeaking as the travel trunk was opened. It made her half-sick to think that a stranger was touching her intimate garments, putting his filthy hands on her sheer lawn nightclothes, her chemises and drawers. Would he carelessly toss aside the antique cameo brooch that Maman had bestowed on her when she turned sixteen? Gloat over the precious photograph of Annie and her family that she always carried with her?

Elizabeth realized with amazement that what she felt now was more anger than fear. After all, what could ever hurt her again as much as she had been hurt by the death of her beloved Annelise?

The answer was clear: nothing.

Suddenly she was incensed. How dare a thief break into her room, trespass on her property, invade her privacy, and frighten her half out of her wits. By all the saints in Heaven, she wasn't going to lie there in her bed like a sniveling, groveling coward! It was time to put a stop to this nonsense. But first, she needed a weapon.

Her pink silk parasol.

It was all she could think of. A pity, too, because it was bound to get damaged in the scuffle, and it was her favorite parasol. But what had to be done, would be done, Elizabeth reminded herself.

Unfortunately, the parasol was on the ancient table beside the bed, just out of reach. She would have to make a grab for it. In order to do that, she needed a diversion.

She took a deep breath, pushed the mosquito netting aside, and demanded to know: "Halt! Who goes there?"

The shadowy figure by the trunk froze.

Elizabeth snatched the pink parasol from the table, and wielding it above her head like Excalibur, repeated her demand, praying the intruder didn't hear the tremor in her voice: "I said, who's there?"

The thief straightened, turned, and flew past her as if the Devil himself were on his tail, in the process knocking a chair over and hitting the tin of biscuits on the table, sending them crashing to the floor of the tomb.

The door at the front of the chamber was flung open, and the shadowy form ran out into the night. In a flash, Elizabeth was out of her bed and in hot pursuit!

Parasol in one hand, she hitched up her night-dress with the other and chased after the intruder, her long legs and excellent physical conditioning once more holding her in good stead. It wasn't until her bare feet hit the path of crushed rock that she remembered she had not even stopped long enough to put on her slippers.

"Damnation!" Elizabeth swore softly under her breath as she stood there and watched her quarry disappear into the safety of the garden.

By the time she could return wearing adequate shoes and a robe, the thief would be long gone. She exhaled a great sigh, partly in relief, partly in exasperation. There was nothing to be done about it now. She may as well give up and return to her room.

She swirled around, and that was when she saw another shadowy figure behind her. She let out a small shriek and raised her parasol "en garde" in front of her.

Then she realized who it was, lowered her weapon, and exclaimed rather peevishly, "You scared the bloody hell out of me!"

Jack stepped into the moonlight and said in a droll tone, "Out for a midnight stroll, my lady?"

Chapter 13

"**O**r should I say a midnight race?" Jack fell back a step or two, and raised his hands in mock surrender. "Madam, you have me at your mercy. Please do not brandish your parasol so. It could prove a most destructive weapon."

"It could indeed, sir," she said boldly.

He looked down at her and remarked, "You seem to be out of breath, my lady."

The man's powers of observation were keen as always. "I *am* out of breath, my lord," she confirmed.

His curiosity was aroused. "And the reason?"

"Because I was chasing a thief from my bed-chamber."

Jack gave a snort of laughter. "You were chasing a thief?"

"Yes. I awoke and saw someone in my room."

When he saw that she was serious, he lost his smile; his mouth thinned. "Are you certain?"

"Dead certain. The intruder was rifling through my travel trunk. I called out. He ran."

His black brows came together in a disapproving scowl. "And you gave chase?"

She nodded. "I gave chase."

"You didn't use the bellpull in your chamber to call for help?"

She hadn't thought of it, but she wasn't going to admit that to Jack. "If I had taken the time to summon help, the thief would surely have gotten away."

"So you went after him yourself."

"Exactly."

"You little fool!" he hissed, clearly frustrated with her. "You could have been hurt."

"The thought had occurred to me."

How could she explain to Jonathan Wicke her progression from fear to anger? From cowering in her bed to pursuing the culprit? Death no longer held any terror for her. Somehow she had survived that awful night last winter when her dear sister—the one person in the world she had loved above all others—had died in her arms. Now Elizabeth knew she could survive anything.

He clasped her by the forearm and turned her from the front to the back and then to the front again, his gaze scanning every inch of her. "Are you harmed in any way?"

"No," she said composedly. "I am quite all right."

She was, however, suddenly aware of the sheerness of her nightgown, and the fact that it was damp and, therefore, had a tendency to cling to her skin in a most revealing manner. Her nipples responded to the cool night air by puckering up against the fine linen material. They were clearly visible, even in the moonlight. Indeed, she was conscious that Jack had been staring at them with the oddest expression on his features for several minutes.

It was suddenly an effort to breathe. "Is there anything wrong, my lord?"

He reluctantly raised his eyes to her face. "Did the thief take anything?"

"I don't know," she answered truthfully.

"Was there only one?"

"I only saw the one," she said, recognizing how feeble and naive that sounded.

"I will return to your room with you," Jack volunteered, taking her by the elbow.

She uttered a weak protest. "There really is no need."

"That," he insisted, an edge of steel under-lining each word, "is a matter of opinion. What if there were two thieves, and the other is still ransacking your belongings?"

Elizabeth suddenly felt utterly stupid. The pos-sibility had not occurred to her. "I didn't think of that," she confessed.

"Well, I did."

Jack was quite out of patience with her, she could tell. It was apparent in the set of his jaw, the rigidity of his mouth, the unbending appear-ance to his head and shoulders.

"I don't like to impose, my lord. You must be

anxious to return to your own room." She looked around the shaded doorways to the caves, wondering which was his.

Jack read her mind; it was uncanny. "My accommodations are next door to yours."

"Next—door?"

"It was once the tomb of a village overseer named Kha."

"Husband of the Lady Isis?"

"Yes." He crooked a brow in her direction. "How did you know?"

"I am sleeping in the Lady Isis's burial chamber."

"Kha must have done well for himself. It is unusual they each had a tomb. Usually a whole family, including married sons and daughters, would have been buried together."

"Together throughout eternity," murmured Elizabeth. "There is something rather comforting about that."

But Jack wasn't listening to her romantic ramblings. He was too busy berating himself for his failure to come to her rescue.

"I was right next door. If I had been in my room," he was muttering, "instead of taking the night air, I would have heard your screams."

Elizabeth didn't understand. "My screams?"

"When you spotted the intruder."

She assumed a regal posture and sniffed indignantly, "I did not scream, sir, when I spotted the intruder, or at any other time. *We* do not scream."

His mouth quirked. *"We?"*

"We women of courage and backbone, sir," she said, a shade haughtily.

"Ah, I see."

Somehow she doubted very much if he did.

"Neverthless," Jack continued, "I will sleep better tonight once I have checked your room for myself."

"As you wish, sir."

"You did warn me, you know," he said as they retraced her steps to the tomb of the Lady Isis.

As long as her legs were, Elizabeth still had to run to keep up with him. "I did?"

A muscle in Jack's face started to twitch, betraying the depth of his emotions. "You said there would be other attempts made to frighten you off."

She stopped dead in her tracks. "Do you think this incident is related to the one in the museum?"

His eyes looked angry. "Yes, I do."

She cried out softly, "The same beast who shut me in the mummy case was in my bedchamber tonight?"

He didn't bother to cushion the blow. "I'm sorry, Elizabeth, but it was very likely the same villain."

"Mother of God!"

"Someone is playing games with you, my dear girl, albeit nasty games," said Jack, in a very hard, dry voice. "I intend to see to it that they're stopped."

Elizabeth only half heard the veiled threat in Jack's tone. She was worried about her diary and the secret notes hidden within the binding. What if there had been an accomplice, and he'd searched her possessions while the first thief had deliberately lead her on a wild-goose chase?

"We must hurry," she urged, and slipping from Jack's grasp, took off at a run.

She raced through the open door of Lady Isis's tomb and made directly for the bed, feeling under the pillow for her precious diary. Her fingers touched smooth, cool leather, and she breathed a sigh of relief.

Jack followed on her heels. "What the devil?" he exclaimed, seeing her bent over the bed. "What's going on here, Elizabeth? What haven't you told me?"

She snatched her hand from beneath the bed pillow and declared, as she turned around, a guilty expression written on her face, "Nothing."

Suddenly he loomed in front of her: a tall, dark, handsome stranger dressed in an exotic robe, a pair of traditional trousers, and black boots polished to a sheen. In the pale moonlight his hair was inky black, his skin a burnished gold. She was reminded, not for the first time, that Jonathan Wicke was the most beautiful human being she had ever seen.

And the most dangerous.

"You may close your mouth now, Elizabeth," he said with a sardonic smile.

She snapped her mouth shut.

He advanced toward her. "Now, my dear, I want the truth."

"The—truth?" Her voice broke.

He came closer. "The whole truth."

She fumbled for the oil lamp on the table beside the bed and made a small production of lighting it. Once the room was illuminated, she felt much better.

"I can't tell you the whole truth," she said as calmly as she could. "I promised."

Jack gave a noncommittal grunt. "*Who* did you promise?"

"Myself."

"Yourself?" That obviously wasn't the answer he'd expected to hear.

Elizabeth nodded, her hair brushing back and forth across her shoulders, reminding her that her braid had come undone sometime during the chase. "I promised myself that the first person I would discuss it with is Papa. I made a sacred vow. Surely you wouldn't want me to break a sacred vow."

Jack started to say something, then changed his mind. "No. I wouldn't."

"Besides, it doesn't have anything to do with you."

Jack mumbled under his breath. It sounded remarkably like "I wish the hell it didn't." But she must have heard him wrong.

Elizabeth reached out and dared to touch his bare arm. "I'm sorry. I wish I could tell you."

"So do I."

"Don't be angry with me."

He blew out his breath expressively. "I'm not angry with you."

"You're disappointed in me."

"No."

"What is it, then?"

His blue eyes shimmered in the lamplight. "It's this whole bloody business."

"I don't understand."

"I know you don't."

The tension in the tiny room was thick enough to cut with a knife.

"I-I'd better clean up the mess the thief made," Elizabeth said, dropping to her hands and knees in front of him.

"I'll see to the blasted biscuits," snapped Jack, hauling her unceremoniously to her feet. "You check your trunk and see if anything was taken."

He righted the overturned chair and scooped up the broken biscuits from the floor of the tomb while she methodically went through her belongings.

"Everything seems to be here," she told him several minutes later.

Jack watched as she closed the lid of the travel trunk. "Apparently you scared the thief off before he could get his hands on whatever it was he was looking for."

"Apparently."

He folded his arms across his chest and leaned back against an ornamental column. "You're not going to tell me what it is, are you?"

"What it is?" she responded evenly.

"What the thief wanted."

"I don't know," Elizabeth swallowed, aware that her face was burning, "for sure."

"But you have some idea."

She lowered her voice to a near whisper. "I have some idea."

Jack expelled an exasperated breath. "God knows, most of us have our share of secrets.

I've got mine. I guess you're entitled to yours."

She moistened her bottom lip. "Thank you, Jack."

"For what?"

Elizabeth paused for a fraction of a second before answering, "For not forcing me to tell you."

His face darkened. "I've never forced a woman to do anything against her will."

It was true, but they both knew he was a persuasive man, and one who was fully capable of using his powers of persuasion on her.

Jack straightened with a leisurely grace. "It is time for me to say *bonne nuit*, my lady. I don't think you'll be bothered anymore tonight, but I will be right next door if there is any further trouble." He turned to leave.

"Jack—?"

He paused with his hand on the open door. "Yes."

"I wish you wouldn't go."

"It's the middle of the night, Elizabeth."

Her breathing shuddered in her lungs. "I know."

"Are you afraid to stay alone?"

"No."

He was very quiet; his face was masked by darkness. "You're only seventeen years old, Elizabeth. I don't think you know what you're saying."

"I'm nearly eighteen, and I do know."

Jack stepped back into the bedchamber and closed the door behind him. "What is it you want?"

You, she wanted desperately to tell him. *I want you*.

She faced him squarely. "I want a kiss."

He looked casually intrigued. "A kiss?"

"Yes," she gulped as fear returned. But this was fear of an entirely different kind. This was fear of the unknown that always existed between an inexperienced woman and a man of the world.

There was sensual awareness in every bone and muscle of his body as Jack sauntered toward her, taking his own good time.

"Your hair is even darker in this light than I imagined it would be." Only after she said the words did Elizabeth realize their significance.

Jack seized upon her slip of the tongue. "Have you pictured me in your bedchamber?"

She was quick to deny it. "No."

He slanted her a sideways glance. "That day in the Great Pyramid we vowed never to play games with each other. Do you remember?"

"Yes."

"We agreed to always—"

"—speak the truth," she finished for him.

"Let us be truthful with each other now, Elizabeth."

She hesitated and then told him what he wanted to hear. "I have imagined you in my bedchamber."

"And I have often pictured you in my bed. I desire you as I have desired no other woman." Jack stopped directly in front of her, reached out, and cupped her face in his palm. "You keep me awake at night, my luscious lady. Do I haunt your dreams as you do mine?"

Elizabeth's tongue was glued to the roof of her mouth. She couldn't speak; she could only nod her head.

"Do you dream of my kisses, my caresses, my wild English rose?"

She wanted to deny everything he was saying, but she couldn't. God help her, she couldn't. It was true. All true.

He was seducing her with his words. "We seem destined, you and I, to meet at midnight while the rest of the world sleeps."

Her hands made supplicating gestures. "I cannot sleep."

"Nor can I." He stroked the stubble on his chin. "We never finished your lesson in lovemaking, did we?"

She held her breath. "No, we didn't."

"The Great Pyramid was neither the time nor the place," he said, taking her hand.

"Indeed, it was cold and dark, my lord."

"Our clothing was a problem, too, as I recall."

"You recall correctly."

He exerted pressure on her hand, pulling her closer. "But it would not be a problem tonight."

"No—" she slowly let out her breath "—it would not."

"Your nightdress is very sheer," he said, lifting one eyebrow.

Elizabeth could feel his hot gaze on her. Her heart began to slam against her chest. "Yes, it is."

"The material is damp and it sticks to your body. I can clearly see the outline of your breasts and their darker centers. They are like rosebuds with morning dew clinging to their tips."

He raised his hand and brushed his fingers across first one nipple, then the other. Then the caress was repeated using the gold ring on his middle finger. Elizabeth could feel the smooth, cool metal through her nightdress. It did strange and wonderful things to her insides. Her stomach lurched. Her body tingled. And so it began again. The myriad sensations Jack could create in her with his touch.

"Is it always like this between a man and a woman?" she wanted to know as she began to shake with reaction.

His voice was a rasp. "Is *what*?"

"This thing that happens between us. Your manhood grows huge and hard. Your skin is beaded with perspiration. Your breathing changes; it becomes fast and shallow. I feel dizzy. My flesh is on fire. Every inch of my body, from head to toe, is sensitive to the slightest touch. My breasts swell at the thought of your caress. And . . ."

"And . . ."

"And there is a warmth and dampness between my legs."

Jack did not bother to disguise the pleasure her confession gave him. He groaned and admitted, "It is rare and wonderful when it happens to both the man and the woman."

"Then it doesn't always happen?"

"No."

"With most men and women?"

"With only a lucky few."

"Then it is rare and wonderful."

"Yes," he assured her.

"What do you suppose it means?"

"It means that we are just right for one another, my lovely Elizabeth," Jack muttered in a husky baritone. "It means that we excite and enflame and arouse and desire each other. That we want to make love to each other."

She did not ask him if it also meant they loved each other. She was not prepared to face that complication. She was already feeling slightly demented as it was. "Is it wrong to feel passion like this?"

He had obviously had enough of conversation. "Hush, my sweet. It feels so good, it can only be right."

The moon slipped behind a cloud; the night shadows closed in around them, but neither noticed.

Jack framed her face between his hands and stared straight into her eyes. "Shall we pick up the lesson where we left off?"

"Yes."

"Do you want to learn more about what happens between a man and a woman when they make love?"

She ached to know. She quickly nodded her head.

Jack made a strangling sound that rumbled deep in his chest. There were suddenly beads of perspiration on his brow. "You do test my self-control," he growled.

"I do?" she said with an air of unassumed innocence.

"Lord, Elizabeth, don't you have any idea how much I want you?"

Her throat was aching. "No."

"Do you want me?"

Want him? She wasn't sure what he meant, but somehow she knew she would surely die now if she did not get him. "Oh, yes, I want you, Jack."

He gave a fierce, tight smile of satisfaction and dropped his hands lightly to her shoulders. With a slightly rough fingertip he traced a line from her throat to her nape. Then he threaded his fingers through her hair and murmured, "Your hair is glorious."

"Th-Thank you, my lord."

He gripped a handful of long, luxuriant strands and brought them to his chest, brushing them back and forth across his bare skin. "It's like silk," he marveled.

"Th-Thank you, my lord."

"It is the color of the rarest rubies: there is a fire deep down in its heart. With just a touch, it seems to burn my flesh."

"Th-Thank—"

A solitary finger was raised to her trembling lips. "Do not thank me again, my sweet girl. Instead, run your fingers through my hair and tell me what is in your heart."

Elizabeth reached up and tentatively touched the thick mane of blue-black curls. Her mouth formed an O in surprise, and she grew bolder. "It *is* like silk."

"Thank you, my lady."

She was filled with a sense of wonder. "It's so soft. Like a whisper."

"Thank—"

She pressed the palm of her hand against his mouth. "The hair here—" she stroked the stubble on his chin "—is short and rough. While here," she said, walking her fingers across his chest with a gentle gait, "it is again as soft as the finest silk." Then she looked closer and frowned in puzzlement.

"What is it?" asked Jack.

"My lord, does a man have—" Elizabeth swallowed hard "—nipples?"

He choked on his own saliva. "Of course he does."

"Do they grow hard and protrude from his chest when he is . . ."

"Sexually aroused?"

Her cheeks flamed. "Yes."

"Why don't you touch one and see what happens?" he suggested.

Elizabeth located a small, nut brown tit that was neatly hidden by the dark hair sprinkled across Jack's muscular chest. She reached out and gave it a quick poke with her forefinger: it reacted instantly, curling up into a tight bud. A second foray was made; this time she lingered, teasing and testing the nub of rigid male flesh. The results were impressive.

"Why, that is amazing, isn't it?" she exclaimed with rapt fascination.

"Damn amazing," Jack gritted through his teeth.

She could detect the strain in his voice and was immediately concerned. "Oh dear, have I harmed you?"

"Harmed me?" he snickered.

"Have I hurt you in some way, my lord?"

There was a glint in his blue eyes when Jack claimed, "Yes, you have hurt me, my lady. Now you must kiss it and make it better."

It was a kind of game, Elizabeth realized belatedly, but it was a game she found she didn't mind, in the least, playing.

Going up on her tiptoes, she dropped a swift kiss on the angular jut of his jaw. "Is it better now?"

"I'm afraid not."

"It isn't?"

"No, you must kiss the exact spot you hurt."

Her mouth dropped open. Surely Jack didn't expect her to kiss his chest. He couldn't want her to press her lips to his bare flesh, perhaps even feel her tongue touch the small brown nipple. "I beg your pardon, sir."

Jack slanted her a crooked smile. "Never mind, my sweet, innocent Elizabeth. I realize it's all new to you. I'll gladly show you how."

With that, he reached out and traced the delicate bone just above her neckline. Somehow his fingers became entangled in the silk ribbon on the front of her nightdress, and as he tugged free, he also loosened her bodice. The next thing Elizabeth knew, her gown was down around her waist, and her breasts were bared.

"My lord!" She tried to cover herself.

"No." Jack captured her hands and held them away from her body. "Don't hide from me."

She watched him watching her. He couldn't keep his eyes off her breasts. They rode high and firm on her rib cage. They were proud and milky white, silky and smooth as satin, with rose red tips that eagerly puckered and grew and hardened under his intent study.

Elizabeth's pulse was racing. First her heart was in her throat, then it seemed to tumble all the way down to her feet. And she ached—oh God, how she ached!

Jack touched her, and she threw her head back as a low, impassioned moan rushed past her parted lips.

"Oh dear, have I harmed you?"

She was dazed. "Harmed me?"

"Have I hurt you in some way, my lady?"

It was the game again. Now she understood. "Yes, you must kiss it and make it better."

He quickly brushed his lips along her cheek in a most chaste fashion. "Is it better now?"

"No."

"It isn't?"

"You must kiss the exact spot you hurt."

Jack bent her back over his arm and lowered his head. She could feel the warmth of his breath on her sensitized skin. She wanted . . . she needed . . . she ached for . . .

"Jack, help me!" she cried out in pain.

He lightly touched the tip of his tongue to the engorged nipple. Then he nuzzled her with his mouth, his cheekbone, even his chin, rubbing back and forth, using the abrasive stubble as an erotic tool. But it was not enough, not nearly enough, and just as a pathetic whimper of need escaped her lips, he finally took pity on her and took her fully into his mouth.

Instinctively Elizabeth arched her back and

drove her nipple between his teeth. The serrated edges nipped that most sensitive, womanly flesh. He moved back and forth, from one breast to the other, giving both an equal share of his attention.

Then he settled down and drew her deeper into his throat and suckled on her long and hard. She could feel the corresponding erotic pull deep down in her womb. Suddenly she wasn't at all the kind of woman she had thought she was. She wasn't practical. She wasn't sensible. She did not have both feet always on the ground. She wasn't a creature of the mind; she was a creature of the senses. She was wild and free and as natural as the heat of the desert under the burning sun, and as cool as the desert night under a slice of pale desert moon. She had never imagined in a thousand lifetimes that lovemaking would be like this.

Lost in the excitement and thrill of Jack's caress, Elizabeth barely noticed when her nightgown was slipped over her hips and she was lowered onto the bed. It was only when roughened fingers moved to her bare legs that panic set in.

"My lord . . . Jack . . . what . . . ?"

"Do not fear, my wild English rose. It is but another of your lessons," he murmured in a soothing tone.

Still, she struggled a little as he came down beside her. There was no mistaking the familiar bulge in his trousers. She knew it well by now.

"Jack," she gasped, "are you going to put it inside me?"

He gently pushed the damp hair back from her

face. "No, my sweet innocent, I'm not. Oh, we will have our satisfaction this night, you and I, but you will still be a virgin after we have eaten and drunk our fill."

She told herself to stay calm. "Is this possible?"

"Entirely possible," he reassured her. "I can give you what you seek. I can take what I need. And you will still be as pure 'as unsunn'd snow,' my lady."

She did not know how this could be, but she trusted him to be telling her the truth. After all, had Jack not always done so? Indeed, was he not the only one to speak honestly to her of these matters?

He began to stroke her, arouse her, excite her as his fingers blazed a pathway from the hollow at the base of her throat, down between the ivory silk of her breasts, across her abdomen, causing her to take in her breath sharply, before descending to the valley between her legs. Just when she would have uttered a protest, Jack began to kiss her, slipping his tongue between her teeth and plumbing the depths beyond.

"Remember what I once said to you about the intimate kiss imitating that most intimate act between a man and a woman?" he whispered at her bare shoulder.

"Yes, I remember," she murmured languidly.

"This is the next lesson, my sweet. Hold on to me." With that, he drove his tongue into her mouth again, and somewhere in the midst of the erotic kiss, he tested the slick honey between her thighs and slid his finger into her body.

Elizabeth's eyes flew wide open. Her head came off the pillow. "Jack!"

Then the slow burning began, deep down inside of her, somewhere she'd never been before, somewhere she had not known even existed. It burned warm at first, then the fire grew hotter and hotter, until it engulfed her, threatened to consume her and eat her alive.

She was overcome by the most incredible sensations. She was tight and his finger seemed to fill her. She was moist, so he could easily slip in and out, and somehow she knew that it was a substitute for his manhood.

Then an exquisite tension began to build, and suddenly she was afraid. "Dear God—"

"Hush, darling girl, don't worry," murmured Jack. "What you are feeling now is perfectly normal and very wonderful. Soon you will know what it is to die in my arms and come back to life again."

With that he drove his finger into her faster and deeper. He rubbed his thumb against that most sensitive part of her, and she was spiraling higher, ever higher. Of their own volition, her hips rose off the mattress.

Then there was an explosion, and Elizabeth shattered into a thousand tiny shards. The impact was felt from the chattering of her teeth to the tingling in her toes. She gave a hoarse shout: "Jack! Hold on to me, Jack!"

"I'm here, sweet. I'm here."

Then it was over.

But it would never truly be over. It would always be there, tucked away inside her, next to her heart, hers to remember, hers to cherish, hers forever.

It was some time later, with her face nestled against his chest, her arms around his waist, that Elizabeth asked Jack to explain.

"You are a passionate woman, Elizabeth. But you know very little about your own body. Tonight you received sexual pleasure and sexual gratification. The tension in your body built to the point of no return and you were forced over the top, reaching your climax."

"You were right. It was like dying and coming back to life again," she said in a bemused tone.

He gently brushed a stray wisp of hair from her face. "I know," he said, smiling.

Suddenly Elizabeth realized that his manhood was still large and hard; it pressed insistently against her leg. "But what of you?"

"It is of no consequence."

"Of course it is of consequence," she said, pushing herself up onto her elbows. "Did you reach your gratification? Did you have a climax?"

He shrugged. "Tonight is for you. There will be other times for me."

"But you have given me so much, my lord. Why can't I give you a little of it back? You did say there were ways to make love that would insure my virginity." She blushed. "Not that I set such a high value by that dubious commodity."

He frowned and informed her in no uncertain terms, "But Society does. And so do I. I will not make love to you in that way."

"But there are other ways," she reminded him. "You said so yourself."

His gaze was heated. "Several."

"Show me."

Jack eased himself off the bed and quickly undressed, letting first his *kuftan*, then his trousers and underclothes, fall unheeded to the floor of the tomb.

Elizabeth watched, her eyes growing wide at her first glimpse of his manhood. It was even more magnificent than she'd imagined from the bulge in his trousers. "My lord . . ." she exclaimed breathlessly "you are huge!"

He couldn't resist teasing her. "Didn't you once tell me that Trout the gardener said you were blessed with the gift of a green thumb?"

"A green thumb?" Whatever did her gardening skills have to do with his body?

He laughed, and it was a delightful sound. "You, my dearest Elizabeth, have the ability to make things grow."

"I did that?" she said, stunned, indicating the size of his manly protrusion.

"You did this," he confirmed as he rejoined her on the bed.

She went to him willingly, and with a soft sigh, wrapped her arms around his neck and lifted her face for his kiss. One kiss led to another, and soon he was touching her between her thighs in that pleasurable way that was nearly pain.

Then he took her hand and placed it on his shaft. It was surprisingly smooth and soft; yet it was as hard as steel. It was the most amazing thing Elizabeth had ever beheld.

"Now I will touch you as I did before," he muttered, sinking a finger into her.

She was just as eager to touch him. She explored his shaft, tracing a bulging vein on the underside with her finger, exclaiming over a drop of dew that appeared magically at its tip, marveling at its strength and its vulnerability.

"You mustn't be shocked, Elizabeth. I would not want to offend you."

"You couldn't possibly offend me no matter what you did," she assured him. After all, he knew her body better than she did herself.

Jack poised himself over her, his broad shoulders blocking out everything but his presence. She placed her hands on his chest as he slipped the hard length of his swollen shaft between her thighs.

"I will not hurt you," he promised.

"I know, my lord. Will you find your satisfaction?"

"Yes, if you will permit me to move back and forth between your long, lovely legs."

The friction was hot and slick between their two bodies. That strange, wonderful feeling began anew in Elizabeth. She put her head back, and Jack's name was on her lips when she climaxed a second time.

Then she was aware of Jack arching his back and giving a triumphant shout as he shuddered and thrust once, twice, three times between her parted thighs. The honeyed essence flowed from her woman's body and mingled with his on the sheets; it was hot and wet and musky.

Elizabeth awoke as a new dawn broke across the desert sky. The bedcovers were rumpled and smelled of lovemaking. She buried her face in the pillow: Jack. It was his scent that lingered there.

She reached out and discovered she was alone. Jack must have returned to his room before daylight could bring discovery. Last night was their secret; it must remain so.

She finally opened her eyes and turned her head. She took in a tiny gasp of air. How in the world? Beside her on the pillow, morning dew still fresh on its petals, was a single red rose. . . .

Chapter 14

He had seduced her; now he must do the honorable thing and marry the girl, Jack acknowledged to himself as he restlessly paced the deck of the *Star of Egypt*.

First things first, of course. The first order of business was to arrange an engagement between Lady Elizabeth Guest and Lord Jonathan Wicke.

Naturally his bride-to-be would be informed of his decision before the steamship reached its final destination in a week's time. He intended to speak to Elizabeth on the very subject, and several others while he was at it—she really must refrain from running about in her nightgown in the dead of night—as soon as he could manage a moment alone with her.

Once the *Star of Egypt* had dropped anchor at Luxor and the Valley of the Kings, he would make an appointment with her father and officially request the young lady's hand in marriage. It would all be done properly and by the book.

Lord Stanhope was certain to give the match his blessing. After all, he, Jonathan Malcolm Charles Wicke, was not without prospects. He had acquired a sizable fortune, a reputation for honest dealings, as well as something of a name for himself in this part of the world. And he was the son of a duke, albeit a slightly disgraced son.

Besides, the girl had as much as admitted to him that her own prospects for a suitable marriage were slim. There had been no Season in London—unlike the elder daughter, whose debut, he understood from the original agent's report, had been a stunning success. Indeed, it had resulted in Lady Caroline's marriage to a marquess. From all indications, it was unlikely that the younger daughter would *ever* have a Season.

" 'A complete waste of time and money.' Isn't that the opinion you once expressed to me, my sweet, unassuming Elizabeth?" muttered Jack, under his breath.

In the early morning light, his eyes were a steely blue as he paced the deck at a furious rate, working off the excessive energy that had plagued him since first boarding the steamship in Alexandria.

He was not a sailing man; he never would be. A ship was too confining, too restrictive for him. He craved the freedom of wide open spaces, endless blue skies, and drifting dunes as far as the eye could see.

And he yearned for the feel of his lovely, surefooted, long-limbed Scheherazade beneath him, her warm flesh between his thighs, her silky mane clasped in his hand!

Deemed too temperamental and spirited for most men to handle, the snow white mare had been a gift last year from Prince Ramses. They rode the desert together, he and the lovely Arabian thoroughbred, his black hair and robes and her white coat in stark contrast to each other as they swept at breakneck speed over the sands of the Sahara.

A wicked grin worked at Jack's mouth. Elizabeth was like his favorite mount: long-limbed, lily white, rare in temperament and spirit, elegant in manner, a thoroughbred, to be sure.

The girl would be furious, of course, if she knew he was comparing her to a horse. Yet she had said it herself. She was too outspoken. Too headstrong. Too impulsive. And too tall.

For most men.

But not for him. Elizabeth Guest would suit him well enough. Well enough, indeed.

After all, he was twenty-six years old. It was time he married. Ramie was six months younger, and as befit a royal prince of the tribe, he already had three wives and, at last count, thirteen children.

Black Jack turned and retraced his steps from the ship's bow to its stern, nodding his head and muttering to himself, since the ever-faithful Kareem was not in attendance to act as his soundboard: "Yes, this match with Lady Elizabeth will do me quite nicely. I see no reason why the betrothal cannot be settled quickly and neatly."

After all, it was his duty to set things right, Jack told himself. He had taken advantage of the girl's ignorance, and he must pay the price.

For he'd been less than honest with Elizabeth when he had claimed that she was still as pure as "unsunn'd snow." The truth was, the bloom was off the rose. The goods were damaged. An innocent had been compromised.

It was his fault, of course.

But he was a gentleman, and therefore, he was ready and willing to accept the blame for what he had done. He would not shirk his responsibilities. He would do his duty, fulfill his obligations. He had gone into this affair with both eyes wide open. He had known exactly what he was doing when he volunteered to teach the lovely Elizabeth the ways of the flesh, to introduce her to the secrets of physical passion.

She had turned out to be a most adept pupil.

There was no going back now, even if they wished to. And he, for one, did not. If anything, Jack was looking forward to continuing her lessons. He itched to get started. The idea of some other man picking up where he had left off was repugnant. Nay, more than repugnant. It was intolerable.

Elizabeth was his.

And she would remain his until he decided otherwise. That was the way of the desert.

Besides, according to tribal custom, she was ruined for any other man. He'd seen to that. Somehow the thought did not displease Black Jack.

Beyond that, there was no reason he couldn't kill two birds with one stone. He would marry Elizabeth, take her to his bed, and, by the gods, he would finally take his fill of her!

At the same time, he would keep his sacred vow to Prince Ramses.

For, sooner or later, the girl would confide in him, telling him what he wanted to know, giving him the information he sought, the information men had been willing to steal for, kill for, even die for since ancient times. He would know where the great pharaoh, Merneptah Seti, was buried.

Elizabeth wondered if the legends surrounding Merneptah Seti were true.

One legend claimed that the great pharaoh had possessed the prowess of ten men and had never been bested in battle.

Another alleged that Merneptah Seti—unlike the kings who came before and after him in the Black Land's long history—had married but one wife, the beautiful Nefetari. It was written that he refused exotic slaves by the thousands, favored daughters, even royal princesses offered him by other nations seeking Egypt's alliance.

But the legend that haunted historians and treasure seekers alike, the legend handed down from generation to generation for thousands of years, the legend that had driven Elizabeth's own father into the desert again and again, was of the riches purported to have been buried with the great pharaoh. Riches beyond compare. Riches beyond any man's dreams.

And the greatest of these was the statue.

Elizabeth bent over the writing desk in her stateroom and studied the copy of the rare fragment of papyrus. She had found it among her beloved papa's notes dating from his first journey to Egypt thirty years before.

For the most part it was a lengthy and tedious list of funereal objects: so many pairs of beaded sandals, so many bracelets and anklets, clothes of every kind and description, mirrors and cosmetics, shaving equipment, boxes and chests, games and musical instruments, palettes and paints, chariots, weapons, ceremonial daggers and swords, furniture, thrones, jars and baskets, dozens of statues of Seti himself, rendered in gilded wood, diorite, ivory, and ebony.

It was a meticulously detailed, if incomplete, list that had been forgotten, she was convinced, by Papa long ago.

As she had a hundred times before, Elizabeth translated one particularly obscure passage, tracing the hieroglyphs with her forefinger as she read aloud: "To praise and pay homage in this life and in the life to come, to that most glorious and great Merneptah Seti, Horus Incarnate, son of Amon-Re, the resurrected Osiris, King of Upper and Lower Egypt, Uniter of the Two Lands, on this the first day of the month of *Tybi*, at this the Festival of the Tail, Nek the Goldsmith is paid—" the amount of coin was obscured by an ancient smudge, as well as several words thereafter "—a solid gold *shabti* with eyes of semiprecious stones to be housed in a gilded shrine of gold on a silver-encased sledge . . ."

A solid gold statue.

Elizabeth's heart was pounding with excitement, as it had the first time she realized what she'd stumbled upon.

"Imagine a treasure of such magnificent proportions," she murmured to herself. "Of course, the centerpiece would be the golden *shabti.*"

And whoever unearthed the tomb of Merneptah Seti would find the shrine and the statue!

Treasure.

Men and women of adventure, of heroism, sometimes of greed, they had all searched for treasure buried beneath the shifting sands of the Sahara, the currents of the ocean, even the green hills of England.

It was a way of life, looking for the royal trappings of the ancient pharaohs, the rich loot of sunken ships, the sword of Arthur, the Holy Grail, the sacred shroud of the Savior Himself.

There was always a lost thing, a lost time, a lost place, cut off from the rest of the world. The quest for the lost had a raw, seductive beauty for some, like her father—like herself, reflected Elizabeth. It was sensual, alluring, dangerous.

Treasure.

It filled her daydreams and her night dreams. It excited her as nothing else did, or ever could. With the possible exception, she admitted to herself with a blush, of the shattering culmination of Jack's lovemaking.

So lost in thought was Elizabeth that when two short raps sounded on her stateroom door, she nearly jumped out of her skin.

"What in the world?" she murmured, bewildered. It was not yet sunrise, and she was still wearing her wrapper and nightdress.

Stashing the copy of the papyrus under her diary, she went to see who it was. She pressed her mouth close to the door and whispered, "Who's there?"

"Jack. I must speak with you."

She opened the door a crack. "Can't it wait, my lord? I have just risen. I am not dressed to receive visitors."

"It can't wait."

"But—"

"I insist on speaking with you now, Elizabeth."

She executed a convincing yawn. "I think not, my lord."

"I think so, my lady."

If only his voice didn't carry so in the quiet morning air, she would ignore him altogether. As it was, Jack's booming baritone could wake the dead.

Elizabeth gave a sigh of resignation and opened the door a fraction of an inch. "Hush, my lord. Please keep your voice down. Everyone will hear you."

"Then let me in and they will not."

She caught a glimpse of his expression and hesitated. Jack seemed calm enough. One might say unnervingly calm. Even suspiciously calm. She did not completely trust his motives. "To what purpose, my lord?"

"I must speak to you concerning a private matter."

"Concerning a private matter?"

"Perhaps a *secret* matter is more to the point."

She drew in her breath sharply. There were several "secret" matters between herself and the gentleman. None of which she would want made known.

He had a flash of temper. "Dammit, Elizabeth, let me in!"

"This is highly irregular."

"Now," he shot back, "or I will be obliged to let myself in."

She knew he meant it. He was perfectly capable of making good on his threat. One swift, well-executed kick with his black boot, and the door of her cabin would splinter like so much tinder for the fire.

"Damn you, Jack," she swore as she granted him entrance.

His smile was triumphant. "Good morning to you, too, my lady."

The stateroom suddenly seemed too small. The unmade bed and her state of dishabille created an uncomfortable sense of intimacy. Elizabeth tried not to squirm.

With as much dignity as she could muster under the difficult circumstances in which she presently found herself, she sniffed and announced with genuine regality, "You've gotten your way, sir. You're here. Now, please say whatever it is that you have to say and leave."

Jack was in no hurry. He leaned back against the doorframe and casually folded his arms across his chest. "You have been avoiding me, my sweet."

She gave him a frosty glare. "Surely you didn't threaten to beat down my door at dawn to tell me that."

He smiled indulgently. "No, I didn't."

Her fists were clenched at her sides. "Well?"

"It has taken me almost a week to find you alone."

"We are on a ship full of people," she pointed out.

He gave an indelicate laugh. "That's never stopped us before."

Wisely, she chose to remain silent on the subject of their past midnight rendezvous. "I would like to get dressed now, my lord."

Jack sauntered past her, plunked down on the edge of her unmade bed, stretched out his muscular legs, casually intertwined his long fingers, leaned back among the pillows, and drawled, "Don't let me stop you."

"Don't be absurd."

He contemplated her without a change of expression. "I have seen you naked before."

She saw red. "I do believe, my lord, that you're deliberately trying to be offensive."

Her unwelcome early morning visitor disregarded the insult. "And you have seen me naked and fully aroused."

Her gasp was audible to both of them. "Now, sir, you have succeeded in being offensive."

"Which brings me to the reason I'm here."

"Because you are offensive?"

He bounced to his feet and said briskly, "Of course not, you silly goose."

"Then why?"

"I thought we should have it settled between the two of us before we reach Luxor."

"Before we reach Luxor?"

"I will speak to your father, then."

"Speak to my father? Speak to him about what, pray tell?"

"Our betrothal."

Elizabeth opened her mouth to speak, but nothing came out. She blinked several times in rapid succession, sank into the chair beside the desk, and finally directed a frenzied whisper toward him. "Our betrothal?"

Jack looked down at her in cool appraisement. "You must learn not to repeat every question I ask you, dear girl. It is a most annoying habit of yours."

Elizabeth fought a crazy urge to laugh in his handsome face. "Why would I marry you?"

"I thought the reason would be obvious." For a moment the man hesitated, then he shrugged his shoulders. "The reason is quite simple really. A few nights ago we were in bed together. We were naked and we made love. We behaved as husband and wife, even though we are not."

She sucked in a startled breath. "I'm afraid I still don't understand."

"It's time to pay the piper, my wild English rose. We are going to become engaged. After a respectable period of time, we will be married."

She found herself staring at him in utter amazement.

When it became apparent she wasn't going to respond, Jack went on. "I'm afraid I have compromised you."

Elizabeth shot out of the chair and began to pace the cabin, her sheer nightdress billowing around her bare legs, her pulse suddenly wildly erratic. "Of course you haven't."

"I have and I apologize."

"You haven't, and an apology is unnecessary."

"Yes."

"No," retorted Elizabeth. Panic was beginning to set in. Jack simply would not listen to reason.

He sighed dramatically. "I have seduced an innocent young girl, and now I must pay the price."

The man was like a bulldog with a bone clenched between his teeth.

"There is no price for you to pay, sir. You did not seduce me. I acted of my own free will."

He stood his ground, refusing to budge so much as an inch. "I did seduce you. I'm totally to blame."

Elizabeth marched up to him and stabbed his chest with her finger. "You are not to blame. Do you hear me? How many times must I repeat myself?"

Jack was immovable. "The bloom is off the rose. The goods have been damaged. An innocent has been sullied."

That stopped her cold. "I thought you said I was unsullied."

"You are and you aren't," he lamented.

She knitted her brows. "I don't see how I can be both."

He paused and, with a lift of linen shoulders, said, "You are too young and inexperienced to understand these things."

Elizabeth had run out of patience. "Am I or am I not a virgin?"

He waved the issue aside. "In a manner of speaking, I suppose one could say—"

She repeated the question a little louder. "My lord, am I or am I not a virgin?"

"That isn't the point."

"That is precisely the point."

Jack uttered an impatient noise. "You're arguing, my dear Elizabeth, on the basis of a technicality."

"Facts are facts, sir."

"Not in this case."

She opened her mouth to speak, but no words came out. It was several minutes before she whispered, in an attempt to console herself as much as anything, "Either way, it doesn't matter. Virgin or not, I don't wish to marry you."

Jonathan Wicke was taken aback. "You don't wish to marry me?"

"Not you or any man, my lord. In the first place, as you have been so kind as to point out, I'm too young."

His steely eyes narrowed. "And in the second place?"

Elizabeth nervously wetted her lips with her tongue and drew in a deep breath. She had always thought she would like to be shorter. For the first time in her life, she actually wished she were taller, for Jack was towering over her, his blue eyes in a rage.

She swallowed and began. "I told you that night on deck. I want to live life to its fullest, to travel the world, to have many grand adventures before I marry."

"Being married to me will be a grand adventure, I promise you," he said dryly.

"I don't doubt that, my lord."

"Good. Then it's settled."

"I'm afraid not." Elizabeth gave him a quick sideways glance and added hurriedly, "While I believe you would make a wonderful lover—"

"Yes—"

"I fear that you would *not* make a wonderful husband."

His features tightened and grew black with anger. "You're a child. You know nothing of men and women. You have admitted as much yourself."

"But I am learning," she reminded him.

"And you will continue to learn once we are married," Jack stated emphatically.

"I cannot marry you."

"You can and you must."

"I won't."

"You will."

They had reached a temporary impasse. The two of them stood there in her stateroom, squared off like challengers in a duel, weapons drawn, waiting to see which of them would get off the next shot.

Elizabeth was furious with him. Her breath was coming in great gulps. She was shaking from head to toe—in anger.

Jack had not asked her to marry him, he had demanded that she do so. There had been no sweetly spoken words of love and passion, but only mention of obligation and duty.

The man had all the finesse of a rutting bull let loose in a herd of cows. He had the manners of a camel driver. He was dictatorial, uncouth, and pigheaded.

And he could, Elizabeth thought with genuine relish, go straight to hell!

Perhaps she was a hopeless romantic, but she wanted it all. And someday she would have it: a handsome young man standing nervously before her, pledging his devotion, swearing his undying love, vowing, if necessary, to crawl across the burning desert sands on his knees for her. Such a man was her dream, and one day she would find him.

Her mind was made up. "You can't force me to marry you, my lord. The answer is an emphatic no."

There was a look of pure fury on Jack's face. His brows snapped together. "My lady, you are a most exasperating female."

"Because I won't agree to marry you?"

"Because . . ." He wanted to wring her neck; Elizabeth could see it in his eyes. "Because you simply are."

"This conversation, my lord, has come to an end." She dismissed him with a curt but excruciatingly polite nod of the head. "I wish you a good morning, sir."

Jack stomped to the door and flung it open, nearly tearing the wood from the frame. "Do not mistake my intent, madam. One way or the other, we will be married." The cabin door slammed shut behind him, rattling on its hinges.

Elizabeth stood there and stared after him, wondering if she had just done something very foolish or very wise.

Chapter 15

He was a dunce.

A dolt. A dunderhead. A tomfool. A shallow-brain and a thick-wit.

He was an imbecile. A dotard. A driveling idiot.

He was muddleheaded, addlebrained, moronic, and a thorough jackass.

There was no end to the names Jonathan Wicke called himself in the next several hours. He was a caged lion, pacing to and fro, wearing a path from the door of his stateroom to the bunk, from the bunk to the writing desk, from the writing desk back to the door.

"You're a bloody fool, Wicke!" he swore at himself out of frustration. "You handled her all wrong."

He could see that clearly now. Elizabeth was

220

a young woman of gentle breeding. Hers had been a privileged and sheltered upbringing; a life filled with music and culture, gardening and books. A quiet life. A contemplative life.

A boring life.

But it was not for him to judge. Like a clod, he had barged in and run roughshod over her delicate female sensibilities, that was the point. He had treated her like one of the earthy women of the tribe, or, worse, one of the doxies of his youth. She was obviously neither.

He had made a grave tactical error.

Several.

He'd given her no time to get used to the idea of an engagement between them, let alone marriage.

He should never have called her a silly goose to her face, or implied that she was a child who knew nothing of men and women.

Worse, he had forgotten the pretty words. A lady liked to hear pretty words from a gentleman. She liked to be wooed. She liked receiving poems and presents and posies.

To his credit, the rose on her pillow had been an inspired gesture. The "morning after," Elizabeth had given him sweet, secretive smiles every chance she'd had. He should have remembered the lesson of the rose. As it was, he was all the way back to the bloody beginning.

Or worse.

Now he would have to play the gallant, the besotted fool, the repentant lover, wooing the girl in earnest, even courting her.

And courting Elizabeth, he acknowledged, was going to be no bed of roses. Jack only hoped he had the patience and stamina, for she was bound to lead him on one hell of a merry chase. The thought was enough to drive a man to drink.

He opened the liquor cabinet in his stateroom, but quickly discovered the cupboard was bare. Things were simply not the same when the ever-attentive Kareem wasn't here to look after him. There was only one solution to his problem. He finished dressing for the day and headed for the ship's lounge.

He had his choice of tables. The room was deserted at this hour of the morning. Most of the passengers were either still abed, or breakfasting in their cabins.

"Brandy, my good man," he called out to one of the uniformed waiters. "A full bottle and a large snifter."

Both magically appeared in front of him. Jack poured himself a drink and took a sizable swig, letting the distilled spirits slide smoothly down his throat.

He had never been any good with the ladies, came the morose thought as he peered over the edge of the partially filled glass. Oh, he was good with women, damn good. But any man worth his salt knew there was a world of difference between a woman and a lady.

Ladies were a law unto themselves.

His blessed mother, may she rest in peace, had been a lady from the top of her perfectly coiffed head to the tip of her perfectly turned silk slipper. Indeed, it was often said there was no greater lady in the north of England than the Duchess of Deakin.

They had all adored her.

His father thought the sun rose and set in his beloved Clara. He worshiped the ground on which she walked. Whatever his Clara wanted, his Clara got.

What Clara wanted was children.

They had two sons in quick succession. Lawrence, who was born exactly nine months to the day after their wedding, and Jonathan, who followed two years later. Unfortunately the duchess's delicate health prevented her from having any more children after that. It was the great sorrow of her life.

"Or was I the great sorrow of your life, Mother?" murmured Jack as he downed the rest of his brandy and quickly poured himself another.

He had been a grave disappointment to his mother; he knew that better than anyone. Yet she had *not* thought him the black sheep of the family, and always met his thoughtless actions and selfish deeds, his boyish pranks, even his dismissal from Cambridge, with nary a word of condemnation, with only love and approval.

God in Heaven, he missed her!

She had been gone six long years. Jack took another swallow of his drink. Six years ago today to be exact. Of course, he hadn't found out until months afterward since he was halfway around the world as she had lain on her deathbed and called his name.

His father, the duke, and his elder brother blamed him for their beloved Clara's death.

Everyone did. It had never been said in so many words, but Jack knew. They had never forgiven him.

He had never forgiven himself.

Black Jack emptied the brandy snifter and stared into the bottle of dark amber fire. How long he sat there, he never knew. It was the voice of André Polonski that finally penetrated his melancholy.

"Having a short one before luncheon?"

It was barely nine o'clock in the morning, and both men knew it.

"Go to hell," muttered Jack, without looking up.

"Thank you all the same, but I've been there, and frankly, I didn't care for it," countered the dapper man dressed in gray cashmere, maintaining, surprisingly, his sense of humor. "Do you mind if I join you?"

Jack grunted, "Suit yourself," and poured another round of brandy. He had wisely lost count of how many glasses this one made.

André Polonski signaled to the waiter behind the brass and wood bar at the far end of the ship's lounge, and a second bottle and a second glass magically appeared on the table. He neatly tipped the elegant vintage and studied the label for a moment. "Ah, Napoleon brandy. Is there any finer?"

Jack chose not to reply.

His uninvited guest tried again. "May I inquire whether we are drinking to celebrate or forget?"

"Women!"

"Ah, to forget."

Jack was unaware that a muscle in his face had

started to twitch. "Damn nuisance."

"I couldn't agree with you more." Polonski poured himself a brandy and tossed it back in a single motion. He returned the glass to the table and explained, as he poured a second, "I would usually sip a brandy of this caliber, in order to savor its flavor, but under the circumstances, I believe I have some catching up to do." He raised the filled snifter to the morning light. "Of course, the distinction of a fine brandy depends partly on the quality of the wine used and partly on the method of distillation, but principally on the type of wood."

Black Jack frowned. "Wood?"

"Yes, the type of wood in the barrel in which the brandy is aged."

A grunt was his only response.

"Cognac matures most satisfactorily in casks of Limousin oak, of course." This statement was met with silence. "The true connoisseur, however, prefers Armagnac over Cognac. Although I find the former brandy a little heady for my personal tastes."

Jack looked up and declared in a rough tone, "I never bloody well liked you, Polonski."

Intelligent if slightly dissipated gray eyes held his. "I never bloody well liked you, either, Wicke. But, odd as it may seem, we have a great deal in common."

Black Jack polished off his liquor and insisted, "Explain yourself, sir."

The count made himself comfortable before he spoke. "To begin with, we are both exiles from our own countries."

"True enough."

"We both possess meaningless titles that do little more than obtain us the necessary credit at our tailor's and the occasional invitation to a luncheon or a weekend house party."

"True again."

"By the by, may I be so bold as to suggest that you take the name and address of my tailor? You may tell him I sent you." An elegant arch of the man's brow said the rest.

Jack laughed with genuine amusement. "I prefer native robes to European suits. I'm afraid it shows."

The stiff formality of André Polonski's reply contained all his disapproval. "Indeed, I'm afraid it does."

In spite of himself, Jonathan Wicke found he was interested in his drinking companion's opinions. "What else do you believe we have in common?"

"We appreciate beautiful women."

"What man doesn't?"

"I assume we both know the answer to that," said his counterpart with a sophisticated and world-weary twist to his mouth.

"Egods, Polonski!"

Blithely he went on. "We not only appreciate beautiful woman, but we enjoy them."

"Sometimes," Jack qualified.

"Sometimes." The pale gray eyes were exceedingly shrewd. "Do I detect a hint of impatience?"

"You do."

"Perhaps even aggravation?"

"Definitely."

Polonski smiled, showing perfect white teeth; but there was something rather unpleasant about the smile. "Perhaps it is time for me to volunteer to take the lovely Lady Elizabeth off your hands?"

"Not if you value your life," shot back Jack blackly.

The count paused, then added carefully, "I didn't realize she was your private property."

"Well, she is."

"Is the lady aware of that fact?"

"She will be."

"I see." It was a very astute observation. "And if I should choose to ignore your claim on her?"

Jack leaned forward in his chair and stated with deadly intent, "I wouldn't if I were you."

"Of course," said Polonski with his usual dry wit, "I am not you. That is the whole point."

Blue eyes squinted in anger. "You know damn well what I mean. Keep away from Elizabeth."

"And if I don't keep away from the lady, what will it be? Fisticuffs? Pistols at thirty paces? Swords? Weapon of choice? Or will you simply beat the bloody hell out of me with your bare hands?"

A feral grin from Jack was all the answer required.

The count shook his handsome head. "You really have become a heathen, Wicke."

"Yes, I have."

The man sighed. "Fortunately, my 'interest' lies elsewhere."

"Amelia Winters."

Polonski arched a brow in surprise. "You noticed."

"I noticed."

"I'm sleeping with another man's wife, and you're trying to bed an innocent young girl." Then, sardonically, "We do make a fine pair."

Jack laughed darkly and muttered under his breath, "We're both bastards by temperament, if not birth."

André Polonski swirled the amber-colored brandy around in his glass. "Of course, if one wishes to get technical about it, I am also a bastard by birth."

"I've known plenty of both kinds in my life," Jack said carefully, trying not to slur his words. "Seems to me that it's more a matter of character than which side of the sheets a man happens to be born on."

There was a touch of cynicism in his manner as André Polonski related his story. "My mother was—is—a lady, English actually, although her name shall remain unmentioned. My father already had a wife when they met and formed their 'liaison.' Divorce was out of the question, of course."

"Of course," echoed Jack.

"As fate would have it, my father and his wife could have no children. Eventually I was acknowledged as his rightful heir and inherited the ancestral titles and lands."

"Lucky for you," muttered Jack thickly.

The count's forehead creased a moment perplexedly. "Not so lucky, I fear."

"Not so lucky?"

He sighed in resignation and spread out his hands in a dramatic gesture. "Ours was a small country, wedged between Austria and Hungary. There had been internal strife for some years. The peasants grew more and more restless and finally revolted. The royal family and the aristocracy were forced to flee for their lives. I got out in the dead of night with the clothes on my back and little else."

Black Jack shoved his chair back, staggered to his feet, circled the table, and gave his drinking companion an affable pat on the back. "Damned shame."

"Yes," André Polonski agreed inebriatedly, "it was a damned shame."

Jonathan Wicke grabbed his own bottle and poured the other man a splash of brandy from it. "Let's drink to poor homeless bastards like us."

They clinked snifters, and repeated the toast with a somewhat grudging but newfound respect for each other. "To poor homeless bastards like us."

Both gentlemen were in their cups by luncheon, and had to be assisted to their cabins by members of the ship's staff. Their absence for the remainder of the afternoon was noted briefly by the other passengers. But it was the season, after all, to make merry. Tomorrow was Christmas Day, and the *Star of Egypt* was scheduled to land in Luxor.

Chapter 16

❧✦❧

It was unlike any Christmas Elizabeth had ever spent before, or would ever spend again, that Christmas Day as the *Star of Egypt* dropped anchor at Luxor, the legendary city once known as Thebes.

The company disembarked, their baggage to follow by oxcart, and made their way in horse-drawn carriages to the cluster of buildings near the northern edge of town: Colonel and Mrs. Winters, Count Polonski and Georges, Lord Jonathan, minus his ever-faithful Kareem, Alee, Elizabeth, and Colette.

The row of stone houses with ancient colonnades behind them was their first view of the great temple of Karnak: home to the king of the gods, Amon-Re, and every king since for over thirty-five hundred years.

Each pharaoh had added onto the vast temple complex, building and rebuilding, columns here, gateways there, an avenue of sphinxes with curly-horned rams' heads, sanctuaries of fine pink granite, statues and pylons and courtyards, until the total covered nearly two hectares, five acres.

And it was nearly all in ruins.

Elizabeth adjusted her parasol and accepted the hand offered her as she descended from the carriage.

"This house is for your use, *sitteh*, although I fear it is not grand enough for an English lady."

"The house is fine, Alee," she assured the young Egyptian. "I'm sure I will be very comfortable here."

They entered through the front door; it was of heavy wood, a rare commodity in a desert country with virtually no natural forests, and painted a most peculiar shade of blue. Elizabeth found herself in what would be described in an English home as the drawing room.

There were hand-woven carpets on the floor, a horsehair settee prominently placed in the center of the room—Colette feared it was infested with vermin of every size and description, and by the second day in residence, insisted on disinfecting it herself—large, tasseled pillows that one presumably sat on, since they were piled knee-deep on the floor, and sundry odds and ends of furniture, pottery, tapestries, and brass ornaments.

It wasn't the furnishings, however, that interested Elizabeth. What she found fascinating were the actual construction blocks themselves.

"Alee, where did the stone come from that was used to build this house?"

The handsome young man frowned. "The stone, *sitteh*?"

Dropping her reticule and parasol on a low table, she made a closer inspection of the walls. "Why, these blocks are from the temples. Look, there are inscriptions here and here," she pointed out. "God in Heaven!" she exclaimed, her hand flying to her mouth.

Alee became agitated. "What is it, *sitteh*? What is wrong?"

"Milady, you have gone utterly *blanche*, white as a ghost. Are you ill?" inquired Colette, with genuine concern for her young mistress's well-being.

"I'm fine. I am not ill," Elizabeth hastened to assure her companions. How could she make them understand? It was wondrous and yet it was deplorable. It was sacred, yet profane. She was equally thrilled and horrified. "Do you have any idea what is depicted on this wall?"

They shook their heads.

Her hand was trembling as she reached out and touched the beautifully carved relief. "Here is the cartouche, her name engraved upon it. This is part of her face and gown; while in front of her, in traditional pharaonic dress, is her son by Julius Caesar, Caesarion."

"Julius Caesar, milady?"

She nodded and quickly translated the hieroglyphs. "The scene shows the queen making her offerings to the goddesses." Elizabeth took a deep breath and announced with incredulity, "It is the most famous of all the Cleopatras: Cleopatra the Seventh. It is *the* Cleopatra."

"*Mon Dieu*, on the wall of our *maison*?" exclaimed Colette Duvay.

"Yes, on the wall of our house. These stones should be returned to the temple at Karnak," declared Elizabeth. "Surely someone is trying to put the pieces of the puzzle back together and restore the ancient buildings to their former glory."

"There are those working on such a project, *sitteh*." Alee was no less impassioned than she, as he went on to explain. "There has always been a shortage of building materials in Egypt. The local peasants care little for our history; they can neither read nor write their own language. Their daily life is a struggle to simply exist, to put food on the table and clothing on their children's backs." Then he straightened his youthful shoulders and said, "It is up to us, to those who understand and appreciate the legacy of the Ancients, to protect and preserve the heritage of this great land."

Elizabeth regarded him with newfound respect. "You are right, of course. It will be done by dedicated and capable Egyptians such as yourself."

The young man gave her a brief but polite bow. "Now I must excuse myself and see to the other guests."

His hand was on the doorknob when she called out to him, asking the question that had been uppermost in her mind since the moment the ship dropped anchor. "Alee, where is my father? When will I see him?"

"Our—Lord Stanhope went to the excavation site before dawn, *sitteh*, as is his daily custom. He left word that he would return for tea."

Her face dropped. "Not until teatime?"

He was gentle with her. "It is his custom."

"Thank you, Alee. I understand," said Elizabeth.

Although, in truth, she did not. It had been three long years since she had seen Papa. She had come thousands of miles by train, ship, horse and carriage, donkey, even camel. Somehow she had expected her father to meet the *Star of Egypt* as it docked, or at least be there to greet her on her arrival in Luxor. She could not hide her disappointment.

"Do not distress yourself, *sitteh*. It is simply his way," said Alee in parting.

The instant the door of the stone house closed behind him, Colette began muttering to herself as she inspected their rooms. "*Où est-il? Il est votre père. Quelle honte! Quel outrage!*"

Elizabeth felt a lump begin to form in the back of her throat. She tried to swallow the bitter tears. "Please, Colette. Papa doesn't mean to hurt people. Truly."

"This I know. Obviously I do not mind for myself. It is you, *chérie*, that are hurt by his neglect."

She took a swipe at her damp cheek. "Alee is right. It is simply Papa's way."

"Ah, *mon petit chou*, pay no mind. I will unpack our things and have this house *propre* by teatime. I must inspect the bedchambers first," she declared, heading for the back of the abode.

Colette was scarcely out of the room when a tentative knock sounded on the blue wooden door.

"That will undoubtedly be our trunks. I'll see to them," Elizabeth called out to her companion.

She opened the front door and was surprised to find a young boy of ten or eleven standing there, a small box clasped in his hands.

"*Sitteh?*"

She nodded. "Yes."

He held the box out at arm's length and indicated she should take it from him.

Apparently there was no accompanying note. "But who is it from?"

The boy shook his head; it was obvious he did not understand her.

Elizabeth tried again, anyway. "Who gave the box to you?"

The youngster's brown eyes were blank, then they lit up and he began to chatter animatedly. Now she could not understand a word he was saying.

She thought for a moment, then raised her arm above her head. "Man?"

He frowned, nodded vigorously, and repeated, "Man." He jumped into the air, reaching as far as he could to show that it had been a very tall man.

"Black hair?" she enunciated, pointing to his own dark locks.

The boy grinned and nodded his head again.

A tall man with black hair.

It could only be Jack.

Motioning with her unencumbered hand, Elizabeth instructed, "Please wait here."

She disappeared inside to get a small coin from her purse, but by the time she returned, the messenger boy was gone.

Elizabeth closed the blue door and carried the small, carved chest to a table beside the settee. She examined the outside and judged it to be alabaster, Nineteenth Dynasty, pharaonic, and of some considerable worth. The etchings on the sides and the top had been done by an exceptionally skilled artisan. It was a simple, but beautiful box.

Unsteadily her heart began to pick up speed. She reached down and raised the lid. For a moment she was puzzled, but just for a moment.

Then Elizabeth began to smile with delight as she removed the small onyx object from the box. It was a perfect miniature black sheep. . . .

Elizabeth had wanted her reunion with Papa to be private, rather than public. But it was not to be. The entire company was gathered in the main guesthouse for tea when his horse and buggy pulled up outside.

At first, as she watched through the window, she did not recognize the new arrival. She saw only a middle-aged man dressed in dusty robes, who, when he threw back his hood, appeared to be prematurely aged by sun and sand. His hair was long, shaggy, and pure white in color. His skin was like brown leather. His eyes were narrowed in a permanent squint.

She only realized it was her father when she saw Alee rush out to tether the team of horses.

What would Papa say to her after all this time? What would she say to him?

With genuine trepidation, and a growing sense of excitement, Elizabeth rose to her feet and hurried to the vestibule to greet him.

Avery Guest, the sixth Earl of Stanhope, came striding through the front door of the guesthouse in a billow of voluminous robes and knee-high boots covered with red desert dust. He muttered in Arabic to the handsome young Egyptian at his side. Then he glanced up, spotted her, and stopped dead in his tracks.

His mouth dropped open. "Lizzie?"

Determined to maintain her dignity at all costs—she would not, so help her God, give in to the tears burning at the back of her eyes— Elizabeth sunk her teeth into her bottom lip until she tasted blood. "Yes, Papa."

He gave her a long, measuring look, but made no move toward her. "You've grown up."

"Yes, I have," she said in a husky voice.

Suddenly Lord Stanhope's deeply tanned face dissolved into a remorseful smile. "You're not my little Lizzie anymore, are you?"

"No, I'm not, Papa."

She hadn't been his "little Lizzie" for years. It was simply that he had not been there to see her grow up, changing from child to girl, from girl to woman. And he had not been there when she'd needed him most. It was his choice. But it had resulted in a loss for both of them.

Her father had changed as well in the intervening years, of course. Elizabeth remembered him as tall, handsome, dashing. A gentleman from head to toe, immaculately groomed and dressed in the latest sartorial fashion as befit his station in life. Now there was a stoop to his shoulders, and she was nearly as tall as he was.

Papa had become an old man.

Lord Stanhope stroked his chin in an absent-minded gesture, and she noticed the red dirt embedded under his nails. "How long has it been, Elizabeth?"

"Three years."

"Three years? That long?"

Closer to four, damn you, she wanted to shout at him. But she held her tongue.

His expression bore no trace of an apology. "Then you must be nearly . . ."

"Eighteen, Papa. I will be eighteen in the spring."

"Old enough to be a woman."

"I am a woman," she said in a low, earnest voice.

He gave her a rueful smile. "Of course you are. And a beautiful one, too."

Elizabeth blushed with pleasure.

It was the first compliment her father had given her since he had declared one day—it must have been five or six years previous—that at least she showed signs of not ending up like her elder sister, Caroline, who was an utterly useless female, caring only for gossip, fashion, frivolous pastimes, and young milksops who dared to call themselves men.

After that incident, Lord Stanhope and his elder daughter had rarely seen eye to eye on anything. Indeed, Caroline hadn't bothered to invite him to her wedding, even though at the time, he was in England on one of his rare visits home.

Surely it was all water under the bridge now, rationalized Elizabeth as her father shook the desert dust from his boots. Any minute now he would ask after Maman, or Franklin, or Caroline, or, at the least, poor sweet Annie.

Instead, Lord Stanhope suggested, "We'd better not keep the others waiting. I could use a cup of tea. My throat is dry as a bone."

Elizabeth took a step toward him and, lowering her voice so only he could hear her, stated, "I must speak to you in private, Papa, on a matter of utmost importance."

He made a vague, airy gesture with his hand. "Perhaps over a cup of tea."

She fixed him with large, reproachful hazel eyes. "It must be in private."

"In private, of course," he said, after the briefest of pauses. "We'll have a talk soon."

"It must be soon."

"It will be. I promise."

Elizabeth's spirits plummeted. She recalled all the other promises made—and broken—in the past. Papa was forever making promises he did not keep.

I promise you'll have a white pony for your seventh birthday.

I promise you can accompany me to London on my next trip.

I promise I'll be home for Christmas this year.
I promise this time I'll say good-bye before I leave.
I promise.
I promise.
I promise.

Elizabeth no longer believed in promises. She hadn't believed in them in years.

Promises only broke your heart.

The young Frenchwoman's voice murmured in the desert night to her lover, "I promise, *cher*, I will tell milady soon. *C'est plus facile à dire qu'à faire;* it is easier said than done. We have been together for many years, she and I. I am not just her maid; I am her friend, her confidante."

The young man held her close and whispered fervently in her ear in several of the languages in which he was fluent, "But I love you! I adore you! I want to marry you. We must decide and leave soon, before it is too late. The ship sails for Alexandria before the end of next week. We will be home by spring."

She sighed dreamily. "Spring in Marseilles."

"On a winding little street by the sea, we will have our own shop with rooms above. It will be a chance to live our own lives for the first time."

"I know. I know," she cried softly.

"One day we will have children."

"Children," she repeated with a sense of wonder.

"I love you, *chérie*."

"And I love you," she vowed. "I will tell milady soon. I promise."

*   *   *

"I promise you that my husband knows nothing about us," the woman purred in a sultry voice as she slipped silently through the night toward his waiting bed.

She was already partially undressed, having divested herself of her clothing as she glided provocatively across the bedchamber. The man was aroused by the sight of her half-nude form; that was obvious from the way he was watching her.

His gray eyes were riveted on her high, firm breasts as she unlaced the front of her corset. His gaze followed the long, shapely length of her legs as she slowly and provocatively rolled down the pale pink silk stockings and tossed them aside. His eyes lingered on the rounded derriere when she turned her back to him and slipped out of her lacy drawers.

Not out of modesty was her back turned—they both were aware of that—but to deliberately reveal another view of her perfect hourglass figure.

She stood before him in all her natural glory and stretched her arms above her head.

"You are a vain cat, Amelia," he laughed huskily.

She wasn't about to deny it. "So I am."

The handsome man rolled onto his side and propped himself up on the bed pillows. "I'm not so certain that your husband knows nothing, however."

She sashayed to his side and, bending over him, let the tips of her breasts trail along his bare chest. Her nipples puckered prettily. "Hulbert is getting old and he is stupid."

"Stupid or very shrewd." He pulled her down on top of him and ran his hand along her bare back, admiring its perfection. He dropped a kiss on her shoulder. "I wonder which."

She touched her mouth to his, sliding her tongue in and out like a cat lapping cream. "I promise you, Hulbert knows nothing, and I promise that he will do whatever I ask."

He showed his white teeth in a sardonic smile. "You are a bitch, Amelia,"

"And you, André, are a bastard."

The count laughed. His voice was low and husky and full of sexual promise. "Perhaps that is why we are so well suited to one another."

Her deft hands found him and began to work their magic on his body. "I don't think it's the only reason," she said as he groaned with pleasure.

Chapter 17

"**P**apa, I must insist on speaking with you alone," Elizabeth informed him for what had to be the tenth time since she had arrived in Luxor the previous week.

Without bothering to glance up from the piece of ancient pottery he was examining, Lord Stanhope replied, with his customary vagueness, "I promise we'll have a talk soon."

Elizabeth planted her hands on her hips and refused to budge from the hut that served as his makeshift workshop. "Now, Papa. It must be *here* and *now*."

She finally got his attention.

He carefully set aside the shard of canopic jar, removed his spectacles—although how he could see through the layer of fine red dust that always seem to coat the lenses was beyond her—and looked straight at her. It was not the first time Elizabeth had noticed how tired he appeared.

"All right," he said without enthusiasm, "we'll talk."

"In private."

The earl uttered a succinct word or two in the native dialect and motioned to the workers toiling over baskets filled with pieces of pottery similar to the one he'd been studying. One by one they quickly vacated the hut.

"You've gotten your way, daughter. We're alone." He ran a weary hand over his myopic eyes. "I suppose you want to discuss the countess, or Franklin, or perhaps Caroline—"

She meant no disrespect, truly, but despite her best intentions, Elizabeth lost her patience with him.

"They're your family, Papa. Don't you care what happens to them? Don't you want to know if they are well, or happy, or even alive? Don't they mean anything to you?"

He had the decency to appear chagrined. "Of course they do."

She wanted to say, *What could they possibly mean to you, Papa? You haven't seen any of them in years. You never even bothered to come home after Annie died.*

"You haven't said a word about Annie—" Elizabeth broke off, surprised at the bitterness in her own voice.

Lord Stanhope lowered his head for a moment. "I didn't know what to say."

"You could have asked if she suffered in the

end. You could have told me that you prayed she died peacefully in her sleep." Her voice softened. "You could have shed a tear, one tear, and mourned the fact that a sweet angel like Annie is gone from this earth."

"I was afraid to," he said wearily, admitting defeat.

"Afraid to? Why?"

He took a monogrammed linen handkerchief from his pocket—Elizabeth recognized it as one of several she had given him for Christmas many years ago; only, now it was stained a permanent dull brown from sand and sweat and desert dust—and watched as he made a muddle of trying to clean his eyeglasses.

"I suppose—" he gave up on the spectacles "—because I didn't want to hear the answers."

All of a sudden Elizabeth felt like weeping. In the space of a heartbeat, she and her father had switched roles. She had become the parent, he the child. It would never be quite the same between them again.

Her voice was full. "Oh, Papa, you're fifty-seven years old. How long do you think you can keep running away from life?"

"I'm not running away from life. Only from the life I knew in England."

That, at least, was an honest answer.

Elizabeth sighed, and absentmindedly picked up the top of an ancient jar from the worktable. She studied the lid for a minute, murmuring half to herself, "*Duamutef.*"

That got Lord Stanhope's attention. "What did you say?"

She glanced up. *"Duamutef."*

Her father's eyes narrowed. "What do you know of *Duamutef*?"

She shrugged. "He was one of the four sons of the god Horus. In the ancient process of mummification, the heart and the kidneys were replaced inside the body shell of the deceased, but the other internal organs were stored in jars, each with a special head: the falcon held the intestines; the human got the liver; the baboon, the lungs; and *Duamutef*, the dog, the stomach."

For the first time since her arrival in Luxor, there was a spark of interest in Papa's eyes when she spoke. "You've been reading in my library."

"Yes."

A guarded "I'm surprised the countess allowed it."

Elizabeth danced around the issue. Her face turned several shades of pink and she poked about in the dust with the toe of her shoe. "Well, it is possible that Maman didn't realize exactly what it was I was reading."

Her father grinned and suddenly looked twenty years younger. "You never told her, did you?"

She swallowed. "No."

Obviously Lord Stanhope couldn't quite believe what he was hearing. "She had no idea?" he said, incredulous.

"None."

"She still doesn't?"

"Not as far as I know."

He laughed out loud. It was a delighted sound; a childish sound. "Believe me, if she realized you were even the slightest bit interested in Egypt,

she'd be screaming from the ridgepole of Stanhope Hall itself." The earl cleared his throat
and tried to regain his dignity. "Metaphorically
speaking, of course, since the countess does *not*
scream."

Elizabeth pursed her lips and said, with utter
seriousness, "You must understand, Papa. I did
not like sneaking behind Maman's back. Truly. It
was just that one day I stumbled upon a book by
Belzoni and began to read it, and I couldn't seem
to stop. . . ."

"Your secret is safe with me," he promised,
chuckling and shaking his head.

Elizabeth sighed. "I didn't ask to speak with
you alone in order to discuss Maman, or my
reading on the subject of Egypt, or at least not
directly. It is about an entirely different matter altogether. I need to talk to you about—"
she lowered her voice to a confidential whisper
"—Merneptah Seti."

He was still chuckling. "Merneptah Seti?"

"Yes, Merneptah Seti."

The earl wiped a tear or two of merriment from
his cheeks. "My Merneptah Seti?"

"Yes, *your* Merneptah Seti, if you will." Why
wasn't Papa listening?

His eyes were twinkling. "Have you been reading about him as well?"

"He was a pharaoh of the late Nineteenth Dynasty, believed to have ruled from 1201 to 1192
B.C., husband of the beautiful Nefetari, named
for the wife of the Great Ramses. They had four
children together before she died from the fever.
Seti mourned her for the rest of his life, refusing

to ever remarry," she recited.

Lord Stanhope nodded his white head with approval. "You always were quite bright. Certainly the best scholar among my children." He added as an afterthought, "Although in the case of Franklin and Caroline, and even poor, sweet Annie, I'm afraid that wasn't saying much." He slid his dusty spectacles back on the bridge of his nose. "Excellent, Elizabeth. Excellent."

"Papa—"

He looked up, peering over the steel rims of his eyeglasses, and gazed out the tiny window on the opposite wall of the hut. There was nothing as far as the eye could see but an endless horizon of brown sand and brown desert. "Why, I can still picture you standing in the schoolroom of Stanhope Hall, your back as straight as a rod, while you recited the kings and queens of the realm from Aethelred to Victoria with the same absolute determination and accuracy."

"Papa—"

"I'm very proud of you, little Lizzie."

"I'm not little Lizzie anymore," she shot back, her frustration growing.

"That's right, you aren't, are you? You're all grown-up now."

She brought her impatience under control. "Papa, I need to talk to you about Merneptah Seti."

For an instant, he appeared confused. "I thought you already had, my dear."

Unshed tears burned Elizabeth's eyes, but she refused to give up; she refused to give in. It was too important. This time there was too much at stake.

She tried another tact. "You have been searching for Seti's tomb for thirty years, haven't you?"

Something ignited behind the earl's tired eyes. "Yes, and this time I'm certain that we are searching in the right place. The pottery shards we have been uncovering are from that period, as well as the rock shavings. If we dig in the exact spot, we're bound to come upon the stela and the entrance to Merneptah Seti's tomb. I know we're close. I can feel it in my bones." He was rambling, oblivious to her presence. "There are so many cracks and crevices in the Valley of the Kings, but he's there. I know he's there. I can almost *feel* him."

She had no choice.

Elizabeth straightened her shoulders, took a deep breath, and blurted out, "Papa, I believe that you're looking in the wrong place."

Lord Stanhope lifted his head slowly and stared into her eyes. "What did you say, Lizzie?"

She swallowed hard and said it again: "I believe you are looking for Seti's tomb in the wrong place."

At first her father seemed merely taken aback. She even thought he was going to laugh. But he didn't. When he spoke next, she could hear the disbelief mingled with anger in his tone. "You're a child barely out of the schoolroom. What would you know about such things?"

As a matter of fact, she knew a great deal about

such things, Elizabeth wanted to inform him. The problem, of course, was going to be finding a way to convince Papa. Like most men, he could be so stubborn and pigheaded.

"I have been reading and studying—"

He cut her off sharply. "Reading and studying," he scoffed, his voice rising half an octave. "I have spent my entire life in this desert. And let me tell you something, experience is what counts." He was actually huffing and puffing with indignation.

"I meant no insult, Papa."

Lord Stanhope ignored her attempt at an apology. "You're a young female with a little knowledge, and a little knowledge is dangerous."

"I agree, but—"

Her father reached out and patted her patronizingly on the head, even though she stood every bit as tall as he. "You shouldn't be filling your pretty head with matters that are better suited to mature men and scholars."

Elizabeth couldn't believe what she was hearing. Dear God, not Papa, too! She had thought he would be different from the others. She had been so sure.

"But, Papa—"

"You said it yourself, daughter. You are nearly eighteen and a woman. It's time you were thinking about marriage."

"Marriage?"

His manner was unyielding. "Caroline was married by eighteen, as was your mother and your grandmother. Best thing for a young woman, really. Keeps her out of mischief."

"Out of mischief?" she repeated, stunned, her jaw dropping nearly to her chest.

The earl was in his element now, pontificating. "The man should be older in both years and experience, naturally."

Her mouth was still agape.

"You're a spirited girl, with a considerable will of your own. Unfortunate tendency in a female, but what's to be done about it? That seems to be one of the troubles with young women today. You will simply need the firm hand of the right man."

Elizabeth snapped her mouth shut. Then opened it again long enough to say, "The right man?"

Her father seem fixated on the subject now that he'd thought of it. "I have several acquaintances here in Egypt, as well as a number back in England. I'm sure we could manage to find some suitable gentleman for you to wed."

Her tongue was thick in her mouth. "Some suitable gentleman."

"Perhaps the son of an earl."

Her own words came back to haunt her. The ones she had declared to Jonathan Wicke that first night on the deck of the *Star of Egypt*: *I cannot bear the prospect of a future in which I am expected to marry the son of some innocuous earl, bear my husband an heir and a spare, and then blithely initiate a long string of love affairs as do the other members of the Marlborough House Set.*

Desperate, she tried again. "Papa, I do not wish to marry at this time. I want to stay here in Egypt with you and help find the tomb of Merneptah Seti."

"Impossible."

The heart was going out of her. "Impossible? Why?"

"This is no place for an Englishwoman," he said, his voice dry and brusque.

Elizabeth felt as if she were suddenly in the midst of one of her dreadful nightmares, only she was wide-awake. "Then why did you send for me in the first place?"

Lord Stanhope wrinkled his brow and muttered under his breath, "Did I send for you? How odd, I can't seem to remember. . . ."

"You wrote a letter to Maman last summer."

He frowned. "Did I? Last summer? Are you certain?"

Elizabeth's lips thinned and went white. "Of course I'm certain. You requested that Colonel and Mrs. Winters act as my chaperons since they were on home leave and about to return to Egypt," she recounted.

He shrugged his shoulders as if it was of no consequence to him either way. "Then I must have done so."

"Oh, Papa . . ." she cried softly.

The earl gave the spectacles on his nose a nudge. "I have wasted quite enough time discussing the subject of your marriage, Lizzie. I must get back to my work. There are important things I need to attend to. I'm on the verge of discovering Merneptah Seti's tomb, you see."

Elizabeth's shoulders slumped in defeat. Her hand was already on the doorknob of the hut when she finally looked back at the stranger who had been her father.

Jack's prophetic words echoed in her mind: *"On this Journey up the Nile, which we call the River of Life, be careful what you seek, Elizabeth. You may find more than you had bargained for."*

She closed the door behind her and went in search of the one man who had never lied to her.

Chapter 18

It was a bold-faced lie.

"Frankly, no, I hadn't given an engagement between us another thought," said Jack.

Elizabeth appeared crestfallen and nervously fingered the saucer beneath her cup of now tepid tea. "I see. I suppose it's only natural that you wouldn't have, my lord. I quite understand, of course."

Jack leaned back in the corner of the atrocious paisley-covered sofa that dominated the drawing room of the guesthouse in which he was staying, and arched a dark, sardonic brow in the girl's direction. "Are you trying to tell me that you're having second thoughts, my lady?"

"You—" Elizabeth broke off, whether as a result of nerves, or a simple lack of breath, he was not to know "—might say that."

"I might?" He couldn't keep the amusement out of his tone. It was obvious that the lady was dashed uncomfortable. It was equally obvious that she had something on her mind. He wondered what it was.

She finally looked him straight in the eye, and there was no trace of humor or caprice in her expression. Whatever she was about, she was *deadly* serious.

"I find myself in a most precarious position, my lord," she said.

"Indeed?"

She nodded.

He waited.

Elizabeth seemed to be choosing her words. "I would like to strike a bargain with you."

The situation was getting more intriguing by the moment. "A bargain?"

Again there was hesitation on her part. "An exchange, if you will."

In spite of himself, Black Jack was fascinated. "Do go on, my lady," he prompted.

"I will agree to supply you with certain valuable information, and in exchange, you will provide me with protection," Elizabeth said, and now her voice was brisk and businesslike.

Jack sat bolt upright. "Protection? Has there been another incident? Has someone else broken into your quarters, Elizabeth? Why didn't you tell me immediately?"

She quickly reassured him that was not the case. "It isn't that kind of danger, sir."

His blue eyes narrowed. "Exactly what kind of danger is it, madam?"

After a moment she explained: "If I do not become engaged to you, my lord, I'm very much afraid I could find myself betrothed to some gentleman of whom I know nothing."

He didn't like it. "Why is that?"

She sighed. "Because Papa has gotten it into his head that I should be married."

"Not an unheard-of sentiment for the father of an eighteen-year-old daughter," Jack tossed off with a nonchalance he wasn't feeling.

"I'm afraid that isn't the worst of it." There was genuine alarm in Elizabeth's eyes. "There is something not quite right about Papa."

"Not quite right?"

"He isn't well," she said, her voice shaking slightly.

"I did think he appeared tired," he agreed, stroking his chin.

"I don't mean ill in that sense." Tears suddenly pooled in her eyes. She rummaged around in her reticule for a handkerchief, but came up empty-handed.

Jack reached into his coat pocket and presented her with his own finely monogrammed linen. "Here."

"Th-Thank you," she stammered, dabbing at her damp face.

Black Jack hated it when a woman cried. It was so—messy, and they did look the very devil afterward. Except, of course, that tears only seemed to enhance Elizabeth Guest's beauty. And he found himself wanting to put a reassuring arm around her. Most peculiar. Most peculiar, indeed.

His tone was interrogative. "Exactly what do

you mean when you say your father isn't well?"

Elizabeth twisted the handkerchief in her hands. "Sometimes when I talk with Papa he seems perfectly normal and lucid. And then there are times—" tears welled again and trickled down her cheeks "—like this afternoon when I think he has gone quite mad."

Jack extracted the teacup from her trembling grasp and set it on the table in front of them. "I believe this situation calls for a medicinal glass of brandy."

He went to the sideboard and poured a generous amount of amber-colored liquor in a glass, and pressed it into her hands. She took several sips and coughed.

Then watery eyes gazed up at him. "Aren't you having any?" she inquired with a delicate hiccup.

Black Jack wasn't about to confess that the very thought of alcohol made his stomach turn since that morning aboard the *Star of Egypt* when he and André Polonski had drowned their sorrows together.

"Perhaps later. Right now I want you to explain about Lord Stanhope."

Elizabeth took another sip of medicinal brandy and said in a small voice, "Do you remember the night I told you about a sacred vow I'd made?"

He wasn't likely to forget since it was the same night they had made love, if incomplete love, in the tomb of the Lady Isis. "I remember."

"I couldn't tell you the whole truth about why someone would be searching my bedchamber because I had to discuss it with Papa first."

"And did you?"

"I-I tried," she murmured brokenly.

Jack paused with his hand on the sofa cushion between them. "What happened?"

"He didn't believe me," she told him, her voice shaking with emotion.

There was more to the episode, he was damn certain of it. "Your father didn't believe you?"

"Oh, Jack, Papa wouldn't even give me a chance to explain. He dismissed me as a child barely out of the schoolroom. He said I should leave important matters to gentlemen and scholars, and not trouble my pretty little head about such things." She took a swipe at the furious tears on her cheeks. "That's when he started to talk about marrying me off to the son of some earl, claiming it would keep me out of mischief."

For a moment only, a lopsided grin flickered across Jack's face. He clearly recalled Elizabeth's feelings on *that* subject. The lady had very definite opinions about English earls and their sons.

Then he shook his head in disgust.

There was no fool like an old fool, and Stanhope was an old fool!

His daughter undoubtedly knew more about the Black Land and its history than most of the so-called archaeologists and Egyptologists who had cluttered up the countryside since the time of Napoleon.

Only last week Alee had come to him and related with great pride that the *sitteh* had instantly recognized the stone blocks used in the construction of the guesthouse in which she was residing. According to the young Egyptian, Lady Elizabeth had translated the hieroglyphs with far more skill than even Lord Stanhope himself possessed.

Alee had also mentioned the *sitteh*'s concern for restoring the temple of Luxor. That was where the stones belonged, she had told him. That was their rightful place.

Maybe Elizabeth would understand, Jack tried to convince himself as he sat beside her on the sofa in his bungalow. Maybe he could confide in her about his mission for Prince Ramses and the tribe.

Maybe.

But not yet.

There was too much at stake.

"That is why I wish to strike a bargain with you, sir," came the intrusion into his thoughts.

Jack's eyebrows rose fractionally. "Exactly what did you have in mind?"

The girl's face was flushed a most becoming shade of pink, whether from the unaccustomed imbibing of spirits, or merely a slight case of embarrassment over the situation in which she found herself.

"For your part, you would pretend to be my fiancé," she declared freely.

"Only *pretend*?

Elizabeth took another sip of brandy and suggested in an almost cheerful tone, "Naturally, it would be an engagement in name only."

"I see."

"It is intended to put Papa off the scent, if you get my drift?"

"Oh, I get your drift, all right."

"In exchange—" she took in a deep breath and let it out again "—I will tell you a secret."

"You will tell me a secret," he repeated, verbatim.

Elizabeth took a thorough look around her, then lowered her voice to a theatrical whisper. "Papa is looking in the wrong place."

He said not a word.

She expounded, apparently assuming that she had not made herself clear. "Papa is looking in the wrong place for Merneptah Seti."

It was the best news Jack had had in weeks!

He was very careful with his next question. "How do you know?"

The girl dropped her voice even lower. "Because I know where Merneptah Seti is buried."

Brandy was tolerable enough once you'd had a sip or two, Elizabeth decided as she polished off the glass of medicinal liquor.

"That was quite good," she remarked to her host as she placed the empty glass on the table beside her teacup.

"Would you care for a bit more?" he inquired smoothly.

She gnawed on her bottom lip. "Is it too early in the day, do you think?"

"It is never too early in the day for a good brandy," he said dryly, rising to refill her glass.

"Thank you," she said politely as Jack returned with her drink.

"You're welcome."

Elizabeth sighed and stated with a previously unknown flair for the dramatic, "How bloody awful!"

Jack was caught off guard. "The brandy?"

"Oh, no, the brandy is quite delicious actually," she chattered as she indulged in another sip. "I meant how bloody awful to spend thirty years of your life looking for something and then not having the sense to recognize it when it's right under your nose."

"I couldn't agree with you more."

"They say, 'Pride goeth before a fall.' "

"Do they?"

"Actually," she pointed out, "the proverb says: 'Pride goeth before destruction, and an haughty spirit before a fall.' "

"Does it?"

"Yes. It's right there in Proverbs sixteen:eighteen."

Jack's expression was neutral. "Well versed in the Good Book, are you?"

"Nanny."

There was a question in his tone. "Nanny?"

Elizabeth sighed. "Nanny has always been a stickler when it comes to reading one's Bible verses." She stared down into the half-empty snifter of brandy. "She would never approve."

"Of drinking spirits?"

"Oh, no, Nanny always keeps a bottle in her room for those special occasions when a little something is required."

Jack seemed to be paying her the closest attention. "Special occasions?"

"Toothache."

"Of course."

"Very good for the vapors."

"I expect so."

She felt the heat rush to her face. "Certain ah-hum female problems."

"Quite," he replied with equanimity. "What would Nanny never approve of?"

"Papa." Elizabeth proceeded to explain: "She was his nanny first, you know. A long time ago."

"Nanny must be getting up there in years," Jack observed as he poured himself another cup of tea.

She thought long and hard, and then concluded, "Nanny wouldn't admit to it, of course, but I believe she must be every bit as old as Trout."

"They would make a fine pair," he muttered.

"Oh, but they do. Trout and Nanny are man and wife. They have been married for nigh on sixty years."

"Well, I'll be . . ."

She wrinkled up her brow. "You'll be what, my lord?"

He regarded her with a nonplussed expression, then sat back, laughed heartily, and said, "I will be happy to pose as your fiancé, Elizabeth."

She was duly grateful. "Thank you, my lord."

He corrected her gently. "Jack."

"Thank you, Jack."

"Now, in regards to your part of the bargain . . ."

Although she felt a bit muddled by the influence of the brandy, Elizabeth knew what she must do. Merneptah Seti was her only bargaining tool. The one thing of worth that she possessed was the knowledge in her head and in her diary. And, unlike Papa, she was no fool.

She laid out her plans. "Once we have convinced my father that he no longer need concern himself with marrying me off to some pompous son of a—"

Opportunely, the man seated beside her cleared his throat.

"—then I will lead you to the tomb of the Great Pharaoh."

There was a moment or two of silence.

She sensed the curiosity that finally drove Jonathan Wicke to ask, "How do you know what no one else has been able to figure out in hundreds, indeed, in thousands, of years?"

She hesitated, weighing his question. "It is, my dear man, the result of research and study and . . ."

"And . . ."

"And a woman's intuition."

That, apparently, was the last thing Jack had expected her to say.

"A woman's intuition?" he burst out.

Elizabeth lifted her chin, looked regally down her nose at him, and proclaimed, "The truly intelligent man never underestimates the power of a woman's intuition."

To herself, she thought, *Queen to king's knight four. Check. Checkmate.*

Jack was still muttering to himself when she proposed, "Shall we seal our bargain with a handshake, sir?"

"A handshake?" he replied in a vexed way. "I

think not, my dear lady." He edged closer to her along the paisley sofa, deftly plucked the glass from her hand, and took her into his arms. "A bargain such as ours should be sealed with a kiss."

With that, Jack covered her mouth with his.

It was a sweet and intoxicating kiss. It was a gentle and provocative kiss. It was a kiss full of promise, of things yet to be. His breath was warm and wonderful, like the best French cognac, its unique bouquet wafting across her face.

"I like kissing you," Elizabeth murmured as Jack nibbled at her throat.

"And I like kissing you."

"I like the other things we do, too," came the whispered confession.

"So do I."

"Are we very wicked?"

Jack laughed; it was a gritty, masculine sound. "I certainly hope so."

Elizabeth gave a slightly intoxicated giggle. "So do I."

"I think, my dear fiancée, that I must fetch Colette to see to you. You've had a bit too much brandy."

She pouted. "No."

"Yes," he countered firmly.

"I would like some more, please. It is quite delicious."

"You've obviously had more than enough already."

Elizabeth eyed him with feminine suspicion. "Are you aware, sir, that you have an unfortu- nate tendency to behave in a highhanded manner? One might even go so far as to say an over-bearing manner."

"Naturally, I am wounded by your low opinion of me, madam."

"What are you going to do about it?"

Jack shrugged his broad shoulders. "Nothing. Absolutely nothing."

"That's what I mean," Elizabeth declared, struggling to her feet. "Without exception, men are stubborn and pigheaded and refuse to listen to reason."

"How fortunate for us, then, that we have you ladies to point out to us the error of our ways," he said amiably, steadying her with his arm.

She was still thinking about that one when a knock sounded on his bungalow door.

"Excuse me, my dear." Since Kareem was not in attendance, Jack had little choice but to answer the summons himself.

It was Amelia Winters.

Without preamble, she demanded to know, "Is Lady Elizabeth here?"

"Yes." But Jack did not extend the woman an invitation to step inside.

"I must speak with her immediately on a matter of utmost importance."

Jack seemed more amused than offended by Mrs. Winters's bad manners. "That may be somewhat difficult."

"Why?"

"I'm afraid that my fiancée has had a bit too much brandy to drink. Indeed, I was on my way to secure Mademoiselle Duvay's assistance when you knocked."

"Your fiancée?"

Somehow it sounded very official and irrevocable when Jack said it.

"You may be the first to congratulate us. Lady Elizabeth and I are officially engaged to be married."

The woman recovered admirably, as she always seemed to. "Of course. Congratulations, Lord Jonathan. My best wishes to you both."

Elizabeth called out from across the drawing room. "Thank you, Mrs. Winters. Most kind of you."

Her chaperon tried to maneuver around the rather formidable obstacle of Jonathan Wicke, but it was to no avail. "I really must speak with you, my lady. It is important."

"You may tell me," said Jack, "and I will relay the message to my betrothed."

Amelia Winters gave him a sweetly sanguine smile. "If you insist."

He gave her an equally polite smile in return. "I do."

"Then you may inform your betrothed of this, my lord. It seems that she has been deserted."

Jack's expression never altered; he simply stood there and waited for the woman to finish.

"We have just discovered that Georges and Colette have run off together. It seems that the young couple has eloped. . . ."

Later Elizabeth lay in her bed and read Colette's farewell letter again. It brought both tears of sorrow and tears of joy to her eyes. She was going to miss her friend, naturally, but this was Colette's

chance at love and happiness, and how could she
refuse her that?

She would remember always the last few lines
of the young Frenchwoman's letter:

Chérie, when you find the right man to love,
never let him go.

And know that I will hold you next to my
heart until the day I die.

Yours,

C.

Not for the first time, nor the last, Elizabeth
cried herself to sleep.

Chapter 19

Hulbert Mathias Winters had never forgotten the night he had his first woman.

The occasion had been his thirteenth birthday. There had been a big family celebration at Pelly House, and his dear, sweet grandmother had presented "Bertie" with an antique saber—he had been at military school for several years already and been wanting one rather badly— and a leather-bound edition of Pepys.

He still had the saber; he had never bothered to even read the Pepys.

The colonel sank back into the plethora of pillows on the floor of the so-called sitting room of the desert bungalow and sipped his port.

It was indulgent of him, he knew. The port was imported and expensive, but then, he had expensive tastes, and this was the way he preferred to end his day. Or, in this case, his evening. For the hour was past midnight, and Amelia had long ago gone to her bedchamber.

Hulbert Winters put his head back against the soft, sensual material of the pillows and let his mind wander. A scoop of blue-veined Stilton with his glass of port—now, that was enough to start a man salivating.

The full, rounded breasts of—Dara, yes, that had been her name, Dara. The memory of those dark, dusky teats made a man's mouth water, as well.

Over forty years later and he still got hard just thinking about that night. He had always assumed the jade was a gift from his father and his uncle, but he had no actual proof.

All he knew was that his grandmother would have had a bloody conniption if she had ever found out. . . .

He stretched out on top of the bed sheets, enjoying the sensation of crisp, cool linen against his naked adolescent flesh, and folded his arms behind his head.

It hadn't been much of a birthday, as birthdays went. He hated these "command performances" at Pelly House. But his father had made it clear: He had better damn well do as he was told if he wanted that horse next year when he turned fourteen.

So he had been the perfect little gentleman all evening, promising himself that next year would be better, that next year he would have his own horse and his own saddle and perhaps a bit of money of his own, as well.

Perhaps his grandmother would pop off and die, and remember him in her will. Of course, even if Grandmama did intend to bequeath him part of her estate, he would undoubtedly have to wait for the money until he came of age.

Blast! It was bloody inconvenient being so young and so poor. He hated it!

Through the damask curtains hanging at the window, Bertie could see streaks of summer lightning flash through the sky. The distant rumble of thunder followed, then rain, buckets of it; it started coming down in torrents.

He didn't hear the door open; it was the faint gaslight from the hallway that gave away the fact that someone had entered the guest room where he always slept.

"Who's there?" he whispered, his heart beginning to pound like a brass drum.

"Bertie?" It was an unfamiliar, uncultured accent.

He hesitated before he answered. "Yes."

"May I come in?"

He still didn't recognize the girlish voice. He wasn't sure what to say. "Why?"

There was a quaver in the admission: "I-I'm afraid of the storm."

He drew the covers over his lower body, suddenly aware of every nerve ending from his scalp to his groin. "Suppose you can come in, if you want."

There was the soft scurry of bare feet on the thick Persian carpet, the rustle of bedcovers, and a dip in the mattress as the wench slipped in beside him.

He felt a little ridiculous asking the question, but he did. "Who are you?"

"Dara," she murmured, moving closer to him.

"Dara?"

"I work for your grandmother in the kitchens. They needed extra help tonight, so I was one of 'em chosen to serve your birthday dinner."

Now he remembered. He had watched her every chance he'd had during the six-course meal. She was small and slender, exotic in appearance—a touch of some South Seas island in her mixed blood, no doubt—with surprisingly large breasts. He remembered wondering what color her teats would be.

"I remember you," he admitted, swallowing with extreme difficulty, hoping she couldn't read his mind; at the same time almost wishing that she could.

Bertie supposed he should ask what she was doing this far away from the servants' quarters, but he didn't. He was afraid if he said anything, the girl would leave.

And that was the last thing, he realized, he wanted Dara to do.

"How old are you?" he asked instead.

"Nearly eighteen. I think."

"I'm only thirteen."

"I know. Cook told me."

He wasn't sure what to say next; he took a stab in the dark. "Can you read, Dara?"

"Nup, but I'd like to be learned."

"Can you count?"

The wench brightened. "Yes." Adding, "Course, I can only recite my numbers to ten." She curled up beside him and slipped an arm around his waist. Then she slowly moved her hand lower and giggled. "You're a mighty big boy for your age."

Bertie found he could not breathe.

All of a sudden Dara tossed back the bedcovers and propelled herself across his body. Hitching up her nightdress, she unceremoniously plunked her bottom down on his belly, one leg on either side of his. He could feel her warm flesh right through the skimpy material of her shift.

She reached out and touched his face in an almost tender gesture. "You'll help me, won't you, Bertie dear?"

He managed to nod.

"Now, I want a straight answer," purred the jade as she bent over him in the semidarkness. "You mustn't make up lies just to make me feel better."

"I won't," he croaked.

For some reason, that made her laugh. "Promise?"

"I promise."

"Cross your heart and hope to die?"

Bertie nodded, and made the sign over the left side of his chest.

The buxom wench pouted and drawled in a sultry voice, "Do you think my breasts are too big?"

He shook his head and managed to find his voice. "N-No."

"God's truth?"

"God's truth."

"No fib?"

"No fib."

"Swear?"

He nodded. He could swear with a clear conscience. He was absolutely certain, in fact.

"Mayhap you should take a better look afore you swear, Bertie." With that, Dara raised her slender arms and drew her shift over her head in a single, sweeping movement. Without a second thought, she tossed it on the floor of his bedchamber. "What do you think now?"

Bertie didn't think he had ever seen anything so beautiful in his entire life.

Dara's breasts were round and full, just as he had imagined. The tips were puckered, as if she'd been out in the cold, or rubbed up against a piece of coarse burlap material. They were reddish brown in color, like ripe berries. Indeed, they looked good enough to eat.

His mouth drooled to taste her. His hands itched to touch her.

Dara read his mind.

She leaned closer and whispered in his ear, tracing the outline of his lobe with her tongue, "You can touch me if you like, Bertie."

He was tentative at first, but he reached out with one finger and gave her nipple an experimental nudge. Then he covered one breast with his hand and awkwardly squeezed.

She leaned closer until her brown teats were nearly brushing against his lips. "You can take me into your mouth if you wish, Bertie."

He began to salivate. "Are you certain?"

"Course I am." She laughed softly in the back of her throat, and it was a sound he took delight in. "Let me show you how. Relax and part your lips a mite more. There." She inserted one hard, berry brown nipple between his teeth. "You can nibble a bit till you get the knack of it. Then we'll try all kinds of things."

Before long Bertie was all over the girl with his hands and his mouth and his tongue. She called him a quick learner and moaned every now and then in a low, husky voice that sent chills spiraling down his spine.

He had touched himself before in the dark of night, but when Dara took his rigid member between her lips and began to suck on him, he gave a hoarse shout and spurted instantaneously into her mouth.

The girl nonchalantly licked her lips, dropped a musky kiss on his mouth, and started again.

It was turning out to be one bloody hell of a birthday!

Dara was undoubtedly the best birthday "present" he had ever been given, mused Hulbert Winters as he sipped his port. His father and his uncle had chosen well. He had occasionally wondered since then if they had "tried out" Dara first to be certain she was just the kind of present a thirteen-year-old novice needed. But he had never asked.

It was enough to have the memories.

Hulbert finished off his port and staggered to his feet.

Amelia.

His eyes narrowed slightly when he thought of his "wife" and partner.

It wasn't often that he could service the gutter-snipe like he had been able to in the beginning. After all, he wasn't a young man anymore, and her sexual appetite was voracious. But tonight there would be no problem in that department. He was already as hard as a rock.

The colonel stumbled across the carpet and headed toward the bedroom Amelia had claimed as hers the first day they had arrived in Luxor. He thought of knocking and decided against it. He could damn well enter her bedchamber any time he pleased. He threw open the door.

The room was empty.

But he knew where to find her, thought the colonel as he closed the door again and made his way through the bungalow and out into the clear desert night. He knew where to find her.

He knew exactly where Amelia was.

Chapter 20

⌒⌒◯◯⌒

The sound of Amelia's sultry voice through the half-open window told the colonel he was right.

She was with Count Polonski.

At least she was in Polonski's bungalow, and since the hour was nearly one o'clock in the morning, he seriously doubted if the two of them were having tea and cake together.

Swaying on his feet—he would be the first to acknowledge that he had consumed a considerable amount of port tonight—Hulbert Winters braced one hand against the ancient stone block wall of the building and used the other to cautiously push open the shutters. He now had a clear view into the drawing room of a bungalow that was nearly identical to the one he and Amelia were occupying.

Facing in the direction of the window, André Polonski was seated on a red velvet sofa that looked as if it had come straight out of a London bawdy house. He was fully clothed and, as usual, impeccably groomed: clean-shaven, not a hair out of place, his cravat as neatly tied as it had been that morning. Apparently the elopement of Georges and Colette had not had disastrous results as far as the count's appearance was concerned.

Amelia, on the other hand, was clad in her nightdress and wrapper. She was kneeling on the floor between the gentleman's legs, her shapely back to the window.

The colonel had had enough experience with the guttersnipe to know exactly what she was about. Her arm was moving up and down in a pumping motion, as if she were churning butter, only, of course, Amelia was anything *but* a milkmaid.

Although, to be sure, Hulbert reflected with a twisted and thoroughly depraved smile, the she-cat was fully capable of "milking" a man dry.

He cocked his head and listened to their conversation.

André Polonski spoke first. "Do you really think the girl knows anything?"

In a husky voice usually reserved for the boudoir, Amelia answered, "She must."

"Has her father confided in her, then?"

Hulbert could almost picture the Cheshire-cat grin on Amelia's face. "I don't think Lord Stanhope has anything of import to tell his daughter. I believe it is the girl who knows something."

He had to hand it to Polonski; he was one cool customer. The colonel detected only the merest rise in the man's eyebrows.

He wondered what else, however, was "on the rise."

"So Lady Elizabeth is the key."

"I'm almost certain of it," stated Amelia as she bent over and buried her head in the man's lap.

Hulbert felt the stirrings of sexual excitement begin all over again. He had still been half-aroused when he had staggered out of their bungalow in search of the errant hellcat. Now he could clearly hear her smacking her lips and sucking on the count's undoubtedly rigid flesh.

Polonski reached down and pressed her face deeper into his crotch. "You do that very nicely, my dear." He blithely went on. "I would like to ask you a question or two. You may simply shake your head one way or the other in response. No need to stop what you're about."

Amelia gave a nod, immediately recognized, as she would, that the movement was erotically stimulating to the man, and gurgled in the back of her throat.

"Egods, you do do it expertly," gritted the count through clenched white teeth. A sheen of perspiration broke out on his forehead. "Tell me," he said, with some degree of difficulty, "do you believe Lady Elizabeth knows the location of Merneptah Seti's tomb?"

A nod of the blond head drove his hardened shaft deeper into the trollop's mouth.

Polonski inhaled sharply. The sound was audible even to the colonel. It was a moment or two before the younger man seemed to regain control of himself. "You—you mentioned that you had searched, or had tried to search, the girl's room the first night we slept in the caves. What were you looking for?"

Amelia lifted her head. "The little bitch has notes and maps stashed somewhere."

The handsome man on the sofa sat up straighter. "What?"

"You heard me. She has notes and maps stashed amongst her belongings."

Polonski reached down, slid his hand inside the front of Amelia's nightdress, and began to caress a breast. Her head fell back, and a low animal moan issued forth from her parted lips. The wrapper and nightgown were pushed off one lily white shoulder. Then her lover caught her bared tit between his finger and thumb, squeezing harder and harder until she cried out with pleasure that bordered on pain.

Hulbert licked his lips licentiously. This was even better than sitting in the dark remembering Dara. This was even better than poking the hellcat himself. It took a lot less energy, for one thing.

But there was something else: He found it quite exciting and stimulating to observe another man in flagrante delicto with his supposed wife. He wished he'd thought of it sooner. . . .

Amelia was attempting to explain. "A few weeks ago Hulbert and I were taking a late night stroll on the deck of the *Star of Egypt*. We happened to notice that a lamp was still burning in Lady Elizabeth's cabin. We glanced in the window and saw that she had fallen asleep over her desk." The blonde pushed his hand away and covered her breast as much as to say, *business before pleasure*. "We could see sheets and sheets of thin paper covered with handwriting, drawings, and hieroglyphs. Naturally we wanted to take a closer look, but the girl awakened at just that moment. So we had to bide our time until we reached the caves."

"You are the sly one, my dear."

They both knew he meant it as a compliment.

Amelia was clearly pleased. "Since I'm smaller and quicker on my feet—and since Hulbert is in his cups every night from that expensive port he swills—it was only logical that I be the one to steal into her bedchamber to try to find the papers."

"And did you find them?"

"No," she said crossly. "The damnable girl woke up. The next thing I knew, she gave a great shout, jumped from her bed, and chased me from the tomb."

André Polonski put his handsome head back and laughed with genuine amusement. "Now, that is a sight I would like to have witnessed."

Amelia must have given him a tweak with her sharp claws, for he let out a startled gasp. "I'm glad you find me amusing, my dear count."

He was no longer laughing. He cleared his throat and said, "So you believe the daughter is the key."

"I'm certain of it."

"You must know the legend as well as I do. It is said that the tomb of Merneptah Seti contains a god-king's treasure beyond the scope of any mortal's imagination." The man began to thread his long, sensual fingers through the kneeling woman's hair. "It could all be ours, my darling."

Her voice vibrated. "All ours?"

Rhythmically he stroked her blond tresses. "We could steal Elizabeth Guest's papers, including the maps, find the treasure, and live like royalty for the rest of our days."

Hulbert Winters watched as Amelia turned her head in profile. She was licking her lips, the greedy little bitch.

"We could live anywhere we wanted," she murmured.

"We could have several houses: one in London, perhaps another in Paris, or even Vienna."

"We could travel anywhere we wished."

"Around the world." They both laughed. Polonski reminded her, "We're still young, but it would be more wealth than even we could spend in a lifetime."

"More than even we could spend?"

"I would buy you only the finest and the rarest jewels. A woman with your beauty was meant to wear rubies and emeralds in her hair, diamonds in her perfect and delicate ears, precious pearls around her throat." Polonski encircled Amelia's long, slender neck with his fingers. His voice was mesmerizing. "You were born to be a queen among women, an empress."

Amelia eagerly agreed. "Yes. Yes."

The count's nearly colorless eyes narrowed. "What of your husband?"

She shrugged. "What of him?"

"Will you leave the colonel?"

There was not a moment's hesitation on Amelia's part. "Yes."

"Will he be any trouble?"

"Not if we act first. We must get a look at those papers in Lady Elizabeth's possession," she insisted with a sense of urgency. "Something tells me that she has the information we need to lead us directly to the tomb of Merneptah Seti."

André kept a perfectly straight face this time. "Did you truly steal into her room at the caves?"

"Yes."

"Then I have a confession to make, as well. After you and I arranged to 'accidentally' meet at the Antiquities Museum in Cairo, I hired a local thug to put a scare into Lord Stanhope's daughter. The thug was to follow the girl and act upon any opportunity that presented itself. As it was, she wandered off by herself, and he managed to push her into a mummy case and shut the door."

"How very naughty of you, André."

"The original idea was that *I* was to come to her rescue and she would be eternally grateful to me. Then I could use her gratitude to form a relationship with her."

"Something went wrong," she surmised.

He nodded. "It was Wicke, I presume. He must have found her first. Remember how secretive they were when they rejoined us that day?"

"Yes, now that I think about it, I do," the blonde said, tapping her bottom lip with her fingertip. "I had supposed he'd stolen a kiss from the chit."

"Apparently he's done far more than that if the two of them are now officially engaged."

"Bastard!" she hissed.

"No, my dear Amelia, I'm the bastard," the count said with self-deprecating humor. "You must know what you're getting into if you join up with me. I want you to go into it with your eyes wide open." His hand slid from her neck to her gown as he again eased the delicate material off her shoulders. "You really are a lovely creature."

Raising her up beside him, he began to flick his pointed tongue back and forth from nipple to nipple. Then he drew her into his mouth and suckled long and hard. She put her head back and moaned.

The bastard was skilled, acknowledged Hulbert as he avidly watched from outside the window. Polonski knew what to do with a woman, that was for damn certain. He had the she-cat eating, literally, out of his hand.

"Oh, I know what I'm getting into," whispered Amelia. "You are the best lover I've ever had."

"Coming from you, that is a compliment," said the count sardonically.

She offered no apologies or explanations. "I am what I am, André."

"And I am what I am, Amelia."

"Do we have a bargain?"

"We do."

"Shall we have some of that delicious champagne now to toast our newfound partnership?"

Polonski poured them each a glass, and they raised their drinks in a toast. "To us, my dear Amelia."

"To us," she echoed, taking a demure sip of her champagne.

Then she greedily finished off her drink, plucked the glass from André's hand, and set it on the table. She pushed him down on the sofa, and her deft fingers quickly went to work. Within several minutes she had Polonski undressed and stretched out nude beneath her. She straddled his body, her long blond hair and diaphanous night-dress flowing around him like a wispy cloud.

"André?" she purred his name.

He hesitated. "Yes."

She reached out and touched his face in an almost tender gesture. "You'll help me, won't you, darling?"

He nodded.

"Now, I want a straight answer," she said as she bent over him in the semidarkness of the bungalow. "You mustn't make up lies just to make me feel better."

"I won't."

She laughed. "Promise?"

"I promise."

"Cross your heart and hope to die?"

André laughed again deep down in his chest—it was apparently not the first time they had performed this particular scenario—and made a sign over his heart.

Outside the bungalow window, Hulbert Winters began to squirm uncomfortably. His face turned a furious shade of red. The bitch was acting out his fantasy, his memory of that first night with Dara!

He should never have told her. He should have known she couldn't keep a secret. He wanted to reach out, put his hands around her neck, and squeeze until she turned blue, until her eyes bulged, until the last breath was wrung from her lovely rotten body.

The colonel listened as Amelia drawled in a sultry tone, "Do you think my breasts are too big?"

André quickly shook his head and said, "No."

He had obviously already learned that a man never knew where Amelia's games would lead him. But her games were never dull, and they were often very interesting.

"God's truth?"

"God's truth."

"No fib?"

"No fib."

"Swear?"

The she-devil remembered every single word he had related to her, realized Hulbert Winters as he observed the couple in front of him.

He would get her.

In the end, he would make Amelia pay.

Meanwhile, he discovered he was as hard as he ever recalled being. In some sort of perverse way, this was the most exciting sexual experience he had ever had. He was watching his own dream. He was watching another man and woman act it out. He was outraged. He was furious. He was painfully aroused.

André nodded. "I swear."

"Perhaps you should take a better look before you swear, my dear." With that, Amelia raised her arms and drew her sheer nightdress over her head in a single, sweeping movement. Without a second thought, she tossed it on the floor of the sitting room. "What do you think now?"

Her breasts were round and full; the nipples were pink and perfect and puckered. They were a delicious color, like ripe strawberries.

Indeed, Hulbert thought, they looked good enough to eat, and he knew firsthand that they were.

He started to drool; the spittle formed in the corner of his drunken mouth and dripped onto his chin. Suddenly he wanted very badly to taste Amelia. His hands itched to touch her. He wanted to tease her until she cried out again and again for him to finish what the other man had begun.

He could see that André Polonski was devouring her with his eyes, feasting upon the sight of her luscious form.

Amelia leaned closer and whispered in his ear, tracing the outline of his lobe with her tongue: "You can touch me if you like."

The younger man was tentative at first, playing the scene as they had no doubt rehearsed it many times before. He reached out with one finger and gave her already distended nipple an experimental nudge. Then he covered one breast with his hand and awkwardly caressed her.

Amelia leaned closer until her pink tits were brushing back and forth across his lips. "You're such a big boy, such a good boy, you can take me into your mouth if you wish."

He began to lick his lips like a wolf about to pounce on an unsuspecting hare. "Are you certain?"

"Of course I am." She laughed softly in the back of her throat. "Let me show you how.

Relax and part your lips a little more. There."
She inserted one hard, pearlized nipple between
his teeth. "You can nibble a bit until you get the
hang of it. Then we'll try all kinds of things."

"Will we?"

They seemed to depart from the script at this
point. André was all over Amelia with his hands
and his mouth and his tongue. She called him a
quick learner and moaned every now and then in
a low, husky voice that sent chills spiraling along
the colonel's spine.

He reached down and took hold of himself.
Whether she knew it or not, Amelia was going
to bring satisfaction to two men tonight.

And when the blonde slid down along André
Polonski's body and expertly took his turgid flesh
between her lips and began to feast on him, the
colonel was forced to stifle the hoarse shout that
sprang to his own lips.

Amelia raised her head some minutes later,
nonchalantly licking her lips.

Colonel Winters adjusted his trousers and prepared to slip away into the night toward their
bungalow. While he had to admire, perhaps even
applaud, Amelia's technique, Polonski could have
her and good riddance!

They weren't going to trick him. He knew their
game now. And he would, the colonel thought
with a sly smile, have the last laugh.

Chapter 21

*E*lizabeth *was in love.*

It was foolish of her. It was unwise of her. It was very probably dangerous for her.

And it was entirely out of her hands.

She had simply awakened this morning, several weeks after her engagement was announced to Jonathan Malcolm Charles Wicke, and known it was true.

Her fiancé was well aware that she "fancied" him; there had been no way to disguise the passion that flared between the two of them whenever they were alone. But Jack would certainly have the last laugh if he were ever to discover the depth of her feelings for him.

After all, *she* was the one who had refused his initial offer of marriage. *She* was the one who had insisted that their engagement be no more than a pretense in order to prevent her father from handing her over to some milksop whose idea of a stimulating evening was a "rousing" game of whist, or the latest gossip about who was bedding whom. Everyone in Society knew it was not a game of "musical chairs" at most country-house parties, but of "musical beds."

Yes, Elizabeth was in love with Jack, but she was determined that he would never know.

Of course, the fact that he was turning out to be a consummate actor wasn't making it any easier for her. Jack was playing the role of the devoted fiancé to perfection: He spent nearly every waking moment in her presence; he paid her every attention; he bestowed small gifts upon her at the slightest whim; he kissed her deeply, passionately, and often, because he insisted a woman looked "kissed" or "unkissed," as the case may be, and surely she wanted their betrothal to appear genuine. Somehow she found she could not argue with his logic.

Besides, she enjoyed kissing him. Indeed, she looked forward to it at every opportunity. Although there had been no repeat of the glorious lovemaking they had indulged in that night in the caves.

Much to her disappointment.

Indeed, Jonathan Wicke had been the perfect gentleman since their engagement.

It was most annoying.

Elizabeth stood at the window of her bungalow and watched the three men in the distance: Papa, Alee, and Jack.

It was first light. Her father and the handsome

Egyptian youth were loading some newfangled surveying equipment, just arrived from England, into Papa's horse-drawn buggy. Jack was standing nearby, arms folded across his broad chest, black brows furrowed into a scowl, his stance speaking of both frustration and anger.

Papa had said no again.

Each day for the past two weeks, she or Alee—the young man had become her staunch ally in such matters—had asked her father for permission to visit the excavation site where he was working in the Valley of the Kings. And each day he had adamantly and unequivocally refused her request. He insisted that the desert was no place for a girl.

This morning Jack had decided to speak to Lord Stanhope on her behalf. He knew, perhaps more than anyone, how much it meant to her.

Yes, Jack's gifts—a finely woven cotton shawl from his own farm and looms, a fragment of ancient papyrus, a rare book on desert vegetation and animals—that had been presented daily were thoughtful and appreciated, but he knew what she yearned for: Elizabeth wanted to visit the Valley of the Kings, to share her father's lifelong work, to have him accept her as an intellectual equal.

It was the one thing she wished for above all else.

It was the one thing, it seemed, that no one could give her.

She saw Jack throw up his hands in disgust and head for her bungalow. She didn't need to see his face to know that it wasn't good news.

She sighed and watched the other two men a moment longer as they worked side by side. There was something she couldn't quite put her finger on. Something about Alee and Papa . . .

Then she was distracted by Jack's approaching figure. The morning sun glinted off his right hand and drew her attention to the gold ring in the shape of an ankh that he always wore on his middle finger.

Perhaps someday Jack would trust her enough to tell her the true significance of the ring.

Perhaps someday she would trust him enough to share her own secrets.

But trust was something that had to be earned, and until that day came—if it ever did—the two of them would continue with the fragile truce they had declared.

They had been engaged for a fortnight. Wouldn't Jack, indeed, have the last laugh if he found out that she was already wishing theirs were a genuine betrothal?

Would he be angry, or merely relieved, she wondered, if he were to discover that she intended to return to England just as soon as she could make the necessary travel arrangements?

She had come to Egypt. She had seen many wondrous things. She had sailed up the Nile and had found, as Jack had predicted, far more than she had bargained for. She had experienced bitter disappointment at the hands of one man, and passionate love at the hands of another.

The prophetic words of an earlier traveler to the Black Land, quoted by Lady Charlotte that day in the rose garden, came back to haunt Elizabeth now as she stood at her bungalow window: "One wonders that people come back from Egypt and live lives as they did before."

Elizabeth Guest knew she would never be the same. Her life had changed beyond measure. She was not the naive young girl who had begun this journey from Yorkshire just a few short months ago.

She was older and infinitely wiser. She may not have lived life to its fullest in every sense of the word, but she knew the secret females had been discovering since the dawn of time: One was not born a woman; one became one.

She had become a woman.

It was the sound of shouting and frenzied cries for help, along with the thundering of horses' hooves entering the compound, that propelled Jack and Elizabeth from the relative tranquillity of their afternoon tea. The entire party put down their china cups, rose from chairs around linen-covered tables, and quickly made their way out onto the main verandah.

The carriage was being driven at an insane pace by one of Lord Stanhope's archaeological assistants. The earl was in the rear of the buggy, covered by a tarpaulin to keep the intense sunlight off him. His bloodied head was being held by a second assistant, but one glance told the story.

Avery Guest, the Earl of Stanhope, was dead.

One trembling hand fluttered to Elizabeth's mouth. She took a faltering step toward the carriage, but Jack's arm flew out and stopped her.

"You stay here until I have a look," he commanded.

Elizabeth ignored his advice. She inhaled a deep breath and approached the deathly still figure of her father. As if in a dream—nay, surely as if in a nightmare—she reached out and touched his face.

His flesh was warm. But it was the heat of the desert sun that made it so, not the breath of life flowing through his lungs, nor the blood of life pumping through his crushed body.

"Oh, Papa—"

"I'm so sorry," began the man in the back of the buggy.

She looked up at the driver with huge tears pooling in her eyes. "W-What happened?"

"It was an accident; a dreadful, horrible accident, my lady," explained the young assistant. The story was related in bits and pieces that would only later make complete sense. "Lord Stanhope was certain we had located the tomb of Merneptah Seti. There was a narrow ledge of stone high above the valley floor. It seemed to lead into the entrance of a cave. Your father insisted upon crossing first despite all our objections and warnings." The young Englishman was forced to stop and brush his shirt-sleeve across his watery eyes.

The second assistant went on. "The ledge gave way beneath Lord Stanhope's weight. There was nothing we could do. He fell forty, perhaps fifty feet, straight down."

"He did not suffer, my lady," added the first man. "He hit his head on an outcropping of rock almost immediately. He was unconscious the entire time and never knew what happened."

Elizabeth repeated the words as if to console herself and both of them. "He didn't suffer. He never knew what happened."

"The earl was so happy in those last few moments. He was nearly delirious with excitement. He was so certain that his dream was about to come true."

She took her father's lifeless hand in hers and raised it to her lips. "I'm truly glad you died happy, Papa."

After a moment a strong arm encircled her shoulders. "Let me have your father's body carried inside now, Elizabeth. There are things that must be seen to," said Jack.

"Yes. Of course," she agreed, as if in a trance.

One of the young archaeologists mumbled, "Someone must tell Alee that his—that Lord Stanhope has been killed."

"I will," volunteered Jack.

Elizabeth Guest gave herself a small shake—or perhaps she shivered despite the intense heat of the day—straightened her back, and stated, "I will tell my brother that our father has been killed."

Then she turned and, with the grace and dignity of a queen, walked toward the ancient stone house where her half-brother, Alee, lived.

The full impact of the day's events didn't hit Elizabeth until she was preparing for bed that night. She was sitting alone, half-dressed, half-undressed, staring out at the moon.

Of necessity, they had already buried Papa beneath sand and stone, within sight of the Nile and the Valley of the Kings, in the land that he loved above all else.

She had proudly stood beside Alee as he spoke of their father, both in English and in Arabic. She tried to draw comfort from the words of the handsome young Egyptian: "A man is happy if he is living his own life in his own way."

Indeed, Papa had always lived life in his own way.

Her pensive musings were interrupted by a knock at the door of the bungalow.

She answered the summons with uncharacteristic lethargy. "Yes? Who is it?"

"Amelia Winters," was the reply.

Opening the blue wooden door, she managed to inquire, "What is it, Mrs. Winters?"

The pretty blond woman stammered, "I-I'm so sorry about your father, Lady Elizabeth."

She was tired. Bone-tired. And she was frankly not in the mood for condolences from an indifferent chaperon. "Thank you, but as you can see, I was just getting ready for bed."

"I know it's late, my dear, but I thought you might have trouble sleeping tonight. I've—I've brought you some warmed goat's milk to drink. It is supposed to help, according to the cook."

Elizabeth was surprised to see a silver tray with a glass and a jug balanced in Amelia Winters's hands. She hadn't expected such a thoughtful gesture from the woman. Unbidden, tears sprang to her eyes, as they had a hundred times already that day. "How very kind of you."

"You seem exhausted, my lady. Why don't I help you finish preparing for bed and tuck you in as your dear Maman would if she were here?"

Elizabeth couldn't recall the last time her mother had tucked her in, but Nanny had done so for several weeks after the death of sweet little Annie.

Somehow Mrs. Winters insinuated herself into the bungalow and went straight through to the bedchamber, setting the silver tray down on the table beside the bed. "Now, let's get you into your nightclothes, and then I'll pour you a glass of nice, warm milk. You've had a terrible shock, but you will feel better if you get some rest."

"I don't know how to thank you," murmured Elizabeth as she allowed the older woman to take charge.

"There's no need to thank me," said Amelia Winters as she eased the nightgown over her head. "It's a small enough thing for me to do."

Slipping beneath the bedcovers some minutes later, Elizabeth graciously accepted the glass of warmed milk handed to her. "Why are you being so kind?" she inquired, meaning no offense.

The buxom blonde did not appear to have heard the question. "Drink your milk. Every drop, now."

She took several long swallows and felt the warmth all the way down to her toes. How strange. She was feeling quite drowsy already. "The cook was right," she murmured.

Amelia Winters watched with eyes that seemed to shimmer in the lamplight. "The cook?"

Words slurred together. "When she said that

the milk would help me sleep."

Her companion laughed, and it was not a pretty or pleasant sound. "You are a little fool."

Suddenly Elizabeth realized that something was wrong. Dreadfully wrong. "Mrs. Winters, what did you put in my milk?"

"Something to help you sleep."

"Why?"

"We want your diary, of course, and this time I don't want you waking up and chasing after me."

For an instant she roused. "It was you in the caves!"

"Yes."

She mumbled, "It wasn't nice to dig through my personal belongings."

"No, it wasn't. But I'm not a particularly nice lady. Or haven't you realized that yet?"

"Colette warned me that you weren't a lady at all."

The blonde arched a wicked brow. "Colette was right. You should have listened to her." She opened one drawer after another. "I don't suppose you will save me a lot of time and trouble by telling me where you've got it hidden."

"No."

"That's what I thought you'd say."

Elizabeth's arms and legs had grown as heavy as lead. She couldn't seem to move. She could barely lift her head off the pillow. "My diary won't do you any good."

"Of course it will. André and I intend to find Merneptah Seti's treasure ourselves. We can live like royalty on the proceeds for the rest of our days."

That wasn't was Elizabeth meant. There were secrets no one knew. No one but her.

Crucial sections of her notes were written in code. A trick she had learned from Papa long ago as a means of protecting vital information from falling into the wrong hands.

But there was more.

Far more.

"Not right . . . sacrilege . . . cursed."

"I don't believe in all that nonsense about ancient curses, so there is no reason to try and frighten me," stated the woman as she tore into Elizabeth's trunk.

"N-No—"

Amelia Winters turned and speared the girl with a hardened glare. "Do you want to tell me where your diary is?"

"N-N—"

Then she was screaming inside her head: *Jack! Help me, Jack! Don't let her steal my notes and maps!*

It was the last thing Elizabeth remembered. She didn't even have the energy to call out loud. Her last coherent thought was a single word. One man's name was on her lips as she passed into drugged oblivion: *Jack!*

Chapter 22

J ack!
    Elizabeth awoke with a start and sat straight up in bed.

Only, she wasn't in her bed. In fact, she wasn't in a bed at all. She seemed to be reclining on some sort of cushioned pallet on the floor, covered to her chin in a richly embroidered cloak.

She wasn't sure which was worse: the awful throbbing in her temples, or the discovery that beneath the embroidered cloak, she appeared to be wearing nothing more than a diaphanous veil or two.

God forbid! It had been white slavers, after all! She'd been sold into a *harim*. She had become the exotic plaything of a rich pasha.

She quickly lay back down and burrowed beneath the silken covers.

What was the last thing she remembered?

Her father was dead. The painful knowledge shot straight through her heart. It was true. She remembered every sad detail of that day. Was it only yesterday?

No.

Vague images were forming in her mind. Something told her that a considerable amount of time had passed since they had buried Papa, she and Alee.

Alee. Where was her newfound brother? What had happened to the handsome young man of whom she had grown so fond?

Another image began to materialize. This time it was of a blond woman with sharp eyes, eyes filled with malice and ill will: Amelia Winters. Now it was coming back to her in bits and pieces. Her chaperon had brought her warm milk laced with a sleeping potion. She had been drugged.

They had stolen her diary.

Elizabeth pressed the palms of her hands against her temples, and the throbbing eased for an instant.

She had to think. Who had stolen her diary and papers? Not Colonel and Mrs. Winters. No, it had been Amelia Winters and Count André Polonski.

Traitors! Villains! Blackguards! They were untrustworthy, dishonorable, and treacherous.

Jack.

Dear God, Jack would not know what kind of people they were. She must warn him, somehow, someway. She only prayed that it was not too late.

She sat up again. This time slowly and taking great care with her head. That was when she spotted the lovely young girl sitting patiently by the opening of the tent.

Tent?

The floor of the spacious pavilion was covered with thick Persian rugs. Tiny brass bells hung from every protuberance; they tinkled and swayed gently in the breeze, creating a wonderful, ethereal sound.

Intricately woven tapestries decorated the walls. Lanterns were placed here and there at regular intervals, lighting even the darkest corners of the tent, for it was evening. Large pottery urns, elaborately carved tables, and chests of every size and description seemed to complete the decor.

This was obviously the tent of a very rich pasha.

Elizabeth decided to try her voice. She had fully intended to inquire about her surroundings. Instead, she found herself asking, "May I have a drink of water?"

The girl eagerly sprang to her feet. She answered in only slightly accented English: "Of course, my lady. Your wish is my command. Are you hungry? Are you warm? Cold? Do you wish wine, or perhaps you would prefer goat's milk?"

She managed a weak smile. "Just a little water, thank you." She would never drink goat's milk again.

The girl hurried to a nearby table and quickly filled a goblet with water. She presented it to Elizabeth with a small show of ceremony, then immediately retreated in the direction of the tent opening.

Elizabeth raised the goblet to her lips and took a sip. The water was cool and delicious. As the girl raised the flap, she called out to her, "Are you leaving already?"

"Only for a few minutes, my lady. I must inform my master that you have awakened. I will return presently."

Elizabeth finished the water and found herself wishing for more. She had to confess that she was suddenly hungry as well. There was a great hollow feeling in the pit of her stomach. It must have been some time since she had eaten. Perhaps days. She had no idea how long it had been since that fateful visit from Amelia Winters.

There was a platter of fresh fruits and several loaves of bread on the table beside the jug of water. Surely there was no reason she could not help herself.

Elizabeth wrapped up in the embroidered cloak—she was not about to run around dressed in an outfit that consisted of two gossamer squares of material and precious little else—and struggled to her feet. She discovered that her legs were the consistency of quince jelly. She barely managed the short distance to the table before sinking to her knees again.

She had gobbled down a dozen dark purple grapes, savoring their exquisitely sweet taste, and several bites of bread before there was a "knock" on the pole by the opening; the flap of the tent was flung to one side, and a man strolled into the pavilion.

He was no ordinary man.

His long robe and *kuftan* were woven of the finest silk and stitched throughout with gold and silver thread. The handle of the dagger tucked into his sash was encrusted with precious gemstones: diamonds, emeralds, rubies, of a size such as she had never seen before.

His features were carved from an ancient mold: his nose and chin were somehow vaguely familiar and aristocratic in appearance. His eyes were large and dark—the color of blackest obsidian—and bright with intelligence. They were outlined with traditional Egyptian kohl.

Around his neck he wore a collar-plate of thousands of small gold beads that was worthy of a king's—or a pharaoh's—ransom. There were rings on his fingers and bracelets around his wrists, even pectoral ornaments, armlets, and anklets. Elizabeth had never seen jewelry of this magnificence in either the British Museum or in the Antiquities Museum in Cairo.

But it was the color of the man's hair that captured and held her attention.

Red.

His hair was a vibrant, rich, natural shade of red.

"A thousand pardons, Lady Elizabeth, for the intrusion," her visitor begged in perfect, cultured English. "I did not realize you were dining."

She nodded and tried to swallow the piece of bread suddenly stuck in her throat.

"Pray continue with your meal," he said politely. "I know you must be hungry. It is good to see you up and about after your misadventure."

She managed to pour a small amount of water into her goblet and take a sip before speaking. "I do not mean to be rude, sir, but who are you? How do you know my name? Where am I? How did I come to be in this—place?"

The man laughed heartily and held up his bejeweled hands in front of him in mock surrender. "I am Prince Ramses, my dear lady. As to your other questions, I leave the answering of those to your husband."

"My husband?" Elizabeth repeated, bewildered.

"Black Jack."

She still did not understand. "Black Jack?"

Prince Ramses' red brows furrowed into a stately frown; then he smiled and said, "Jack. Or perhaps you know him only as Lord Jonathan Wicke."

Elizabeth tried to stand, but it was still beyond her strength. "Jack is here? Where is he? I must speak to him."

Prince Ramses explained. "Your husband is not here, but we are expecting him to return to camp at any moment." Adding, "He is taking care of some unfinished business."

She grew more agitated. "I must warn him. I need to tell him something about Amelia Winters and Count Polonski."

The prince strolled to the table, plucked a succulent grape from the serving platter, and nonchalantly popped it into his mouth. "As a matter of fact, Mrs. Winters and the count are, I believe, the unfinished business he is seeing to."

Part of Elizabeth was relieved; part of her was

fearful. "Jack knows of their treachery, then?"

"Indeed, he knows it full well."

"Please, sir, tell me, is he in any danger?"

"Not in the least."

"Are you quite sure?"

"Quite." His dark eyes narrowed. "Black Jack is perfectly capable of taking care of himself when it comes to anyone, or anything." Prince Ramses shrugged his gold-laden shoulders. "With the possible exception of a certain beautiful young Englishwoman."

It took Elizabeth a moment to realize that he was referring to her. She blushed a vivid shade of pink.

"Ah, I see that you do love him."

She averted her eyes.

"This is most excellent, Lady Elizabeth. My friend has waited a very long time to marry. I would not want to think of him spending his life without the passion and love I have found with my own wives."

That brought her chin up. "Wives?"

To his credit, he did not laugh at her ignorance. "As has been the tradition among The People since ancient times, I am permitted to marry as often as I choose."

Perhaps it was rude to inquire, but Elizabeth's curiosity demanded satisfaction. "How often have you chosen to marry, my lord?"

"Three times. I have thirteen children, as well. But I am still young. Only twenty-six."

"Jack is twenty-six."

"Yes, I know. We were at school together."

"School?"

"Cambridge."

"I see." Of course, she did not. At least not entirely. Cambridge would explain, however, Prince Ramses' excellent command of the English language.

"Black Jack has not told you everything, has he?" the prince asked.

There was a great deal, apparently, that *Black* Jack had not bothered to tell her.

Were they truly married?

Or was it just another pretense, like their engagement?

And if they were man and wife, why could she not recall the wedding ceremony?

"We've had so little time together," she offered weakly, her head beginning to ache again.

"And there was the tragic accident that killed your father, Lord Stanhope. Please accept my condolences, madam."

Elizabeth bit her lip. "Thank you, sir."

Then she spotted the ring Prince Ramses wore on the middle finger of his right hand.

It was gold.

Pure gold.

In the shape of an ankh: the ancient Egyptian symbol of life.

"My husband—" the word sounded so foreign on her tongue, so strange, yet somehow so right "—wears an identical ring to yours."

"Jack has not explained this to you?"

"No, he has not."

"Some of the story is only his to tell, but I will relate the portion that is mine. You have, no doubt, been wondering about my hair."

She swallowed and tried not to offend the princely man. "It is a most beautiful and unusual color."

"Indeed, it is. In ancient times—I am speaking now of many thousands of years ago—red hair was considered an omen of ill will. The Egyptian born with 'flaming' hair was regarded as defective, or worse, evil." He chuckled and poured himself a goblet of wine. "But that all changed."

"Of course. It must have been Ramses the Second himself who brought about the change in the populace's attitude. It is written that he had red hair. . . ." In a hushed voice, Elizabeth repeated the litany: "Prince Ramses. The Great Ramses." Her eyes grew round as saucers. One hand flew to her mouth. "Then you must be . . ."

With extreme dignity, he nodded his head. "I am the direct descendant of the pharaohs. And this nomadic tribe which we call The People: we are all that remain of the Ancient Ones who once ruled the Black Land."

Elizabeth Guest's heart was nearly bursting with excitement. This was grand adventure beyond anything she could have imagined or dreamt. "You are also the direct descendant of Merneptah Seti, are you not, my lord?"

"I am."

"And the ring?"

"Black Jack and I each wear such a ring as a reminder that he once gave my life back to me, and I once returned his to him."

She was dumbfounded. "You saved each other's lives?"

The prince expounded. "We are and always will

be brothers. Blood brothers. We have been so since we attended Cambridge together many years ago. But that is Jack's story and for another time. For my part, he saved me from an enemy's treachery and an enemy's knife in the back." He intertwined his fingers until one hand was indistinguishable from the other. "We are bound together, Jack and I, for this lifetime and for whatever comes after. I love him above all other men. I value his life more than I do my own. For he is truly an honorable human being."

Elizabeth did not realize she was crying until she tasted the salt of her own tears on her tongue.

Her royal visitor reached out and touched her damp cheek. "Are you certain you love him that much? You would make a wife fit for a king, and I am certain that my other wives would welcome you with open arms."

"I thank you, sir, for your generous offer. But there is only one man for me."

"I hope Jack realizes what a lucky devil he is," murmured the prince. He cocked his head to the side and listened. "And speaking of the devil, I believe I hear your husband now. He has, no doubt, been seeing to his beloved Scheherazade."

"His beloved Scheherazade?" repeated Elizabeth under her breath.

Who in the bloody blazes was Scheherazade?

Prince Ramses turned just as the tent flap was thrown back and Black Jack swept into the spacious pavilion, tossing the hood of his robe from his head.

"Elizabeth, my dearest! You are awake at last!" He was dressed in the traditional robes and headdress of a well-to-do Egyptian, as he had been that first day in the bazaar at Alexandria.

She was so relieved to see him, to know that he was unharmed, that he had not suffered at the hands of the traitorous Amelia Winters and Count Polonski, that she quite forgot for a moment that she was angry with him.

Then she stood and drew herself up to her full height. "Yes, *husband*, I am awake," she said pointedly.

"Now, Elizabeth, I can explain about that," he began.

"While you are at it, *husband*, perhaps you can also explain who your beloved Scheherazade is?"

Ramie slapped his old friend on the back, laughed with utter delight, and called over his shoulder as he exited the tent, "I do believe, old chap, that you may at last have met your match."

Chapter 23

Once they were alone, Elizabeth planted her hands on her hips and, for someone who still appeared a bit wobbly on her legs, demanded in a surprisingly strong voice, "And who, may I ask, is Scheherazade?"

Black Jack didn't know whether to kiss the damn woman or give her a shake.

He had been riding for days without stopping, first to see to Amelia Winters and Polonski, and finally to return to camp and Elizabeth. There had been only brief rests to water and feed Scheherazade; the mare had the heart and stamina of a horse twice her size.

Nay, three times her size.

But he was tired and hungry, and he found that he did not care for the shrewish tone in his wife's voice. Perhaps it was best to let her know

310

from the start which of them was wearing the pants under their robes.

Jack shrugged off his dusty outer *kuftan* and flung himself down onto a pile of pillows. "I am hungry and thirsty. First, I will eat and drink. Then I will wish to bathe. Later we will speak."

"We will speak now."

His eyes narrowed into chips of ice blue sapphires. "I will eat and drink first."

"Who is Scheherazade?"

Black Jack reached out and poured himself a goblet of date wine and broke a loaf of bread in two, taking an entire half for himself.

He tore off a chunk with his bared teeth and began to chew. Every now and then he paused and raised the goblet to his mouth, washing down the bread with a swig of wine, muttering all the while under his breath, "I should have married a woman of The People, a woman who knows how to care for a man who is tired and thirsty, a man who has ridden for two days and two nights without respite to return to her."

Elizabeth sank to her knees beside him. "You rode for two days and two nights to return to me?"

He looked straight into her eyes. "Yes."

"Not to see Scheherazade?"

He frowned. "Of course not. Scheherazade was with me."

The girl's cheeks burst into flames. "You had another woman with you on this journey?" she said accusingly.

Black Jack decided enough was enough. In fact, it was more than enough. "Scheherazade is female, but she is *not* a woman." *Thank God*, he added silently.

Elizabeth was obviously confounded. "Then *who* is she?"

"Not *who*," he corrected, attacking a huge bunch of dark purple grapes, "but *what*."

"*What* is she, then?"

"My horse."

The play of expression on Elizabeth's face in the past ten minutes was one he would never forget. She was angry, then jealous, then relieved, then angry again, coming full circle.

"Your horse?" she shot back.

He nodded; his eyes dancing with merriment.

Elizabeth picked up one of the tapestry pillows and swatted at him. "You deliberately led me on, allowing me to think that Scheherazade was another woman, and she is your horse!"

He effortlessly plucked the pillow from her grasp. "Were you jealous, my sweet?"

"Jealous? Pah, why would I be jealous?"

"Because you want me for yourself."

Her aristocratic nose rose a little higher in the air. "You have obviously gotten too much sun, sir. It has affected your brain and is causing you to suffer from delusions of grandeur."

He put his head back and laughed heartily.

All of a sudden Elizabeth's eyes grew serious. She abruptly changed the subject. "You must tell me, Jack." She clutched at his arm. "Where is my half-brother? Is he well? Is he safe?"

He quickly reassured her. "Have no fear. Alee is both well and safe. He has gone to stay with his maternal grandparents until this whole business is cleared up."

"That is a relief," she admitted, releasing her grip on him. "Alee told me once that his mother had died many years ago during childbirth. With Papa gone now, too, I was afraid he would have no one."

"Alee will be well taken care of. In addition to his grandparents, he has a large extended family of aunts and uncles and cousins."

She picked at the fringe on a pillow. "But I am his only sister."

He gave a decisive nod of his head, his eyes never leaving her. "But you are his only sister."

"Except for the others back in England, of course."

"Except for the others back in England."

Elizabeth seemed to make up her mind about something. "I must visit my brother once this 'business,' as you call it, has been cleared up."

"I will take you there myself."

"Thank you." She looked at him—gratitude clearly readable in her eyes—and offered him a plate of sweet, honey-dipped cakes. "Will you have more refreshments, my lord?"

Black Jack politely declined. "I believe that I have had quite enough to eat and drink, my lady. But I will bathe now and tell you what has occurred with Mrs. Winters and Count Polonski." Adding, as he began to divest himself of his clothing, "That is, if you are interested."

She leaned toward him eagerly. "Of course I am interested. You must not leave out even the smallest, seemingly insignificant detail. I want to know everything."

Jack bit the inside of his mouth to keep from smiling. She was a curious little creature, his wife. He sighed. *His wife.* He supposed *that* would be the next topic of discussion.

"I will try to recall every detail, no matter how minor," he promised her as he began to strip down to bare skin.

"Sir, you seem to be removing all of your clothes," Elizabeth pointed out to him.

What female nonsense was this? "Madam, I am fully aware of that fact."

"But you will be totally—unclothed."

"Indeed, I will be soon. It is the only way I know to bathe properly."

"But—"

"You have seen me naked before. There are no secrets between us when it comes to this."

Elizabeth swallowed, and Black Jack could see that she was trying to keep her eyes averted. But her curiosity quickly overcame her modesty. When he stood before her in all his natural glory, he watched her intently watching him, and he felt his manhood grow hard and thicken until he was fully aroused.

"Cursed affliction!" he swore softly, and was surprised to hear Elizabeth's shy laugh in response.

"Even for the worst affliction, my lord, surely there must be a cure," she said cheekily.

He stepped into the small copper tub and took a goat's skin bag from a hook on the nearest tent pole. He poured an adequate, if not excessive, amount of precious water over his head and let it stream down his body in tiny rivulets. Then he took a handful of pristine white sand from a bowl and began to rub it lightly over his flesh.

"Tell me what has occurred since the last thing I remember, Jack," she urged him as she brushed the dust from his discarded robes and folded them into neat stacks.

"What is the last thing you remember?"

Elizabeth was silent for a moment, then spoke in a near whisper. "It was the evening of the same day Papa died. I was preparing for bed, and Amelia Winters came to my bungalow door with a glass of warmed goat's milk." Her voice grew stronger; there was even a hint of anger in her tone. "She claimed the milk would help me sleep. She was right, of course. The witch had put something in it to make certain I slept."

"Amelia drugged you."

She nodded her head emphatically. "I remember hearing her laugh and say that they planned to steal my diary and maps. This time, she cackled, she did not want me to awaken and chase after her."

Jack's hand paused in the midst of scrubbing the mat of dark hair on his chest. "So it was Amelia Winters in the tomb of the Lady Isis that night?"

"She came right out and admitted it to me." Elizabeth sighed discouragingly. "And now Count Polonski seems to be in partnership with her. I distinctly heard her mention his name: André."

Jack resumed his bathing and continued the story from there. "It was Alee who first alerted me to the fact that something was wrong. He pounded on my door early the following morning. It seemed that he had grown concerned when he could not get any answer from your bungalow." He reached behind him, but there was a spot just below his left shoulder blade that he could not manage. "My dear, I find that I require your assistance."

Elizabeth glanced up. "Yes, my lord?"

"There is one spot just here—" he indicated the specific area on his back "—that I cannot reach. Would you mind?" He held out a handful of white sand.

"Of course not," murmured Elizabeth, rising to her feet. She took the sand from him and tried to rub it around on his flesh below the left shoulder. "There is obviously a skill to bathing with sand, sir, that I have not learned. I seem to be spilling more of it than anything else."

"It is of no consequence," he told her, reminding himself to keep breathing in and out as he felt the butterfly-light touch of her fingertips on him.

"Have I scrubbed the spot you desired, my lord?"

Jack wanted so badly to say no, to shout *no,* to tell Elizabeth exactly where he wanted—nay, *needed*—her to touch him.

He was not a modest man by any means, but he was so near to ejaculating his seed into midair that he was forced to turn his back to her to finish his bathing.

"Anyway," he went on after regaining some semblance of control over himself, "we checked the other bungalows and found they were all deserted. Not only were Amelia Winters and André Polonski gone, but the colonel, as well."

That news caught her by surprise. "Colonel Winters has disappeared, too?"

Jack nodded. "Into thin air."

"Dear Lord, what if some foul deed has been done to the poor man?"

"I think not," said Jack with a sardonic smile.

He rinsed the sand from his body and stood there, all shiny and new, the black hair on his head, the smattering of hair on his chest, that which arrowed down his torso and nestled around his erect shaft, all dripping and glistening with dewdrops. He reached for a clean robe and slipped it around his shoulders.

"What of your bathwater?" She inquired of practical matters for a moment.

"We waste no water here in the desert, especially that which we have drawn from the oasis in order to bathe. The sand will quickly settle in the bottom of the basin, and the water will be used in the laundering of garments, or for the animals."

Her voice was husky. "That is most wise, my lord." Then she returned to the subject of her former chaperons. "Pray, continue with your account of recent events."

His expression changed and his eyes went dark as midnight. "We found you in your bungalow, Elizabeth, and for a time we feared you were not alive."

Jack could not begin to tell her how he had felt in those moments before they realized she was merely in a deep sleep. He had wanted to destroy everything and everyone within reach. He had thought that she was dead, beyond his help, as his mother had once been. He had wanted to kill, or be killed. It made little difference to him which one, or both.

Her eyes grew huge with disbelief. "You and Alee thought I was dead?"

His brusque reply confirmed it. "Yes. Then we realized you had merely been drugged. The glass of milk and the jug were still on the tray beside your bed. But we could not sufficiently rouse you, no matter what we did."

She rubbed her temples. "I seem to have a vague recollection of someone talking to me, forcing me to walk about the room, pouring hot liquids down my throat."

"We tried, but it did no good. All you wanted to do was sleep. So I packed Alee off to his grandparents—much against his will, I might add. I assured him that you would be safe here in the desert with me, that The People would protect you as one of their own. He finally agreed to go. Several of your father's trusted assistants served as his escorts. Once they had safely delivered Alee to his family, they were to return to Luxor and await further orders."

"And my belongings . . . ?"

He truly regretted having to tell her this part. "Your bungalow was in shambles. So I loaded you into your father's buggy and headed directly here to The People. Your safety was my first and only concern."

Her pretty face twisted into a disappointed scowl. "Then Amelia and the count still have possession of my diary and precious papers."

"No."

Her head jerked up. "No?" She became agitated. "Then who does? Tell me quickly."

"Patience, madam; I will relate the whole story to you as I learned it."

Apparently Elizabeth did not notice that the embroidered cloak had slipped off her shoulders, revealing the skimpy outfit beneath.

Patience, Jack. You must have patience as well. It's going to be a very long night. A very long night, indeed.

"Once Alee was taken care of, once you were safely ensconced with The People, then I returned to take care of Amelia Winters and André Polonski." His blue eyes grew cold and hard. "We of the desert know what to do with thieves. The punishment may seem harsh, but that is the unwritten law of the land."

"W-What do you do with thieves?"

Jack knew Elizabeth would be shocked, but he did not mince words, nor did he soften the truth. This was a harsh country, and she must face reality. There was no mercy and no forgiveness in his world for the treacherous.

"He who steals forfeits his hand. He who drinks from or fouls another man's waterhole is left in the desert with nothing to quench his thirst. He who swears falsely against his neighbor has his tongue cut out. He who seduces another man's wife loses his—"

She quickly interrupted him. "I quite understand."

He shrugged his muscular shoulders, and

stretched out on the pile of pillows stacked alongside the table. "It seems that someone else had already tried to mete out the thieves' just punishment for me."

"Please explain, my lord."

"I found Amelia Winters and Polonski on a remote stretch of road between the Valley of the Kings and the Valley of the Queens. They had been left for dead."

Elizabeth's hand flew to her mouth. "For dead?"

Jack nodded. "Polonski had a bullet wound to his right hand, and one to each leg that prevented him from walking. Amelia, for all her faults, had refused to leave him, despite his urgings. She had tried to find some sort of shelter for them, but there was not so much as a twig to provide shade. They wouldn't have lasted another day in the unrelenting heat and sunlight. He had not even left them a canteen of water."

"He?"

"Colonel Winters."

"Colonel Winters!" echoed Elizabeth, obviously stunned by the announcement.

"Hulbert Winters is the true villain of the piece, I am afraid. Amelia and André may be thieves, but the colonel was perfectly willing to eliminate anyone who stood between him and what he wanted."

"Eliminate?"

"Do away with. Murder. Kill."

"God in Heaven!"

"Yes, and what he wanted was your diary and maps, my dear. I don't know how he found out about the lovers' plan to double-cross him and go after Merneptah Seti's treasure themselves, but he did. I can only surmise from what little they were able to tell me that he followed them into the desert, deliberately shot Polonski, threatened Amelia, stole your papers, and left them to their fate."

"But he seemed to be such a kind gentleman. . . ."

"Which, I suppose, all goes to show how deceptive appearances can be."

He could see that she was still trying to take it all in. "Colonel Winters, a killer . . ."

"So it would seem."

She gave him a long, measuring look. "What happened to Amelia and André?"

Black Jack reached out and gave her hand a reassuring pat. "Don't worry. I took them to the nearest village where they could be properly looked after."

Elizabeth chewed on her bottom lip. "Did you turn them over to the authorities?"

He nonchalantly broke a piece of cake into two pieces and popped one half into her mouth and the other half into his own. "No. I did better than that."

"Better than that," she mumbled.

"I left them with a solemn promise."

"A solemn promise?" repeated Elizabeth around the bite of honey-soaked cake.

"I promised Amelia and André that if either one of them ever dared to harm you again, in any way, I would hunt them down and finish what the colonel had started."

Elizabeth choked on her cake.

"I saved their miserable lives," muttered Jack, his eyes black with intent. "But I wouldn't hesitate for an instant to carry out their just punishment."

"My God, Jack."

"It is, my dear Elizabeth, the way of the desert."

Shaken, Elizabeth repeated, "You mean that you would kill them?"

"I wouldn't have to; the sun and the sand and the desert would take care of that for me. But make no mistake about it, I will protect what is mine. And you are mine."

She was convinced, but she couldn't help wondering aloud, "What, do you suppose, has become of the colonel?"

"Colonel Winters will not escape. I shall deal with him another time. It was necessary that I return to take care of my wife."

"Speaking of which . . ."

Jack leaned back among the tapestry cushions and watched her through hooded eyes, as if he had been expecting the subject of their marriage to be raised. "I had to wed you. It was the only way."

Elizabeth couldn't decide whether she wanted to slap the man, laugh in his face, or make love to him. "The only way to do what?"

"This is a harsh land. You had to become mine so I could protect you with my name and within my tent. If I had not done so, every randy buck of the tribe could, and would, challenge me for your favors."

She looked at him askance. "My favors?"

"Your sexual favors."

Despite the cool evening breeze, Elizabeth felt the heat of embarrassment rise to her cheeks. Men quarreling over her? Jack fighting, perhaps killing, to protect her? It was more than she could fathom.

She cleared her throat and decided to clarify matters. "Are we truly married?"

His expression never changed. "According to the laws and customs of The People, yes."

She massaged the sides of her head. "But I don't seem to recall . . ."

"It was a short ceremony and the bride was groggy, to say the least."

"I see."

"Our marriage is not binding outside this culture. I will protect you as long as it is necessary, and then you will be free to return to England."

There was an odd little silence. "Do you believe in the marriage vows we exchanged?"

Jack paused for a fraction of a second before he answered, "I do, but I have lived with The People for many years now. It is different for an outsider."

Elizabeth wanted to know; she needed to know. "In the eyes of The People, am I still considered an outsider?"

The answer came in a dangerously soft voice. "In marrying me, you have become one of The People."

"That is why you knew it would be safe to leave me in their care."

"Yes."

She finally understood what this man had done for her. He had not only saved her life; he had saved her dignity and her self-respect. In taking her, Jack had given Elizabeth back to herself.

She moistened her lips. "I don't know how I will ever be able to repay you."

"There is nothing to repay." Jack extended his long, bronzed arms above his head and yawned. "I have traveled many miles today. I am weary. You have been through much yourself. It is time we slept."

She gazed around the comfortably spacious tent. "Where will we sleep?"

Suddenly there was a sexual tension rekindled between them that had not been present since he had concluded his bath.

"Our pallet is prepared for us," pointed out Jack.

"But there is only the one."

"It is, nevertheless, large enough for two people." A faint amusement crossed his handsome face. "The People consider us to be man and wife. But if it is any comfort to you, my dear, I have no plans to ravish your lovely body tonight. Indeed, I have every intention of immediately falling asleep."

Elizabeth supposed it was of some comfort.

One by one Black Jack extinguished the lanterns until the only source of illumination inside the tent was a pale slice of moonlight shining through an opening high above. They stretched out side by side, but the distance between them was great, indeed.

The night was filled with familiar sounds: the hissing of a camel tethered in the distance, the soft laughter of a man and woman, the whinny of a mare and the answering neigh of her mate, the musical tinkling of the small brass bells suspended throughout the pavilion.

It was some time later—she had no idea how much later—that Elizabeth sighed and whispered into the darkness, "Are you asleep, my lord?"

"No."

"Why not?"

"I cannot sleep."

"Nor can I." Elizabeth turned onto her side. "I thought you had every intention of immediately falling asleep."

She could hear the self-deprecating humor in Jack's low, resonant baritone. "It would not be the first time my best intentions have gone astray."

Searching the pallet between them, she located his right hand. The hard feel of cool metal greeted her fingers. "Prince Ramses wears a gold ring identical to yours. He told me that it is a reminder, that you had once saved his life."

"As he did mine."

"You saved him from an enemy's treachery and an enemy's knife," Elizabeth recalled, hoping it would prompt him to confide in her.

Jack rolled over onto his back and stared up at the ceiling of the tent. "Ramie saved me from my worst enemy."

"Your worst enemy?"

"Myself."

"He saved you from yourself?"

He sighed. "It was many years ago. Ramie and I were at Cambridge together. There was a nasty incident and I was falsely accused of stealing another chap's money. Unfortunately some of the missing coin was found among my belongings. Since I refused to point the finger at the bloke we all suspected was the real culprit, or defend myself—I was an arrogant bastard in those days—I was kicked out of my club and my university. I had dishonored myself and sullied the family name."

Elizabeth gave his hand an understanding squeeze. "Oh, Jack . . ."

"My mother believed in my innocence—she always did take my side, right or wrong, while she was alive—but the duke, my father, considered it the last straw. He made his opinion of me very clear: I was unquestionably guilty. Furthermore, I was the lowest of the low, the blackest of the black sheep, the wildest of the blue-eyed wild Wickes, and beyond all redemption. He had one son and heir: my elder brother, Lawrence. I was nothing; I was less than nothing."

A cold pain lodged in Elizabeth's chest, like a dagger of ice.

"Ramie found me a week later in a dingy London hovel. I'd apparently had no food to eat in all that time and was trying desperately to drink myself into a permanent stupor. Left to my own devices, I would probably have killed myself within a fortnight. He got me cleaned up, informed me that he was returning to his own country and that I was coming with him."

"And you went."

"I went."

"You have been with Prince Ramses ever since."

"I have been with him ever since."

"And when your mother died six years ago?"

"The People gave me a reason to go on living. They became my family."

It was some time before Elizabeth found she could speak, and then it was in a voice scarcely above a whisper. "I believe you were innocent, Jack."

"What would you know of my guilt or innocence? It was many years ago and you had not met me, or even heard of me. You were a mere child at the time."

"You've stated that you were innocent. That is enough for me."

He groaned and warned her. "Oh, my dear, sweet girl, don't believe in me."

"It is too late," she informed him. "I do believe in you. You are an honorable man, and I would trust you with my life."

"But I haven't always told you the whole truth and nothing but the truth."

"That only makes you human."

He took her firmly by the shoulders and brought her face up close to his. "Elizabeth, look me straight in the eyes."

She could clearly see his features and the dark blue of his irises in the moonlight. "I am, my lord."

"Listen to my every word."

"I will, my lord."

"I was deliberately following you that first day in the bazaar."

"I guessed as much, my lord."

"I was on a mission for Prince Ramses and The People. My intent was to discover as much as I could about you, to find out what you knew about the burial place of Merneptah Seti. I would have done whatever was required to gain this information."

"I deduced that fact quite some time ago, my lord. I am not stupid."

He threw up his hands in exasperation. "I didn't used to think you were."

"You cannot insult me, my lord; I have already seen through your game."

"My game?"

"You cannot make me believe you are truly wicked, or the blackest of the black sheep, or the wildest wild Wicke, no matter what you tell me."

He spat out fiercely, his voice growing louder, "I was fully prepared to seduce you, even marry you if necessary, to gain this information."

She gently traced the line of his rugged jaw with the tip of her finger. "You have seduced me. You have married me. But you have not yet gained the information you sought."

He swallowed hard and made a strange kind of strangled sound in the back of his throat. "*Arrrg—*"

"I do not believe that you would make a very good spy, my husband."

"I used to—until I ran into you," he growled.

"Then, as Prince Ramses suggested earlier, perhaps you have, at last, met your match."

"Pah, you are a seventeen-year-old girl!"

"I am nearly eighteen and I am a woman," she shot back. "A *married* woman."

"In name only."

"Then we shall have to do something to change that, won't we?"

Jack went very still. "What did you have in mind?" he asked cautiously.

She insinuated her hand under the sleeve of his sleeping robe and ran it lightly up and down his bare arm, occasionally bumping into the side of his chest, his waist, his thigh. She felt his body twitch in reaction. "I thought we might continue with my lessons."

"Your lessons?" he responded in a hoarse voice.

"You did say that there were many ways to make love, did you not?"

"Yes . . ."

"Well, why don't we try the usual method first and work our way through the others one at a time?"

"But you are a virgin," Jack blurted out.

She could feel her face becoming a bright shade of red. "I know that. But it's not my fault."

"I didn't say it was." His eyes narrowed in reproach. "I once asked you to marry me and you refused."

She sighed, and did not argue with his statement. Indeed, she could not, for it was true. She decided against mentioning his less than amorous approach at the time. "I did."

"You claimed that I would make a good lover, but not a good husband."

"I was wrong."

"You were wrong?"

"Yes, I admit I was wrong. And I have changed my mind."

"Changed your mind!" he softly roared.

Elizabeth arched one elegant chestnut brown eyebrow in his direction. "It is a woman's prerogative."

"By the sacred son of Osiris!" He punched at the pillow beneath his head. "Of all the lame excuses—"

"Hush, my dear husband," she urged, slipping her hand inside the front of Jack's robe.

She began to caress his chest: the smooth flesh over strong bones and even stronger muscles, the tight little brown male tits hidden among the smattering of dark hair, the hard belly below. Then she moved her hand lower and heard him sharply draw in his breath.

"My God!"

"Sir, your affliction seems particularly cursed tonight," she announced.

"Madam, that is not humorous."

"You, of course, would know more about that than I would, my lord. My acquaintanceship with the ah . . . male affliction is quite limited."

"*Quite* limited?"

"Very well. *Very* limited. Indeed, I believe that I can enumerate on the fingers of one hand the times—" Elizabeth tapped her index finger on his erect member as she counted out loud. "One. Two. Three." She paused and consider for a moment, then resumed. "Or is it four?"

"Three or four, it is of no consequence," he ground through clenched teeth.

She loosened the sash of his sleeping robe, and the material fell away; they both had an unobstructed view of his nude body in the moonlight.

"You were right, of course," stated Elizabeth.

"For once," muttered Jack.

"When a man is aroused, it is all out front for the whole world to behold."

"I certainly hope not the whole world."

"Well, only in a manner of speaking, naturally. But he cannot hide his response to a woman, can he?"

"No, he cannot."

"You are very large and hard."

"And apparently growing larger and harder by the minute," he muttered under his breath.

Elizabeth encircled him with her hand and lightly squeezed, taking full measure of his shaft. "I never imagined that a man would be so—"

"Elizabeth!"

It was his tone of voice that demanded her attention. "Yes, my lord, what it is?"

"You must not . . . It has been so long . . . I am on the verge . . ."

Her forehead wrinkled in thought. "Have I done something I oughtn't?"

"It's not that, my sweet," he said tightly.

"You must explain it to me, then, Jack. I am ignorant in these matters, as we both know full well. If you do not tell me, who will?"

He nodded. "I will try."

Elizabeth waited. And while she waited for him to begin his explanation, she stroked his manhood and watched with fascination as several drops appeared on the tip near the tiny opening. In the moonlight, they glistened like dew. She leaned closer and squeezed him again, and was surprised by the shout Jack gave as his shaft leaped in her hand and he jerked: once, twice, three times in a row. A vaguely familiar and musky essence spurted forth from his body.

"Bloody hell!" he swore.

"What's wrong?"

"Nothing."

"Wasn't that supposed to happen?"

"Yes, but—"

"Isn't that the same kind of sexual climax you had when we were in bed together in the tomb of the Lady Isis?"

"Yes, but—"

"Isn't that what happens to a man when he reaches a certain point in his affliction?"

"Yes, but—"

"But *what*, my lord?" she asked in all innocence.

"But that wasn't quite what I'd had planned tonight."

Of course, Elizabeth inquired, "What did you have planned, my lord?"

"I will show you, my luscious lady," he said as he casually discarded both of their robes.

"Jack!"

The two gossamer squares of material were even less of a barrier. They disappeared in an instant.

Once they were both naked and stretched out side by side on the pallet, he said to her in a tone filled with sensual promise, "Now, let us watch what happens to your body, my sweet."

He began at one end—burying his lips in the silky mass of her hair—and concluded at the opposite by delving his tongue into the arch of her foot.

Elizabeth had never imagined that her skin would be sensitized to the merest touch, the slightest caress. She had never dreamt that every part of a woman's body could be so attuned to a man's. The hair at her nape was standing upright. Her arms were covered with gooseflesh. Her nipples were hard, they ached, they approached the threshold of pain. She was desperate to thrust one into Jack's mouth and beg him to suckle her; suckle one and relieve the other with his fingers.

She was already on fire, wanting, needing, seeking, by the time he slipped his hand between her legs and parted the soft flesh at the apex of her thighs. His fingers came away warm and wet with her fragrance. He touched them first to his lips, then to hers. He kissed her, and their male and female scents, the essences of their bodies, mingled.

"This is you. This is me. This is us," Jack murmured as his tongue slipped between her lips and found her tongue. "Taste me. Taste you. Taste us."

"I want us to be as one," she whispered as she wildly kissed him back. "Put it inside me, Jack. Please!"

"Put *what* inside you, sweetheart?"

In sheer frustration, she struck out at him. The blow was ineffectual; it was no more than the touch of a butterfly on a flower.

"Damn you, Jack! Put your manhood inside me."

He stopped teasing her and stared down into her tear-filled eyes. "Are you certain that's what you want, Elizabeth?"

"Yes."

"You will no longer be a virgin."

"I don't care. I want you. I want to feel you inside of me. I want you to be a part of me, filling me, filling all of me."

"Yes!" he responded fiercely. "But first I must stretch you and make the passage as painless for you as I can."

He slid one finger into her, and Elizabeth instinctively arched her back, driving her female mound toward his hand, seeking something, some release that was just out of reach. His thumb ground into her pelvis and she raised her hips right up off the pallet.

"Jack, please! I want! I need!"

"I know!"

He slipped a second finger in alongside the first and drew them slowly apart until she was slick and open to him.

"Now?" she cried out.

"Soon," he promised. "I'll try not to hurt you. But you are so soft, so tight, so new, and I am, perhaps, too hard and too large."

"I don't care. Do it!" she begged him. "Do it now!"

Jack hovered over her for a moment, then he took his shaft in his hand and carefully guided himself toward that desired destination.

He eased himself in halfway and paused, gasping for breath, praying for control.

"Dear God," he exhaled.

"Don't stop," pleaded Elizabeth. "I want all of you."

"Are you certain?"

"I am certain." With that, she raised herself up, impaling her slender body on his.

He thrust fully into her, driving long and hard and deep, burying himself in her sheath. They both gave a shout, whether of triumph, or astonishment, or even of pain, they cared not a whit at that moment.

"Are you all right?" called out Jack.

"Yes." She smiled up at him. "We did it!"

Jack put his head back and laughed. "Oh, my sweet innocent, we have just begun to do it."

Her eyes widened appreciably. "Just begun?"

He nodded and started to move inside her, slowly and easily at first, then with greater vigor. Eventually he was thrusting into her harder and harder, again and again, until Elizabeth felt an unbearable tension building.

"Elizabeth?"

She heard the question he was asking in the way he said her name. "Jack, something is happening to me."

"I know."

"I feel as if I am going to explode."

"Don't be afraid, my love."

"But I am."

"Remember the climax you experienced that night we were together in bed? Well, this is just another one that is bigger and better."

"I'm still afraid," she admitted breathlessly.

"There is no need to be. I'm here. I will hold on to you. I will protect you."

"Promise?"

"I promise."

With that, she put back her head, her lips parted; her mind ceased to function and she became a creature of the night, a creature of the sensual, a creature of pure flesh and blood. Her heart was pounding in her ears. Her skin was on fire. She was about to shatter into a thousand tiny pieces.

As she felt herself go over the edge, she exploded and cried out, "Jack!"

She held on to him for dear life and would not let go even long after she had begun to float back to earth.

Then she heard his hoarse shout and felt him lift his buttocks and thrust into her, emptying himself into her, wringing himself dry, filling her to the brim, calling her name over and over and over. "Elizabeth! Elizabeth! Elizabeth!"

Elizabeth awakened sometime later and found Jack sprawled heavily across her body, his manhood still inside her, his warm breath stirring the stray wisps of hair around her face.

She was the same. Yet she would never be the same again. This was truly the grandest adventure of them all. She could not imagine anything that would compare with the thrill of making love with the right man.

And Jack was the right man for her. She knew it now. She didn't know if he did, or ever would. But she knew.

She had become a woman in every sense of
the word. She had known the great mystery of
the universe, understood the question, and she
comprehended in some part of her heart and soul
what the answer would always be: It was not the
lovemaking, it was the love.

Jack moved about in his semiconscious state
and pressed a kiss into her bare shoulder. His
hand was wedged between them; it made small,
slow circles across her abdomen. He muttered
something, but she did not understand what he
was saying in his sleep.

She felt her breasts brush against the fine hair on
his chest, and her nipples instantaneously curled
up into tight buds. There was a sore muscle here
and there throughout her body, but she cared not
for them.

Her experience with lovemaking was limited
to those few times with Jack, and yet she was
already able to recognize the changes in her own
body, and certainly those in his. She could feel
his manhood swelling inside her, growing to fill
her, those twin sacs below ballooning as well,
pressing between her legs, teasing her flesh, tan-
talizing her with possibilities that were yet to be
explored.

For in the night Jack had whispered secrets to
her: dark secrets, lovely secrets, exciting secrets,
promises of things to come that were erotic and
exotic, things that caused her to blush down to
the roots of her hair and curl up her toes.

He would show them all to her, he had promised. Many he had only heard of, read of, but
they would learn them together. It was the most

seductive thing he could have said to her.

As Elizabeth lay there on their pallet, she realized that awake or asleep, Jack was beginning to move within her once more. This time he took his own good time. He moved slowly, drawing himself entirely out of her body and then guiding himself all the way back in. He took her inch by inch, half inch by half inch, quarter inch by quarter inch.

It was excruciating. It was exquisite. It seemed to go on forever.

At least she wanted it to go on forever, and yet she thought she would surely die if it did.

She prodded his chest with her chin. "Jack, are you awake?"

"Hmmm . . ." was all he said.

"Are you awake, my lord?"

"If I am awake, or if this is a dream, I care not," the man whispered close to her ear. "This is surely as close to Heaven as a sinner like me will ever get."

"This is not Heaven, my lord. This is your tent."

"That is where you are wrong, my sweet wife. This is Heaven indeed."

"Heaven," Elizabeth echoed in agreement.

They reached the celestial heights together again and again. Indeed, they did not emerge from their tent for three days and three nights. Food magically appeared at their door. Necessities were duly removed. They saw no one. Spoke to no one. They were given this time together.

For this, too, was the way of the desert. . . .

Chapter 24

"**G**reetings, master," came a familiar voice from outside the opening to the tent.

"Enter."

"I cannot, master."

"Kareem?" Black Jack was already awake. He sat up on the pallet and drew the embroidered cover over himself and his still-sleeping bride. It was already midmorning, long past the time when he would normally be up and about his business, but he and Elizabeth had spent half the night talking and the other half making love. "Is that you, Kareem?"

"Yes, Most Exalted and Forgiving One," came the muffled reply.

"Come in, my good man."

"I cannot, master."

Jack frowned. "Are you ill?"

"No, master."

"Are you injured?"

"No, master."

"Are you unable to walk for some reason?"

"I can walk, but I prefer to remain here on my knees."

"On your knees?"

"I am unworthy to stand, unworthy to sit, unworthy to *be* in your presence, Most Beneficent One. I cannot bring myself to look upon your face. I am unfit to kiss your hands, or even your feet. I will prostrate myself before your tent and beg your forgiveness."

"Have you gone quite mad, Kareem?"

"Most regrettably, that is not it, either, master."

Jack was beginning to lose his patience with his devoted friend and servant. "What is it, then?" he demanded.

Elizabeth stirred beside him and sat up, rubbing the sleep from her eyes. "What is *what*, Jack?"

"I'm not sure," he confessed to her. "Kareem is outside and refuses to come in. He keeps mumbling about how unworthy he is to be in my presence."

"You must have done something to frighten the poor man," she concluded, reaching for her robe.

"I didn't do anything. Except bid him enter. Honest, my dear."

Jack was on the receiving end of an extremely skeptical look as his wife slipped out the back of their tent for a few minutes.

*   *   *

"How delightful. I see our morning tea and breakfast has arrived," Elizabeth commented upon her return. She looked about the spacious pavilion. "But where is Kareem?"

Jack tied the sash of his robe and muttered, "He is still busy prostrating himself in front of the tent."

She planted her hands on her hips and demanded to know, "What did you do to him?"

"I didn't do anything to him," he claimed with a convincing air of innocence. "How could I? I haven't seen the man in weeks. Not since I dispatched him to Cairo to do an errand for me."

Her ears perked up. "Errand? What kind of errand?"

"I suppose you may as well know now. I had Kareem leave the *Star of Egypt* and return to Cairo in order to see a man who occasionally does some work for me."

"What kind of work?"

"Investigative work. This particular man . . . deals . . . in information."

"A detective. How exciting!"

"Yes, well, Kareem was supposed to obtain certain information from this man about Count Polonski, and Colonel and Mrs. Winters."

"And has he?"

"I don't know. I haven't been able to convince him to come inside to speak to me."

"Perhaps this situation requires a woman's touch," she said, tapping a finger against her bottom lip. "Shall I try?"

"Be my guest," stated Jack, with a sweep of his hand.

Elizabeth approached the opening of their tent. "Kareem . . . ?"

A muffled salutation: "Greetings, mistress."

"Greetings to you, Kareem. It is a lovely morning, is it not?"

"Yes, mistress, it is."

"Did you have a long and difficult journey from Cairo?"

"Yes," he admitted with a dramatic sigh, "it was a very long and very difficult journey."

"Then we are particularly pleased that you have returned to us safely and in good health."

"It is most kind of you to say so, mistress."

"Won't you please come inside?"

"I cannot."

"Why can't you?"

"Because I have failed my master."

"How have you failed him?"

"I was unable to return in time with the information he sought, gracious lady."

She glanced over her shoulder at Jack, then turned back and announced, "He forgives you, Kareem."

"But I cannot forgive myself."

"You must," she insisted kindly but firmly. "We need you."

"Need me, mistress?"

"Yes. There is much to be done, and we will require your assistance."

"Require my assistance? I will, naturally, do whatever I can to help, my lady."

"I knew we could count on you, Kareem," she

assured the man outside the pavilion. Then she lowered her voice. "But we must speak in private, and we cannot do this while shouting at each other from the opposite sides of a tent."

"I understand, mistress."

"Besides, there is a cup of tea and a plate of fresh bread and honey waiting for you here on the table. Your master and I would like you to join us while we breakfast. You can give us a full report while we dine."

"If you insist . . ."

"I do." She turned and flashed Jack a triumphant smile over her shoulder. "Please enter, Kareem."

There was a momentary delay—the man was, no doubt, rising from his knees and dusting the sand from his robes—and then the tent flap was pushed aside and Kareem walked into his master's pavilion.

"It is good to see you again, my old friend and companion," said Jack as he came forward and embraced him. "May the gods be praised for watching over you during your journey."

Kareem gave a small bow and repeated the litany: "May the gods be praised."

They exchanged pleasantries about each other's well-being, the general news from the city, greetings from Jack's numerous friends and acquaintances, and myriad other details before they finally got down to business.

"Please sit here, Kareem, and tell us what you have learned," urged Elizabeth, once all the formalities had been observed.

She had discovered, frequently to her dismay,

that the ways of the desert were often slow and tedious, requiring a great deal of patience. There was a specific way of doing most things, a certain protocol that must be observed. Women were often excluded.

It could be most annoying.

"You may speak freely in front of my wife," confirmed Jack when Kareem was about to begin his report.

"I did as you instructed, master," said the small and now slightly wizened man. "I went to the house on the street beside the old mosque and made the proper inquiries. I was told to return in one week's time."

"And did you?"

"I did."

"What were you told?"

"Count André Polonski has not been involved in illegally smuggling or selling Egyptian antiquities since an incident three years ago."

"Ah . . ." Jack seemed relieved, almost pleased, by the news.

"Indeed, at the time, it was never actually proven that he was a part of any dubious dealings."

"I am glad to hear that."

Elizabeth's eyes grew larger. So *that* was what Jack had been up to: He had sent Kareem to investigate the count!

The report was continued. "Count Polonski, as you may know, lost most of his inherited wealth and familial estates during a peasant revolt in his native country. He was forced to flee, as was nearly all of the aristocracy, with an empty purse and empty pockets."

Black Jack leaned forward in anticipation. "What has been the source of Polonski's income, then?"

Kareem looked around and lowered his voice before answering, "He receives a stipend from his mother."

"His mother!" blared his attentive listener.

"Yes, master, his mother."

Apparently that was the last thing Jack had expected to hear.

"And who is the count's mother?" Elizabeth asked, now deeply interested.

Kareem looked from one to the other and, with a decided flair for the melodramatic, announced, "Lady Charlotte Baker-Finch."

"Lady Charlotte?"

"Lady Charlotte!"

Elizabeth was dumbfounded. "The same Lady Charlotte Baker-Finch whose home and rose garden we visited?"

Kareem nodded his dark head. "The very one, mistress."

"Well, I'll be a—" declared Jack.

"Very likely, my dear," murmured Elizabeth, patting his hand reassuringly, her razor-sharp mind having already leapt ahead to several obvious conclusions.

Obvious to her, anyway.

It was all beginning to make sense somehow. For it had been at the luncheon at Lady Charlotte's that Amelia Winters had made the count's acquaintance.

Kareem continued his recitation. "Lady Charlotte's income is derived from certain holdings in her native England that she inherited from her parents upon their deaths. These include a sheep farm, a number of shares of railroad stock, certain mineral rights—"

"Yes, yes, yes," muttered Jack impatiently.

"There is also purportedly—" the little man shrugged his shoulders with bewilderment, as if he could not quite believe the accuracy of the next bit of information "—a modest but steady influx of royalties from a book the lady once wrote about an Englishwoman traveling in Egypt."

"*Letters from Egypt*, of course," exclaimed Elizabeth.

Kareem seemed at a loss to understand why anyone would pay good money for a book penned on such a subject. "There were also a number of splendid jewels given to her by the count's father, and over the years she has sold them off one by one to support herself and her son."

"Lady Charlotte and Count Polonski..." Elizabeth still could not quite believe it.

"As to the other matter, master—"

She was suddenly all ears. "What other matter?"

"My wife is a curious creature," muttered Jack, man to man, to his longtime companion.

Elizabeth raised her chin a fraction of an inch into the air. "I assume, husband, that you mean I have a curious turn of mind."

"Of course, my dear," he said placatingly, perhaps too placatingly. "What else could I mean?"

In these domestic affairs, Kareem was a wise man. He had no eyes to see, no ears to hear, no tongue to speak. Indeed, he was quite adept at making himself invisible when necessary.

"What did you learn about Colonel and Mrs. Winters?" quizzed Black Jack.

Kareem opened his mouth and related, "First, they are *not* man and wife. There has never been a formal marriage contracted between Hulbert Mathias Winters and one Amelia Stone. They met some six or seven years ago when he was on leave in London from his military post in the Sudan. Apparently Amelia Stone was an actress at the time, and quite a good one, from all reports."

"An actress, how interesting," said Jack.

"Colette was right. Again. Naturally. She said Amelia wasn't a lady," murmured Elizabeth, more to herself than to either man present.

"The colonel did some intelligence work while serving in Her Majesty's army. The only other pertinent information we managed to gather is that both Colonel Winters and Amelia Stone have expensive tastes and have lived beyond their means for years. No one knows for certain how they supplement his military pay." The man discreetly switched to the ancient language, in order not to offend the ears of his mistress, and informed his master, "It is rumored that for the right price, the colonel would sell anything, including the services of his so-called wife."

Elizabeth said not a word, uttered not so much as a single gasp, but the tips of her ears turned bright red, and in the end, that gave her away.

"You speak the ancient tongue!" accused Black Jack.

"No, I do not speak it. I understand a little, that is all," she quickly defended herself.

Her husband was more surprised than angry. "Why did you not tell me?"

"The need, or occasion, to do so has never arisen," she explained meekly, "until now."

"I wonder what other surprises you have in store for me," he said, with what sounded suspiciously like a chuckle.

Her lips twitched. "I think, husband, you will simply have to wait and see, won't you?"

Jack cleared his throat and turned back to the subject of Colonel Hulbert Winters. "So the man has done some intelligence work."

Elizabeth stood and immediately began to clear away their breakfast things as if there was not a moment to spare. "You do know what that means, don't you?"

Both men looked up at her in astonishment. "No."

"It means we haven't any time to waste."

Black Jack must have sensed the urgency in her voice. He unfolded his long legs and quickly got to his feet. "Any time to waste?"

"Most of my stolen notes were written in code, but it is not a difficult or complex one. It won't take a man like the colonel long to figure it out. He may have done so already. Once he has broken the code, he will attempt to find the tomb of the Great Merneptah Seti himself."

Jack swore softly under his breath: "Hell and damnation!"

"My feelings precisely." Elizabeth glanced down at the beautiful but impractical robe she was wearing, and sighed. "If only I had one of my split-skirt dresses. These clothes are useless for the journey we must make."

He arched a black brow at her. "The journey *we* must make?"

There was no hesitancy on her part when she announced, "We have to reach the burial chamber before Colonel Winters and prevent him from stealing the pharaoh's treasure."

"But the colonel has your diary and all of your notes and maps."

"They may have taken my precious papers from me, but they could not take what is up here." Elizabeth pointed to her head. "It is still all in here, Jack."

He just stood and stared at her. Then he issued a warning. "What we are about to undertake could be very dangerous."

"I realize that."

"You know where Merneptah Seti is entombed, don't you?"

Elizabeth nodded.

"Not to speak ill of the dead, but your father was a fool for not listening to you."

"Then you do believe me?"

"Yes. I do." Jack blew out his breath and reached behind him to one of the storage chests. Opening it, he removed a small leather valise. "The rest of your belongings are still in the bungalow at Luxor. There wasn't much time—and it was all in a terrible jumble—but I grabbed a few things I thought you might especially want or need," he explained, handing it over to her.

Elizabeth took the valise and unlatched the top. Inside was the antique cameo brooch that Maman had given her on her sixteenth birthday, the precious photograph of Annie and her family that she always carried with her, a pair of lacy drawers, one split-skirt dress, and a slightly crushed straw hat.

She gazed up at Jack with tears brimming in her eyes. She could barely speak. "Th-Thank you."

"You're welcome," he said softly.

She wiped at her cheek. "I see there is no corset packed," she teased to cover the depth of her emotions.

"Mark my words, someday any intelligent woman will refuse to wear one," said Jack with a grin.

Elizabeth laughed out loud, thinking of a conversation she had once had with Colette on the same subject.

Then Jack was all business again. "We'd better get going. There are many preparations to be seen to before we can depart tomorrow at first light. We will need an adequate amount of food and drink. Horses. Blankets."

"I will see to all of our arrangements, master," volunteered Kareem.

"No, my old friend. You are clearly exhausted. You must stay here in camp and rest with The People. This is one journey I will make without you," Jack told him kindly.

"There is no journey you will make without me, master. And that includes the Final Journey itself. Where you ride, I ride. Where you walk, I walk," insisted the small man. "I am going with you and the mistress."

Chapter 25

"**K**areem was not happy to be left with the horses and the pack animals," commented Elizabeth as she and Jack began their final descent into the great necropolis: the holy burial places in the Valley of the Kings and farther south, in the Valley of the Queens.

"You know as well as I that Kareem is getting too old and was too tired to hike up and down these rugged hills. He will be far safer and of far more use to us as a watchman."

They paused at the summit of the western bank and looked out across the desert valley with its sheer-sided stone cliffs and thousands of natural cracks and crevices. There was no sign of life except a solitary vulture winging its way overhead and a scruffy jackal picking a path through the hot, loose rocks.

Elizabeth secured the ribbon of her straw hat more firmly under her chin, and pointed to the west. "This is the way."

"Tell me, why are we headed into the Valley of the Queens in order to find the tomb of one of the greatest of the kings?" posed Jack as he followed along behind her.

At last, someone who wanted to hear her side of the story; someone who believed that she knew what she was talking about. She had been waiting *years* for just such a person, realized Elizabeth.

"I have devoted the past six years of my life to the study of Merneptah Seti and his wife, Nefetari. I have reviewed in detail every treatise made available to scholars on the subject. I have pored over every word the great pharaoh wrote for his beloved: both in its original language and in numerous and endless translations."

Jack said, "The love poems, for example, that he created in Nefetari's honor. Like the one I quoted to you that first night we met on the deck of the *Star of Egypt*?"

"Exactly."

"And all this review and study has led you to conclude that Merneptah Seti is buried in the Valley of the Queens?"

"Yes."

"Why?"

Elizabeth negotiated a particularly steep path, and stopped for a moment to catch her breath before she answered Jack. "He was the only pharaoh in history, as far as we know, who married once and only once. He refused all other women. Even after Nefetari died from the fever, he never remarried. He remained devoted to her memory until the end of his days."

Jack took a handkerchief from his pocket and wiped the sweat from his brow. "In other words, he was a one-woman man," he said, adjusting the pack strapped to his back.

"That is what the evidence tells us."

"One man. One woman."

She nodded. "For some—a lucky few, in my opinion—perhaps that is the way it is meant to be. There are certain species of animals that mate for life. Why should the human animal be any different?"

Jack shook his head and smiled. "You are truly a romantic, my dear Elizabeth."

"Yes, I suppose I am." But she would never apologize for it again. Not to anyone.

"Where do we go from here?"

She stopped and studied the rugged terrain for a minute, squinting into the bright sunlight and hoping that she was not forgetting any of the landmarks she had memorized from photographs of the area, as well as detailed maps. "If we proceed approximately fifty feet beyond that outcropping of rock, we should spot a short, narrow passageway cut between two folds in the hills. It will lead to the doorway of Nefetari's tomb."

"But if the entrance is that accessible, surely the tomb was found and robbed long ago," he suggested.

"We shall soon see, Jack," Elizabeth called out to him almost cheerfully as she hurried toward the wadi in the cliffs. "We shall see."

She turned at the landmark, and he was right behind her.

"My God, is that it?" he exclaimed.

For there, under a huge overhanging of stone, tucked into the shadows, among piles of debris and rock, was a small opening in the hillside. It would be easily missed, unless one knew exactly where to look.

"I think that's it. I hope that's it." *I pray it is,* Elizabeth intoned to herself.

Jack quickly began to clear away the rubble.

"There's some carving on this block. Can you read what it says?" he inquired, stepping back to give her a clear view of the hieroglyphs.

Elizabeth reached out with her finger and traced the ancient writing contained within the oval, ancient writing reserved only for royalty.

She murmured in a voice filled with emotion, "It is her name: her cartouche."

"Nefetari's?"

She nodded. Too overwhelmed for a moment to speak. "If we can find the fulcrum, the doorway should easily swing open," she told him.

It took even less time than Elizabeth had expected. Jack secured the stone door with a large rock and lit the torch they had brought with them. Then they stepped into the ancient burial chamber of Queen Nefetari.

The walls were covered with wonderful paintings, some of the finest paintings, perhaps, ever rendered for a royal tomb. The colors and the characters were as vivid and as alive as the day the artist put the finishing touches upon his work for the wife of the Great Pharaoh thousands of years before.

But the chamber itself was disappointing. It was nearly empty. There were a few fragments of broken furniture and smashed pottery, an empty coffin—the lid pushed to one side, a strip of shroud ground into the dirt on the floor, a fragment of crushed bone—but no treasure, no jewelry or chests, not a single statue. The room was, for all intents and purposes, empty.

Empty.

"Elizabeth . . ."

"Yes, Jack."

"I'm so sorry, my dear."

"About what?" she asked, turning to him with a puzzled expression on her face.

"As I had feared, Nefetari's tomb was robbed long ago. Like so many others, perhaps even in antiquity."

"Nonsense."

"Nonsense?"

"This isn't Nefetari's tomb."

Jack appeared confused. "It isn't?"

"Of course not, my dear man."

"But—"

Elizabeth strolled around the small chamber, studying the wall paintings as best she could by torch. "I wish we had a mirror, or several mirrors, to reflect the sunlight in here. These are really quite magnificent."

"Elizabeth, what do you mean this isn't Nefetari's tomb?"

"I mean this isn't her tomb."

"Whose is it, then?"

"No one's."

"No one's!"

She tried to explain it to him the best she could. "Nefetari was never buried here, Jack. No one was. It's a perfect example of a false tomb meant to fool any grave robbers who happened to find it— right down to the counterfeit coffin." She picked up a small, white fragment from the floor and examined it for a moment. "I must say, the bone is a particularly nice touch."

He looked at her as if she had taken complete leave of her senses. "If Nefetari was never buried here, then why did we go to so damned much trouble to find the place?"

She couldn't contain her excitement any longer. "Because if my hunch is right—and I'm willing to stake my life on it—then both Nefetari and Merneptah Seti are buried somewhere nearby."

Jack was utterly taken aback. "Where?"

"That's what we have to determine next," she said, meeting his eyes with a challenging lift of her chin.

His voice was easy, but his stance was a study in disbelief, even anger. "And just how in the hell do you suggest we go about doing that?"

"Now, Jack, stay calm."

His voice rose. "I am calm, dammit!"

"There is a logical method for going about this kind of thing."

"There'd better be," he muttered.

"What we're looking for is a false door that isn't really a false door."

He crooked a well-done brow in her direction. "Would you care to repeat that, madam?"

"We are trying to find a panel in the wall, or the floor, or even in the ceiling, that isn't a true panel, but a door leading to another chamber beyond this one."

He took hold of her by the shoulders. "Look, Elizabeth, it is pretty obvious that we got here before the colonel. Maybe he never figured out the code. Maybe he never will. Maybe no one will ever find the real burial chamber. Darling, why can't we leave them in peace?"

"I would, Jack, but now that my maps and notes are out there, somewhere—" she gestured in the general direction of the tomb opening, the valley, the world beyond "—and out of my control, I can guarantee that someone will search until they find this place. And when they do, they may not have the respect for Merneptah Seti and his beloved Nefetari that we do. They'll hack away at the walls and destroy whatever is in their path. All most people see, all most people want, is the treasure."

Jack took off his hat and ran his hands through his damp, black hair. "You're right, of course. I've seen it a dozen times before with other tombs, other temples. A few years ago they even ground up the stone blocks of Cleopatra's 'birth temple' at Erment to provide building materials for a local sugar factory."

"You do understand, then?"

Jack looked straight into her eyes. "Yes. I do understand."

He took his torch and began to examine the walls on the north end of the room. Elizabeth took a smaller torch found amid the debris, lit it, and began on the opposite wall.

An hour later they had found nothing.

"Let's give it a rest," Jack suggested as he propped his torch up in the sand, plunked himself down on the floor by the fake coffin, and took a canteen of water from his pack. "How about a drink?"

Elizabeth sighed wearily and sat down beside him. She accepted the canteen from his hands and held it to her lips for a moment, swallowing just enough water to clear the dust from her throat. For she, too, was learning the ways of the desert. "I didn't think it would be so difficult to find the true door," she admitted, leaning back.

"We'll find it," stated Jack determinedly, leaning back alongside her.

"Jack—"

"Yes."

"Did you feel something—move?"

"Something move?"

"The coffin."

He jumped up and turned around. "Of course, it's the bloody coffin!"

Elizabeth was immediately on her feet, as well. "Do you think so?"

"We'll soon find out." He took a firm stance and pushed as hard as he could against the end of the stone sarcophagus where they had been resting only a moment before.

"Did it move?"

"I don't know," he confessed, stepping back.

"I'll push, too," volunteered Elizabeth.

"On the count of three," suggested Jack.

They planted their feet in the sand, placed their hands on the edge of the square coffin, and counted in unison. "One. Two. Three."

It moved.

Eventually they had the stone tomb pushed far enough to one side that they could make out a flight of steps leading down into a chamber directly beneath them.

"I know this is your discovery, sweetheart, but it's possible that no one has been below in thousands of years. Who knows what is down there?"

Elizabeth gazed intently into his clear blue eyes. "You are going to be all noble and protective of me, and insist that you go first, Jack. Don't. It won't matter, anyway, because I'm going down there, come what may."

He looked at her, and said with equal amounts of masculine admiration and exasperation, "You are a stubborn little creature, aren't you, wife?"

"Yes, I am."

Black Jack was still muttering about being a damned fool for going along with her harebrained schemes as he handed her the lighter of the two torches and took the larger and heavier one in his own hand.

"At the first sign of trouble, any kind of trouble, I want you out of there and up those stairs. And I mean fast. Do you understand?" he growled.

"I understand."

As she descended the flight of stone steps, Elizabeth's heart began to pound with excitement and fear, excitement and fear that the unknown always brought with it. This was, after all, the culmination of all her dreams, all of Papa's dreams, a lifetime of dreams.

She made her way carefully down the stairs, one step at a time. The dark at the bottom gave way before the beacon of her torch.

Then she felt the solid floor beneath her feet. "I'm there, Jack," she called softly over her shoulder.

"I'm right behind you," he confirmed, and she could feel the warmth of his breath stir the fine hairs at her nape.

"Are you ready?"

"I'm ready."

Together Elizabeth and Jack lifted their torches high, and for the first time in three thousand years and more, human eyes beheld the royal burial chamber of the Great Pharaoh, Merneptah Seti, and his beloved wife, Nefetari.

There were wonders to behold beyond the imagination and dreams of any mere mortal: it was an entire palace re-created beneath the sand and stone of the Valley of the Queens!

A palace filled with the finest carved furniture: couches, tables, chairs, thrones, and chests. There were life-size statues, chariots, boats, baskets filled with food, caskets filled with jewels and coins, jars and jugs, bows and arrows, spears, linens and clothing, figurines of the gods, shrines of gold and silver, ebony game boxes, carved ivory flutes, silver trumpets, cosmetics, ivory boomerangs, swords and daggers, ceremonial shields, leather armor, tools, lamps, even the royal bed.

And there, in the center of the palace room, was a single stone coffin.

Elizabeth did not realize she was weeping until Jack dug out his handkerchief and pressed it into her hand. It was some time before either of them could speak.

"You were right," said Jack in a reverent tone, for this seemed, indeed, to be a holy place.

"I was right," she whispered.

"There is greater treasure here than in all the museums in all the cities in all the world."

"Very probably," she agreed.

"But I see only one coffin."

Elizabeth dried her eyes. "Of course."

"It's what you expected to find?"

"Yes."

"Your woman's intuition again."

"My woman's intuition. It hasn't been wrong yet."

"Then what does it tell you now about Merneptah Seti and Nefetari?"

"That they loved each other so much in life, they wished to spend eternity together. Not just in the same burial chamber. But in the same coffin."

"Of course," exclaimed Jack softly, recognizing the truth when he heard it. "They arranged to be buried together. But how did you know?"

"Because I'm a woman. Because I think like a woman. Because I love like a woman," Elizabeth stated, turning to face him. "And if I should die with my next breath, I would want to spend eternity in the arms of the man I love, in your arms, Jack."

He reached for her. "Elizabeth—"

"How very touching and romantic," came the harsh intrusion of a man's voice from behind them.

"Colonel Winters—"

"Damn you, Winters!"

"Turn around slowly and carefully, especially you, my lord. I have a pistol pointed at Lady Elizabeth's heart, and believe me, I won't hesitate to use it."

Chapter 26

"What I want to know, of course, is where is the solid gold statue of the pharaoh that you mention in your notes?" said the colonel, pointing the lethal-looking pistol at Elizabeth with one hand and patting the breast pocket of his jacket with the other. The slight bulge in his coat revealed the apparent current location of her diary and papers.

"I refuse to tell you," she bravely declared.

"Oh, I think I might be able to find a way to convince you otherwise," claimed Hulbert Mathias Winters with a quick, cruel smile.

Elizabeth felt herself recoil. The man was evil; she realized that now.

"I may not be as handsome or as virile as your young lover here, but I have been known to convince women to see things my way."

"Touch so much as a single hair on Elizabeth's head and you are dead, Winters," growled Jack.

"I assume that is a promise, not a threat, Lord Jonathan." A once-distinguished white brow arched in amusement. "Brave talk from the man *without* the pistol."

"Yes, and I've seen how brave you are *with* one," sneered Jack.

The colonel motioned them to back up and give him more room to maneuver. "Find Polonski and Amelia, did you?"

Black Jack's eyes narrowed into two dangerous blue-black slits. "Yes, I did."

"I don't imagine it was a pretty sight."

Elizabeth stiffened.

Surely Jack wouldn't be so foolish as to tell the colonel the couple were still alive. While she wasn't particularly fond of Amelia and André, she had no desire to see them dead, either. If Hulbert Winters were to discover that two witnesses to his treachery had survived, he might, indeed, return and finish the job he'd started.

"No. It wasn't a pretty sight," was all Jack would say.

She breathed a sigh of relief. For Lady Charlotte's sake alone, she was glad André Polonski had lived.

"Jackals get them? Or was it the vultures? Well, never mind. There is a lady present, and we wouldn't want to offend her delicate sensibilities."

"You have already offended my delicate sensibilities, Colonel," she informed her former chaperon. "You, sir, are not the gentleman I thought you were."

"And for that, my dear girl, I am truly apologetic. I had grown quite fond of you, you know. You sit a horse extremely well, and you have always been a jolly good sport. Unlike that bitch, Amelia." He gave her a mocking little bow. "Excuse my language, my lady."

She refused to rise to the bait.

"Now, let me see, what am I going to do with the two of you?" It was obviously a rhetorical question. "I could simply shoot you both dead here and now and be done with it. I believe you, Lady Elizabeth, said something about wishing to spend eternity in the arms of the man you love." The colonel laughed, and it was a most unpleasant sound coming from him. "But bullets can be such a messy business. Polonski literally bled all over himself, all over poor Amelia, the ground—"

Elizabeth felt the color draining from her face.

"Now, now, no fainting, my dear, or I'll be forced to shoot," warned Hulbert Winters.

She straightened her shoulders and faced the villain, white-faced but with perfect posture.

"See, what a little trooper she is, Wicke. You, at least, had the sense to fall in love with a girl with some spunk. That damnable Polonski and Amelia deserved each other, is all I can say."

"Perhaps they did, but that doesn't mean they deserved to die," spoke up Elizabeth.

The man's eyes grew savage. "No one double-crosses Colonel Winters and gets away with it."

"Are you sure that's what really got your goat,

Winters? Or was it the fact that Count Polonski was cuckolding you behind your back?"

"Shut your frigging mouth, Wicke! Or I'll shut it for you permanently. You don't know what you're talking about. Why, the things I could tell you—"

Elizabeth reached out and touched Jack's arm in an appeal. "Please, darling, don't!"

"Keep your hands to yourself, girl." The colonel furrowed his brow in thought. "Although you have given me an idea." He pointed to a length of sturdy cord that was wrapped around a stack of ancient spears. "Get that rope, my lady. I believe I will feel more secure if Lord Jonathan's hands are tied behind his back. No, on second thought, it would be better if I could see his hands at all times. Tie them in front of him."

Elizabeth did not move.

"If you prefer, I'll simply shoot him instead."

The colonel's threat worked. She retrieved the cord and tied Jack's hands as instructed.

"Tighter, dear lady. Much tighter," instructed Hulbert Winters.

"I'm sorry, Jack," she cried out softly when she saw the cord bite into his flesh, cutting the skin, raising bloody welts that made her sick.

"It's all right, sweetheart," he reassured her, without so much as a flinch.

"Now, back to my original question," said the colonel as he pointed the pistol directly at Jack's chest. "Where is the solid gold statue mentioned in your notes?"

"I don't know."

He cocked the trigger.

"I'm not certain," Elizabeth corrected.

He stared at her, his intent clear. "But you have a pretty good idea, don't you, girl?"

"Yes."

"Where?"

"Please, Colonel Winters, believe me when I tell you that if you try to remove the statue from this tomb, some awful consequence will befall you."

"Are you trying to tell me that the place is cursed?"

"In a manner of speaking, yes."

He laughed. "What kind of fool do you take me for?"

"I don't take you for any kind of fool, unless you insist upon trying to leave with the treasure that rightfully belongs to Merneptah Seti and Nefetari."

"Hogwash! Balderdash!"

"But all of the ancient papyri speak of such a curse," she pleaded.

"Of course they do. That's how the ancient kings and queens thought—or at least hoped—to keep grave robbers from breaking into their tombs and stealing everything. It didn't work then and it doesn't work now." He brandished the pistol. "For the last time, where is the statue?"

She whispered, "In the coffin."

"I can't hear you, my dear. Speak up."

"I said, I believe the gold statue is in the coffin."

Hulbert Mathias Winters rewarded her with a smile. It made Elizabeth ill. "Now we're finally getting somewhere. Good thing we tied your hands in front, Wicke. It appears that your lady love is going to require your help in removing the lid of the sarcophagus." The smile disappeared. "Get to work. Both of you. Use whatever means you have to, but get the top of that coffin off."

It took time. They were both covered with dust and sand and sweat before the lid had been moved enough to satisfy the colonel.

"Forgive us," intoned Elizabeth to the two intertwined figures inside the coffin.

Hulbert Winters peered down and chuckled. "By heaven, my girl, you were right. There it is." He reached in with his hand and came out clutching a gold statue of some fourteen or fifteen inches in height. "Magnificent!" he declared as he turned it around. "I can sell it for a fortune and live like a king for the rest of my life."

"You won't live long enough to spend a penny of it," said Elizabeth.

The colonel paused and looked around at the other treasure in the re-created palace room. "I wouldn't want to get too greedy, since I have to carry it out of here by myself. But I can manage a bit more." He pointed to Jack's pack on the floor. "Empty that out and fill it up with jewelry, my lady. And be quick about it," he urged.

She turned toward Jack with tears in her eyes. They both knew what was going to soon occur whether she did as the colonel ordered or not.

"Do what he says, my love," murmured Jack. "You've got to be brave. It will be all right in the end. We'll be together."

Elizabeth picked out the least valuable of the bracelets and necklaces; the colonel would never know the difference. And it was a small enough satisfaction for the sacrilege that had already taken place within the royal burial chamber.

"Here," she said, once she had filled the pack to the thief's specifications.

Hulbert Winters backed up toward the flight of stairs, the pack of treasure slung over one shoulder, the pistol still poised in his hand. "You always were such a pleasant girl and such a damn fine sport, my lady, that I have decided *not* to shoot you and Lord Jonathan."

"You're not going to kill us?" she said from the far corner, astonished.

"Not directly," he replied, laughing, as he climbed up the first few stairs while he kept an eye on them. "I'm going to let this place take care of that little job for me."

With that, Hulbert Winters quickly negotiated the last three steps and began to push the coffin above back into place.

"You son of a bitch!" Jack called after him as the entrance closed, leaving the two of them entombed below.

"Let me get these ropes untied." It was the first thing Elizabeth insisted upon once they were alone. "I'm so sorry, Jack, for getting you into this whole mess."

His hands were freed. He reached for her and held her close to him. "Don't talk. Just let me hold you for a minute." Then he gazed down into her face and murmured, "I should have told you before. Maybe I was afraid to admit it even to myself. But I love you, Elizabeth."

"And I love you, Jack."

They simply stood there and held on to each other for dear life.

It was in the quiet stillness of that moment that they heard the great rumble begin overhead.

Jack raised his head. "What in the name of God?"

It sounded as if the whole mountain was coming down around them, crumbling into a thousand tons, a million tons, of lethal rock. The burial chamber shook. The dust flew through the stale air. But the structure itself remained intact.

"I told the colonel not to try to leave with the statue."

"Do you think he's dead?"

Elizabeth nodded. "I think Hulbert Winters and his ill-gotten gains are buried literally under a mountain of stone."

"Dear God!"

"I warned him that he who removed Merneptah Seti's treasure from this holy place was cursed."

Jack looked at her askance. "Do you actually believe that?"

"I don't know. But I do believe that the tomb was booby-trapped. The ancient architects were very clever with balancing weights and pulleys, false doors and hidden chambers. They were able to devise all kinds of mechanisms to protect the pharaoh and the pharaoh's treasure."

"Yes, think of what the builders of the Great Pyramids were able to accomplish," said Jack as he released her and began to pace the room.

Elizabeth found herself rambling. "I'll be sorry not to see Maman and England again. Nanny and

Trout and the gardens. I wanted to arrange for Alee to attend school at Cambridge if he desired. I had even imagined stopping off in Marseilles on the journey home and checking to be sure that Colette and Georges were faring well in their new life together."

Jack continued silently pacing back and forth, lost deep in thought.

Elizabeth sighed. "I had all kinds of plans to live life to its fullest, to travel the world, to have many grand adventures, and then settle down in the country one day with the right man and raise a houseful of happy, healthy children and a garden full of roses."

"A rose garden." It was the first thing Jack had said in perhaps ten or fifteen minutes.

"Yes, a rose garden."

"And have you met this man, this paragon of domestic virtue whom you will marry?"

She wrapped her arms around his neck and gazed up at him. "I have done better than that. I have already met *and* married him."

"I thought he was nothing more than a dream," murmured Jack as he kissed her thoroughly.

"So did I. But he was my dream, and I knew that one day I would find him." Her eyes filled with tears. "You once told me that making love was like dying and coming back to life again. But I am afraid, my love, that we will die here and not come back to life."

Black Jack looked down at her, and his blue eyes were glittering with intent. "Would you marry me again, Elizabeth, if you were given the choice?"

"In a second."

"Promise?"

"I promise," she vowed.

"I'm going to hold you to that promise, my dear wife, because I believe I know how to get us out of here."

Elizabeth almost fainted. "Get us out of here?" She caught her breath. "How?"

"It was when we were talking about the mechanisms devised by the ancient architects. When they constructed the Great Pyramids, they always built in an escape route, usually a long, ascending tunnel that ran from the main burial chamber to some remote spot on the surface. Maybe. Just maybe the gods will be with us and we can find an escape route out of this place."

They immediately went into action.

"What do we look for?" asked Elizabeth.

"Something like one of your false doors that isn't really a false door," Jack told her. "It will appear to be a natural part of the chamber, and yet something should give it away if we look closely enough."

Elizabeth picked up the small torch and began to search one side of the burial chamber.

Jack took the other torch and started on the opposite wall.

It was a half hour later that Elizabeth cried out, "Jack!"

He came running. "What is it?"

She pointed at the picture on the tomb wall. "Look."

It was a painting of Merneptah Seti and Nefetari, hand in hand, walking together up a flight of stairs toward the Heavens themselves.

"This could be it," stated Jack, looking around for something heavy enough to break through the plaster wall. "I hope they understand," he added as he raised an ancient hammer and struck the first blow. The wall began to crumble.

"I'm certain that they would; that they do," murmured Elizabeth.

Within an hour the wall had been reduced to rubble, and a long, narrow passageway was revealed.

"It won't be an easy climb," warned Black Jack, holding up his torch and peering into the darkness ahead of them.

"I know."

"We have no idea where it leads, if anywhere."

"That's true."

"We may get halfway up and find the way blocked and have no means of getting back down."

"We may."

"But if we don't try, we're going to die down here, Elizabeth."

"I know."

He stopped and wrapped his arms around her waist. "There are worse things than dying with the one you love."

She touched her lips to his. "There is only one thing *better*, and that is *living* with the one you love."

"To life."

"To life," Elizabeth echoed. Then, "Jack, wait, we must do one thing before we leave."

He turned back. "What is it?"

"I would like us to close the lid of the sarcophagus. It seems the least we can do."

When they were finished, Jack started toward the opening and hopefully the freedom that awaited them. He looked at Elizabeth and said, "Come on, darling, give me your hand. It's time for us to go."

Epilogue

Lord Jonathan Malcolm Charles Wicke, the second and recently reconciled son of the Duke of Deakin, stopped beside his wife and slipped an arm around her waist. "Elizabeth . . ."

She turned and gazed up at her husband. She knew that look. She had seen it a hundred times in the past few months. "Yes, my lord," she replied behind her fan.

"Your guests are beginning to bore me, my lady."

"They are *our* guests, my lord, and there are worse things than being bored, as you know full well."

On the pretext of smelling the fresh roses arranged in her hair, he bent over and touched his lips to her bare shoulder. "I know of far better things we could be doing than entertaining guests."

Elizabeth fanned herself and said in a teasing tone, "And what is that, pray tell, my lord?"

Jack looked down at her and murmured suggestively, "Come on, darling, give me your hand. It's time for us to go."

"What will our guests think?"

"They will think we are making our way to the celestial heights," he said with a loving laugh.

"Jack!" exclaimed Elizabeth when they entered their chamber a few minutes later. "What in the world is all over our bed?"

"Roses, my love."

"Roses?"

"Rose petals, to be precise. I promised myself a long time ago that I would make love to my beautiful Elizabeth on a bed of roses."

With all the love in his heart, Jack kept his promise that night.

Author's Note

In the interest of historical accuracy, it must be noted that Merneptah Seti and his beloved Nefetari are my own invention, as is their love poetry.

It is true, however, that the Great Ramses was proven to have red hair, and that up until his time, one born with "flaming" hair was considered evil.

The People are also a figment of my imagination. The closest true descendants to the ancient pharaohs are modern Egypt's Coptic Christians.

Avon Romances—
the best in exceptional authors and unforgettable novels!